ALSO BY LIZZIE POOK

Moonlight and the Pearler's Daughter

MAUDE HORTON'S GLORIOUS REVENGE

———•———

LIZZIE POOK

Simon & Schuster

NEW YORK   LONDON   TORONTO
SYDNEY   NEW DELHI

SIMON &
SCHUSTER
CANADA

Simon & Schuster Canada
A Divison of Simon & Schuster, Inc.
166 King Street East, Suite 300
Toronto, Ontario M5A IJ3

First Simon & Schuster hardcover edition January 2024

SIMON & SCHUSTER CANADA and colophon are registered trademarks
of Simon & Schuster, Inc.

Simon & Schuster: Celebrating 100 Years of Publishing in 2024

For information about special discounts for bulk purchases,
please contact Simon & Schuster Special Sales at 1-866-506-1949
or business@simonandschuster.com.

Typeset in Fairfield by Jouve (UK), Milton Keynes

Manufactured in the United States of America

1   3   5   7   9   10   8   6   4   2

Library and Archives Canada Cataloguing in Publication
Title: Maude Horton's glorious revenge / Lizzie Pook.
Names: Pook, Lizzie, author.
Description: Simon & Schuster Canada edition.
Identifiers: Canadiana (print) 20230509398 | Canadiana (ebook) 20230539300 |
ISBN 9781982181994 (softcover) | ISBN 9781982182007 (ebook)
Classification: LCC PR6116.O55 M38 2024 | DDC 823/.92—dc23

ISBN 978-1-9821-8199-4
ISBN 978-1-9821-8200-7 (ebook)

For Bobby

Murder is, doubtless, a very shocking offence;
nevertheless, as what is done is not to be undone,
let us make our money of it.

"Blood," *Punch*, 1842

Ah, Franklin!
To follow you, one does not need geography.
At least not totally, but more of that
Instrumental knowledge that bones have,
Their limits, their measurings.
The eye creates the horizon,
The ear invents the wind,
The hand reaching out from the parka sleeve
By touch demands that the touched thing be.

Gwendolyn MacEwen, *Terror and Erebus*

The End of Things

Newgate Prison, London
17 JANUARY 1851

L et us begin at the end, shall we? In a cold London square. A murderer is to be hanged and the fuss has lured the pigeons out in their hundreds. Cloaked in the fumes of cheap meat pies, the birds scratch around traders touting wares to the crowds. With silky, silver-green necks bobbing, they puff their chests in the manner of stout grandees, ducking hob-nailed boots and scattered bottles as they squabble and they peck for a taste of scraps.

Dungggggg.

The birds lift as one, dispersing into shards as the bell loudly tolls.

Down below, from Debtor's Door, a reluctant prisoner is led into the bitter air.

An eel-jelly smog hangs low over the Thames. The air is wet, breathing it like shrugging a damp greatcoat onto the body. Old Bailey is swarming with humans, the ripe-sweat stink of twenty thousand or so. Half of London, it seems, is here for the show, for there is nothing like a hanging to lure mankind out of his house.

The crowd emits a low and persistent bawl—drunks bellow at the skies, harlots toss their heads for high-pitched magpie cackles. Small bodies move through the masses unseen, pilfering coins and purses from unsuspecting pockets.

Above them all, on the scaffold, Calcraft takes his mark, and as he does, the crowd surges forwards for a glimpse of the famed hangman. Bodies swell and churn. In the rush, a young woman falls to her knees. Her limbs are quickly, quietly crushed.

"Get your lamentations!"

"The whole horrid confession right here. In print!"

Boys with threadbare trousers thrust folded broadsides into fingers dripping with jewels.

"You've never read nothing like it! No one more deserving of a scragging."

Wide, darting eyes soak up the lurid details, delicate hands clutch at clavicles, and Calcraft takes his horrid hood and tugs it over the head of the murderer. He fastens it with ghastly nimbleness, his crooked fingers well accustomed to the job. He holds out his hand, to be taken by a quivering palm.

Goodbye.

The crowd erupts and the pigeons burst like brass bullets from the rooftops. Six feet below the city, the rats raise oily heads at the din.

The doomed is guided forwards, ankles strapped, a hempen noose slung around their neck. As they shuffle and stumble, the sun arrives at last, peering out from behind its own heavy shroud.

The doomed soul can see its glow through the scratchy cotton of the hood.

Their shoulders drop.

Their breathing slows.

For a stuttering moment they are gilded in light.

The figure leans forwards into its warmth, fingers slowly

reaching out until, without mercy, the lever is drawn. The drawbar falls with a resounding crash, and they drop through the open jaws of the trap.

*

A few miles away, on a quiet hilltop overlooking the city, a hidden figure watches from the trees as a body is buried in a simple wooden casket. It is exposed up here, a few plots already plundered, yellow disinterred bones scattered bleakly among the headstones. It's a grim space. But this had been the only choice, given the circumstances.

There is one sole mourner, a thin, gray-eyed man whose skin has long lost its tautness. The air is cleaner on this hill, fresher than that wretched place down below. But the slow-crawling stink of the city reaches the nostrils eventually.

The casket is lowered without the whimsy of ceremony, and a robin sets up its calling from the branches of an old oak tree. The song is silvery, rose-oil sweet, but is clawed apart and discarded by the breeze. The thin man treads away, and the sky fills with sunlight. An almighty roar carries across from the city.

He bows his head and pulls tight his coat.

It is done, he nods. It is done.

LONDON

Chapter One

Maude

OCTOBER 1850

Ra-pa-pa-pa-pa.

Maude Horton beats a fist on polished mahogany, the sound swallowed by the stark, clean marble of the corridor. Her chest heaves, sweat making thick the dark hair coiled at the back of her neck. Her skin feels damp and oddly exposed here, surrounded by towering portraits of proud, uniformed men. *Hubris captured in brushstrokes*, she thinks. She puts an ear to the door, waits.

Silence.

She bangs again, sparing no thought for impudence, for bad manners, for the sentiment that women should not go around beating fists on doors such as this one. There had been no reply to her enquiries. This had become the only option.

There's a rustling sound, and Maude briefly imagines those inside dressed in embroidered blue, poring over dusty maps and wind charts, cigars clasped under heavy, oiled moustaches.

RA-PA-PA-PA-PA.

Just as she hears the frantic footsteps of the pursuing guard catch up to her, a crack appears at the door and a man with silver hair and the swollen throat of a toad leans forwards to fill it.

"What is the need for this racket?" The medals at his breast wink keenly.

"Commissioner." The security guard arrives breathless. "She dodged right past me. Tried to stop her. Just . . . I just couldn't quite. She said she was one of the new maids!"

"All right, Mason. Stand down. It's hardly the Storming of the Bastille, is it?" The commissioner's eyes flick idly across Maude's simple clothing. "And?" Wiry eyebrows lift almost to his hairline. "What is it that you need?"

She thrusts the paper, marked with an official admiralty stamp, towards the gap. "I'm Maude Horton," she says. "My sister was Constance Horton, and what I need is the truth."

*

Entering the admiralty boardroom is like having a rag clamped over one's mouth. It brings about a dizzying, suffocating effect. Maude steps forwards, careful not to stumble on the carpet, watching as Sir Hancock, admiralty commissioner, crosses the room then turns to face her, arms folded. Everything within these oak-paneled walls has a leaden weight to it: the imposing ceiling, sculpted into octagons; the mariners' tools so intricate they appear as items in a museum. Carvings frame the ornate fireplace—anchors, swords, scepters and telescopes— and over the mantelpiece a large wind dial, the size of a shield, has been painted with a map of the British Isles. A thin, white arrow strikes furiously to NORTH-NORTHWEST.

Maude glances at the long, mullioned windows, yearning for a taste of clean air. Instead, a watery morning light scythes in through the glass, landing on a long, polished table, where several white-haired men are seated. Some are straight-backed with curiosity, others recline like lemurs on overstuffed leather, nonchalant—as if a woman barging her way into the admiralty boardroom at Whitehall is as common as a mouse crossing the floor.

"Ms. Horton's come about an incident on the *Makepeace*. Despie's ship in the Passage." Hancock's words land with a thud. A wan desk clerk takes up a pen and begins his scribbling.

"Although, I'm afraid, Ms. Horton, there is little more to be said on the subject." He looks vaguely at the floor in front of her. "I'm sure you have all the particulars in your letter there"— a cursory wave of the hand—"from the secretariat."

She turns over the piece of paper. Five meager lines written in cursive.

We regret to inform. Misadventure. Regards.

"Particulars?" Her voice sounds small and she feels her chest begin to flush with heat. "With respect, there are no particulars in this letter, commissioner. Only meaningless formality."

Hancock sucks in his cheeks. The lemurs grumble and shift in their seats.

"What is it exactly that you would like to know, Ms. Horton?" The words are soaked in sugar.

The clerk pauses and holds his pen aloft. Gilt lanterns flicker and a dozen pairs of eyes bore into her.

She draws a slow breath.

"I demand to know the circumstances surrounding my sister's death on the *Makepeace*. I demand to know to what exactly this word refers: misadventure." She holds out the paper and taps it, hoping that they do not perceive just quite how violently her finger shakes.

It had offended her, that word, when she first received the letter a few weeks ago. Hollowed out by grief and frantic for answers, she had torn open the report and scanned the few lines within. Her eyes fell on the loaded term, one that can tell any number of stories.

Hancock heaves a sigh. "It can mean many things in the Arctic, Ms. Horton. And while I am grieved to distress you, accidents happen often on such ambitious expeditions. As I'm sure you can quite imagine."

She wants to tear the vile smirk from his face.

"The Far North is an inhospitable place," he continues, "and in such conditions, weaker bodies can just . . ." He flaps his hand again. By weaker, she knows he means female. "Can just . . . fall foul of the environs. It is why we do not allow women on our ships, Ms. Horton."

That, and the fact that men alone on ships cannot be trusted.

"And, I shouldn't think I have to remind you that your sister should never have been aboard the *Makepeace* in the first place. She cheated her way to a berth, she flouted the rules, disregarded regulations, not to mention disrespected hundreds of years of seafaring tradition and history. So, as I'm sure you'll allow, the admiralty can hardly be at fault for what became of her during that journey."

He seems very certain of what she will and will not allow. "What sort of accident occurred?" She will not be distracted by pomp, by old-fashioned notions of swashbuckling men on the high seas. "If you'll oblige me, commissioner. I must push you again on the specifics." A keen ache in her jaw betrays her clenched teeth.

Hancock scoffs derisively, shakes his head, the motion continuing for far too long for someone who knows the answer to the question posed. He makes a few hollow vowel sounds, then looks to the table. A stringy man peers over his pince-nez to study the contents of his glass. Another appraises the ceiling panels most intently.

"I am not at liberty to—"

"She was my sister!" Maude's voice rings off the room's cut crystal. There is a short, collective gasp. She knows instantly that she has made a mistake.

"Ms. Horton." The commissioner's words are clipped now, but his eyes have grown alarmingly wide. "I am not privy to the particulars of every death that occurs in foreign seas. As you can appreciate, there are rather a lot of them, and I have more pressing things to concern myself with here. Not least the running of the entire country's naval operations."

"Something happened out there." She had told herself she would not allow hysteria to take over. She must try and retain her composure. "Something happened that you are not telling me, you are not telling *anyone*, and I will not be brushed aside by a word that has been selected in order to remove any accountability from the admiralty."

Hancock smiles drily.

She has pushed it too far.

"Ms. Horton, I shall have to insist that you—"

"Why is the body not here?"

Hancock indicates to the guard that their meeting is over.

"Why could we not have a burial? Who performed the autopsy?"

"I think you've wasted quite enough of everyone's time. Good day."

The men at the table clear their throats. Mr. Pince-nez strikes a lucifer, lights his cigar, takes a glorious puff.

A sour taste crawls from Maude's stomach to her throat, as the guard stalks across the room. No. She had hoped that if she came here herself, if they were compelled to put a face to the incident, a family member to the "official report," that they might tell her *something*.

"I will find out," she threatens as the guard seizes her shoulder. "I will find out what happened, even if that means locating the crew. Or . . . Captain Despie." Strong hands propel her roughly to the door. "Or anyone with courtesy enough to tell me why and how my sister died."

"As is your choice, Ms. Horton." Hancock locates an armchair, sits, reclines.

Blue curlicues of cigar smoke escape from the room as the guard yanks open the door. He does not release his grip until they have descended several sets of winding stairs, and he has deposited her, with a pert shove, back out into the yard. As she turns, he pulls the double doors together with a satisfied clunk.

Maude's shoulders slacken, and she allows her head to tip backwards, eyes to the sky. The clouds are sullen, as damp as her mood, and she fights the sob threatening to escape from her throat.

She needs action. Not emotions. She has always been the one to assemble a plan, to find the solution. Tears aren't going to help with that.

She straightens her back, smooths down her skirts and crosses the yard, passing cabs and strolling businessmen as she steps out onto the busy thoroughfare. The patter of footsteps behind her stops her in her tracks.

"Ms. Horton!" Someone is calling out. "Ms. Horton!" She turns, eyes shut, bracing herself for her punishment.

Nothing comes.

She blinks open her eyes. Standing before her is the desk clerk, the man who was taking minutes for Hancock. The one with skin so pale his veins show themselves like rivers on a map.

He glances behind him and takes a cautious step closer,

indicating with a slight jerk of the head that he wants her to move into a side street.

"I think not." She is not in the habit of stepping into dark alleyways with strange men. "Can I help you?"

"Ms. Horton, you are quite safe, I assure you." He ushers her with feeling, now. "I want to ensure we are not being observed."

Her curiosity outweighs her caution, then, and she follows him off the street and into a quiet alley pocked with last night's puddles. The walls, she sees, are crawling with lichen.

He leans out, peers both ways down the street, returns.

His body is uncomfortably close to hers, she realizes; the smoke of other men's cigars still clinging to his shirtsleeves. She takes a step back, watching his pale eyes dart with anxiety. She should be nervous too, she supposes, but this stick insect of a man appears incapable of doing any measure of harm to anything.

"Ms. Horton." He speaks out the side of his mouth as if they are being scrutinized by lip-readers. "Forgive the impropriety, but I have something that I believe you are very much going to want to see."

Oh dear. Perhaps she should be nervous after all.

"It's about the *Makepeace*," he stammers quickly. "About what happened to your sister."

Something takes quick light inside of her. She nods her head giddily, yes, grasping for an end to the agony of unknowing. Then, suddenly, she stops.

"Who are you?" she asks tersely. "Why would you help me?" More pressingly, how does she know that she can trust him? Hancock could have sent him out here, given him something to throw her off the scent, to stop her asking questions once and for all.

"I am Francis Heart, clerk at the admiralty secretariat." He waits for a response, then when it does not come: "I am the one who writes everything down." He straightens his collar. "I have had the immense displeasure of working for the commissioner and his officers for the last several years." Maude scours his face as he talks. He appears a few years older than her twenty-five, but something about his eyes is very old. Beleaguered. "You do not know that you can trust me, of course. You can only hope that I am acting in good faith, and I assure you that I am." He barks out a laugh. "That's what I would say if I were not, I suppose. But I sense you are desperate for answers, and I am quite sure that will compel you to take this risk."

It needles that he thinks he knows her, and it needles even more that he is emphatically right. He glances around them, again. Traps and coaches stream down the street just yards from where they hide. "So, you will meet me. Here." He hands her a note card. On it, she gathers at a quick glance, the name of an establishment with which she is not familiar.

"Friday night," he says. "Seven o'clock. Wear something forgettable. This should do just fine." He gestures at her gray cotton dress.

He nods, goes to leave.

"Wait!" she calls. He turns as a crow flaps clumsily overhead.

"What can I expect? If I am to come. If I am to travel to meet you, can you at least tell me what I will find?"

Heart pauses, a look of resoluteness comes upon him.

"A message from your sister," he says, and steps back out onto the busy street.

Chapter Two

When she was a young girl, Maude discovered she had a nose for medicines. The pharmacy, out the back of which she and her sister slept, was always bursting to its seams with scent: the woody undertones of anise oil, the bitter almond bite of benzaldehyde. Maude's talent was most useful for sorting and cataloguing. With just a sniff she could separate a pot of prepared French chalk from a pot of ground cuttlefish bone; divide a resinous myrrh gum from a sticky spermaceti salve, assigning each of them to their rightful places on the shelves. Maude was a cautious child who erred towards safety and order. If a liquid leaked from an unmarked bottle, she could swiftly identify the substance and advise on any precautions that must be taken so that no one in the pharmacy would be harmed.

She got it from her grandfather, of course, this rare olfactory skill. It meant little passed her by. It meant she could usually tell when something, or someone, was pretending to be something that they were not.

She is still trying to make up her mind about Francis Heart.

A message from her sister. What can he *possibly* have meant? Constance is not alive; she did not return with the *Makepeace*.

Maude had spent a long time coming to terms with that. Yet. Here they are—small tendrils of hope that are winding their slow way in. Could there be another answer? Another chapter to the story? Her sister had already fooled a ship full of men. What's to say she isn't somewhere else altogether now? With a new identity, sipping on whisky, laughing at them all from her new life of comfort and riches?

Heart had asked her to meet him on Friday. Four days from now. She will be sent mad with the waiting. She is going to have to turn her attention to something else, another route, another solution. Yes. She will start by determining the identity and the location of the remaining crew of the *Makepeace*, beginning with the ship's surgeon—surely the last man to see her sister's body. For that, she is going to need her grandfather's help.

It's the floral waft of heliotropin, a scent just like hyacinths, that funnels out from the shopfront vents. It twists its way around the creases of her bonnet, gets a hold of her hair, settling into the pores of her skin. *Wound-healing*, Maude thinks.

The sign above the shop window reads HENRY HORTON, DISPENSING CHEMIST, and the reflection blinking back at Maude from beneath it has her rooted to the spot. It is uncanny to look at yourself and see someone else entirely. This face is a conjurer's trick: a set determination of the jaw, a steeliness in the eyes that she knows she doesn't truly own. If she squints, she can encourage smaller hidden details to shift into focus too; a faint scar above the right eyebrow, the memory of a snagged tooth that pushes its way onto the bottom lip. It looks so very much like *her*, like Constance, that Maude half expects the reflection to come to life and step out from the window glass. Instead, a resounding crash barrels out from inside the shop. The image dissolves and Maude jolts back to her senses.

"Grandfather?"

She rushes to the door. The shop is dim and cool, as always. Low mutterings come from the room out back, followed by the sound of broken glass being swept up with a broom. That's a relief. Maude lifts her eyes to the ceiling, smiles. Her grandfather is a talented chemist but a liability when it comes to loose equipment. Around Maude, a few guttering candles trap glossy motes in their beams. The air is damp and sulfurous, the shelves strung with the iridescent lacework of old cobwebs. A large cabinet displays a rainbow parade of bottles—cobalt and brown shifting to bold, alarming green. Behind it, balancing scales stand armored alongside a brass pestle and mortar. The tincture press looms over pill rollers, cork presses, and scalpels laid out like long, silvery fish. It's always been this way, Maude thinks, every surface filled with *something*: toilet soaps, teething syrups, powders for neuralgia, cures for the bad air. She knows the labels by rote, of course, can recite them with nary a glance: strychnine sulphate, rattlesnake oil, iron arsenic acid. There's a pile of prescriptions on the counter; she picks one up and appraises it, the scratchy writing only legible to her and her grandfather now.

Tincturae jalaep, 3ss.; Magnesiae sulpatism 3ij.; Infusi sennae, 2/3 iss.; misce fiat haustus cras manae sumendus.

A simple laxative.

More glass is knocked over. A wet cough. Expletives are muttered, and with a sweep the old man emerges from the dispensary. He is soft yet wiry, drowned in his striped shirt and neckerchief. His eyes are as filmy as stagnant pondwater.

"You're back. Thank the lord." He crosses himself in jest. "I half expected to have to haul you out of a cell at Newgate."

Maude goes to his side. Breathes in his scent of wood shavings and old smoke.

There are ghosts here with them, in the pharmacy. Ready ghouls of grief that lurk in the shadows. They can be summoned by simple, everyday actions—the opening of a jar to release a scent that Constance favored, a customer rattling the entrance bell, stepping inside, asking after her sister. "Where has she been," they demand, "all this time?"

The sisters grew up here, observing the magic of their grandfather at work. They watched as he neatly pressed his pills—crepey hands rolling the paste into the shape of a sausage, laying it across the grooved brass plate and moving the rollers back and forth until the pills rolled out and into the neat collection tray at the bottom. They watched as he perused his chemist's cabinet, each wooden square with its own shining nameplate and a single brass knob, a secret hidden inside. At first, when Constance was eight and Maude ten, newly abandoned by the death of their parents from fever, they'd been timid with their observation—hiding like town mice beneath benches or folding themselves under the counter. Their hands would clutch together, fingers intertwined, as the strange stink of ammonia and oil of frankincense swarmed about the pharmacy. Above them, their grandfather steeled himself and toiled diligently, knowing that continuing without fuss was the only way to knit together the fractured bones of grief. By ages nine and eleven, the girls had found the courage to emerge, hovering near their grandfather's workstation, chewing on their sleeves and watching wide-eyed as he consulted his leather-bound *Pharmacopoeia*. By the middle of the following year, they knew how to read prescriptions and dispense basic medicines.

Henry's clients grew accustomed to seeing them in the shop, some making visits just to see the pharmacy girls, asking them to fetch their oil of earthworm and their everlasting pills.

Henry Horton taught his granddaughters that the world was made up of two things: science and art. Maude preferred the stories of science, the rational, methodical facets of pills and potions: opium mixed with chloroform and cannabis will supress a cough, just as if you distill a globe of coal tar for long enough it will become carbolic acid. Rules, calculations, assessment of risk, and everything in its order is what suited her best. Constance called her a bore, mocked her prim nature. Constance lived for the art of it all, the spectacle. The way copper chloride flares bright blue when held over a flame.

Now, Maude leans her head on her grandfather's shoulder. "I remain a free woman," she announces. "But I need your help." She raises her head, turns to him. "I have a plan."

"Ah. A plan." He reaches for the mortar and tips in a green chalky substance.

"I need to write to the ship's surgeon," she says, ignoring his raised eyebrows. Maude knows her grandfather used to supply navy ships with their medicines, surgeons stopping by almost weekly to fill their chests, ready for sailing. Constance would brighten when they arrived, trailing them round the shop, tugging at their coattails, asking them to where their ships were sailing. "Into the depths of hell," they'd joke, and she'd ask them if it was likely to take them long to get there.

"He'll have performed an autopsy, won't he?" says Maude. "Inspected the body? If we can track him down, we can encourage him to share his report, find some answers." She leans forwards on the counter, rocking on her elbows. Henry has taken the pestle to the chalk and the bowl squeaks in discontent. "I just need to establish *who* that is exactly and how to get a message to him." They share a dubious glance.

Henry was with Maude when they first learned of Constance's death. She can still remember the moment, the sheer physicality of it. The feeling of her legs buckling beneath her.

Constance was never supposed to be on that ship. Maude thinks of that fact often. But she had inveigled herself there anyway, out of stubbornness, impulsivity, and, as far as Maude was concerned, a misguided sense of honor. The *Makepeace* had carried its muster of men to the wild far Arctic north in search of lost British explorer Sir John Franklin. Although it did not only have men on board, did it. Her sister was there too. Constance's berth had come as a result of a trick. A sleight of hand. A flare of bright blue.

She had left a note when she went, had begged Maude not to follow, and it had taken every ounce of strength for Maude not to go tearing towards that dock to haul her sister off the ship and drag her home. But she had to let her forge her own path, make her own mistakes, even though doing so felt like she herself was dying a little inside.

After just over a year at sea, the public learned that the *Makepeace*'s efforts in the Arctic had been unsuccessful. They'd read all about it in the newspapers that summer— following months frozen in, the ship had splintered in the ice of the Northwest Passage and been forced to limp its way back to London without Franklin, without Franklin's men, and without establishing a navigable route through the Passage from the Atlantic to the Pacific. An indelible failure. No doubt about it. But here it was, on its way home, with Constance safe inside. Or so Maude had believed.

She had been dizzied at the prospect, almost sick with

excitement. As she spent agonizing weeks in the shop waiting, she wondered if she would recognize her sister when she finally saw her. With her short hair and her sea-strengthened limbs, Constance would have been living in the clothes of a boy for over a year. She would have seen things Maude could not even begin to imagine. Ferocious ice bears, the open ocean, the dazzling lights of the famed aurora borealis.

When the day came and the ship's sails, wide like the wings of a dragon, broke the horizon at Woolwich, a cautious murmur rippled across the assembled crowd. It was not a hero's return, but family members had come to greet their loved ones, to welcome them home, to warm their tired, Arctic-frozen bones. The boat took its time to dock, and Maude and Henry watched with their hearts in their throats as men waved from the deck. Others scurried about fastening lines and trimming sails with the unswerving focus of soldier ants. She strained her eyes hard, scoured the assembled crew, searching for a ship's boy with the sharp blue eyes of her sister. She'd hoped that, even in the clothes of a lad she might recognize Constance's movements, the way she held herself, the very bones of her.

It did not alarm her, at first, when she could not see her. The remaining crew would be below decks, she assumed, readying equipment, sorting provisions. Eventually, the ramp thunked down and men began to stream out of the ship's great maw, greeting sweethearts, gathering plum-cheeked children into their arms, or else ploughing their way doggedly to the taverns and brothels that lined the docks. At one point, Henry met Maude's eye and smiled. It caused her to shiver. She'll never forget its well-intentioned falseness.

"Jack Aldridge?" She remembered the name her sister had scrawled in her letter when she left. "Where might I find a Jack Aldridge?" she asked. Her voice sounded flimsy against the wide shoulders of the sailors. Most ignored her, others were not quick enough to hide their raised eyebrows. Officers and seamen pummeled past. Some carried sea chests, others rolled barrels, one even balanced what looked to be the tusk of an elephant across his shoulders. She met the eyes of one unfortunate soul, who appeared to have lost the tip of his nose.

"Jack Aldridge? Have you seen him? Jack Aldridge. Ship's boy." She could barely find the will to croak out the words by the end. The man blinked, removed his hat and dipped his head.

"There!" Her grandfather's eyes were on the landing stage. A tall man in a blue and gold coat stood at the top of the ramp, saluting the crowd like a monarch.

"Despie," said Henry. Her grandfather knew a navy captain when he saw one.

Maude tried to push away the faint keening sound that had struck up in her ears. It came at a ghastly high pitch, growing louder and more obnoxious with every second. She swallowed, grasped her grandfather's hand, and he pulled her through the crowd, focused only on that gleaming blue and gold coat.

They weaved their way to the front just as Captain Despie began his parade down the landing stage. He was flanked by stewards, noses high. One of them, Maude noticed with a stone in her gut, carried a pile of folded clothing in his arms.

"Captain Despie," her grandfather called out once they had reached the bottom of the ramp. The man turned his weather-scoured face towards them. He had a broad nose, Maude still remembers, like a mushroom sliced in half. The skin of his cheeks was red and hard like hide.

"Yes, hello! Thank you for the kind welcome. Hello. Hello." Despie continued past, waving to the paltry crowd.

"We're looking for Jack Aldridge," Maude strained her voice, and they watched as Despie came to a stop, moved his hand to the steward's arm to still him too.

The men turned together. Their faces were swept downwards, as if someone had cast a quick palm over them.

"Repeat the name, please," Despie instructed, not unkindly.

"Jack," Maude said in barely more than a whisper. "Jack Aldridge." She wanted to scream her sister's real name. *Constance. Constance. Constance Horton. She is better than any of you. Where is she?*

Despie fixed her with a strange look. *Does he know?* she thought. *Does he know that Jack is not Jack, but Constance instead?* She half expected him to break into a grin and announce how her sister had fooled them all. The sly girl. What a performance. What a trick. An extra medal, just for being so clever.

But the steward behind him, the one carrying the clothes, coughed and took a step forwards.

"It is with grave regret."

That's all it took.

Maude's world shattered to pieces.

Chapter Three

I t's a tavern, the address. Maude turns over the notecard that Heart had given her four days prior. *THE TWO LUNGS*, the scrawl reads. She raises it towards the sign swinging on a hook in the wind above her head. The same words are emblazoned below two pink-painted organs. *An odd name*, she thinks, as she appraises the building's smart exterior.

She glances over her shoulder, not for the first time. She is anxious, she realizes, to be so far from the pharmacy on her own. Before Constance's death, her life had been small, tightly woven—a cat's cradle arrangement with everything intertwined, pulled taut. Her routines were simple: she would visit the butcher's to collect their meat for dinner; to the bakery, three doors down from the pharmacy, for their fresh bread each morning, returning with warm bags that drew her grandfather's face into a picture of bliss. She and Constance might take a walk around the park now and again to fetch herbs for the tinctures, or visit a lantern show nearby, gaze through shop windows at pretty dresses and expensive kid gloves. But she always knew she would return to the pharmacy, as if she were attached by the waist to it with imperceptible string. She had few friends, save for those who called in weekly for their medicines. Mr. Archer sometimes engaged her in conversation about the primroses at Covent Garden Market, and Mrs. Pye, whose husband owned the Britannia Theatre, regaled the girls with tales of tempestuous stage actresses and backstage bickering. But she had no need for friendships beyond that, not really, not when she had her sister and her grandfather to care for. When Constance had died, Maude had retreated into herself even further, finding it a struggle even to make it to Mr. Kirby's for the fresh loaves. Her grandfather had allowed her the inertia, took that short walk to the baker's himself. It is only now, now she needs answers that are clearly being kept from her, that the string around her waist is loosening.

The boards out front of the tavern, she can just make out in the lamplight, are painted in gold and crimson, fine cursive lettering advertising beer, hot food, and comfortable lodgings. A sifted-flour frost has settled on the paving stones and the light that bleeds out from the windows makes it glitter quite beautifully. There are no drunks clustered at its doorways. No harlots. No rogues. No miscreants. No low deeds afoot in the dark embrace of this tavern's shadows. It looks, she assesses, like somewhere that might be frequented by patrons of quality. She glances down at the gray cotton of her dress, pulls her cape-jacket tight around her shoulders, and steps inside.

Her hunch is quickly proven correct. This is no cheap drinking parlor. The chatter swells around her as a cozy hum. Gentlemen in shirtsleeves, waistcoats, and pocket watches flank tables foaming with ale. Some are engaged in what appears to be heated conversation, making drawings, exchanging ideas, chewing over opinions. There's an energy to the room that is hard to define, an air of anticipation, a sharp and caustic bristle. At the back, a low fire crackles in the grate.

The barman, in oyster shirt and thick apron, slicks back his hair with a palm so that it shines in the dim light of the flames.

There are a few women here, she's heartened to see, thankful that her presence will not appear too anomalous. Although she could certainly never afford these sorts of fabrics. Their silk dresses glow with the vigorous hues of courting rainforest birds.

Maude clings to the walls at first, eyes roaming for the clerk's pale skin and slender shoulders. Drat. She cannot see him. Perhaps he is late? She hopes, for Constance's sake, that he has not had a notion to abandon their meeting entirely.

She is reluctant to take a seat alone and so shuffles along the peripheries of the crowd. On the walls, she starts to notice, are the most unusual pictures. Leaning closer she can discern that they are anatomical sketches. It briefly crosses her mind that she might have stepped into some sort of covert resurrectionists' gathering, although these men do not look the sorts to skulk about low haunts for bodies to purloin and hawk. She looks again at the sketches. One fine pencil drawing depicts a body sliced in two to reveal its riverine nerves and veins. Another, in charcoal, details every tiny bone of a child's hand. She glances at the tables. Men, some with graying sidewhiskers, others flush with the glow of youth, joust with words or tear off pieces of paper covered in scribbles, passing them back and forth like gambling tokens. Beyond them all is a small stage she had not noticed when she entered. A table at its center is draped in baize; atop it: a glass contraption, like a lantern, with a long, green tube attached, leading to a metal mouthpiece. It stirs a whisper of recognition inside Maude, but she cannot quite place it. A chair sits beside the table, patiently waiting for its guest.

She turns back to the wall. Each illustration hangs in a fine gilt frame. Dissected bodies splayed out. Bones, eyeballs, and tongues. There: a close-up sketch of each chamber of the magnificent heart. Here: an old woman, quite deceased, her eyes closed, and stitches hacked across her neck. Maude leans in to read the inscription. *"Esther Hibner (or Hübner) executed at Old Bailey for the murder of a parish apprentice (a girl) by ill treatment and starvation. Monday, 13 April 1829."*

She scours the patrons' faces again, a questioning unease sliding from her gullet to her gut. The room is growing busier by the second, men slipping through the door alone or in tight, animated groups. They bring the frigid air in with them. Maude shivers, wonders briefly if she should leave. But she must stay. She needs answers. She is so very close. She is sure of it.

As if called forth by her conviction, the door swings open and through it strides Francis Heart himself. She watches as he nods a few hellos to the tables, then as he lifts that fair head to search for her. Their eyes meet and the clerk gestures at a table towards the back of the room, furthest from the stage. Above it, on the wall, a large metal saw is encased in a polished display cabinet.

"I am glad you came, Ms. Horton." Heart smiles thinly as she takes a seat, then does the same himself. He gestures to the barman with two raised fingers, then rests his chin on his fist and fixes her in the eye. He seems comfortable in this place, never questioning his belonging the way she does. He is a man, she supposes, and men appear to feel comfortable wherever they are; still, she wonders how an admiralty clerk fits into such a place as this.

"My brother is a surgeon." He has sensed her curiosity. "The Royal College is just up the road. They all drink here. Hence the . . . paraphernalia." He waves his hands at the walls.

No body snatchers then, but Maude wonders why he should

want to meet somewhere so public. He could have asked her to wait in another alley. He could have relayed her sister's message four days ago, when they first met. Why here? Why now? The questions needle and she finds herself pulling at the skin between her thumb and forefinger, an old habit.

The barman arrives with two ales. Maude puts the cup to her mouth. It gives her time to think.

"A strange place to meet." She places the cup on the table eventually and wipes the liquid from her top lip.

Heart nods. "Sometimes hiding from the crowds draws more attention than it detracts." He leans suddenly towards her, lowers his voice.

"Everyone has eyes on everyone in London," he whispers, eyes wide, "especially those less salubrious characters, and if that is the case the best way to hide is to not hide at all."

Maude smiles tightly, thinking it best at this stage not to point out that she has no idea who they are supposed to be hiding from. She watches the muscles in his jaw contract and thinks of the illustrations on the walls. Tendons, ligaments, and veins. "No one will remember we were even here," he continues. "Not after tonight anyway." He nods at the stage, to the strange lantern with its tube and mouthpiece. A broad man in a leather apron is setting out a tray of equipment. She squints, makes out a set of needles and silk, a long, sharp blade.

But she must not be distracted. "Mr. Heart, the messa—"

"*GENTLEMEN*," a voice booms from the front of the room. Maude's head whips back to the stage. The broad man is addressing the crowd. "*And a few strong-stomached ladies, I see. How modern. Welcome, welcome to our little . . . presentation.*"

The crowd murmurs and heckles.

"What is this?" she asks Heart, fighting alarm.

"Could be any procedure, knowing this lot," he chuckles.

"I've seen eye surgery before, the resetting of bones, some boring dental work. But if there's ether involved, it'll get lively."

Ether. Sweet vitriol. That must be what the lantern is for. Not a lantern at all; a Squire's inhaler. That's right. She knows ether, of course, is familiar with its uses for pain relief and, increasingly, according to her grandfather, experimental surgery in America. She knows of its other purported effects—its dizzying, hallucinatory qualities when the vapor is inhaled. Not that she has experienced it herself, she cannot imagine such frightful loss of control. But when she was a child, gentlemen would visit the pharmacy to buy ether for their frolics. Honorable men, physicians, surgeons, wanting entertainment for their parties. When they left, Henry would turn to the girls and raise a finger to the ceiling, "They'll be as high as a kite tonight!"

The surgeon, for Maude presumes he is that, clears his throat and raises an arm to beckon his volunteer to the stage. A young man with disheveled hair extinguishes a limp cigarette, staggers towards the table, and reaches greedily for the inhaler. The attention of every man and woman in the room is tugged firmly towards the stage.

That works for her. She turns and presses Heart again.

"The message?"

Jeers volley around the tables as the surgeon rolls back the young man's sleeve to reveal a taut and sinewy forearm.

"The message?" she probes again, more urgently, but Heart has already leaned behind him to reach into the pocket of his coat.

On stage, the man is gulping at the ether, the chamber a great glass proboscis looming in front of his face. His head soon begins to loll, falling heavily backwards, his features slackening, his pale neck exposed. The audience watches with intent, oblivious to the item that Heart hands to Maude under the table, instructing her to keep it there, out of sight.

She steals a glance. It is, as it turns out, a book. She clutches at its hard cover, running her fingers over the leather, searching for clues. The walls of the room seem to have closed in ever so slightly.

"I shall now make an incision of several inches along the fore-arm here."

Maude is possessed with the need to tear open the pages, to know just why she is here.

"The tendons will be exposed and manipulated, but as you shall see, the patient will not experience any pain at all!"

Impressed chatter swells around the pub.

"Yes, yes, then I'll pass round the ether. We'll see what secrets you lot have been hiding."

Maude grips even tighter, as if the book might take flight and hurtle out the door and into the cold.

Heart leans in again, close enough so that she can smell the beer on his hot breath. "The diary you hold in your hands was written by a Master Jack Aldridge, ship's boy, aboard the HMS *Makepeace*."

Maude's heart leaps into a frantic skitter.

"Of course, we know that it was not actually written by a Master Jack Aldridge . . ."

"Why do you have it? How?" Maude demands. Her mind hurtles back to that day on the dock, the steward handing her Constance's clothes. A strange necklace. The way the ground seemed to come apart beneath her feet.

Why was she not given the diary if it belonged to Constance? To "Jack"?

"It was returned to the admiralty office, to Hancock directly, by Captain Despie," Heart explains. "I saw it happen and I knew, then, that it must hold information that they did not like."

The skitter in her chest has broadened to an almighty thud. "What sort of information?"

Heart pauses, flicks his eyes around the room.

"Read it for yourself."

"And here we have the median nerve, and if I just give that a little poke . . ."

Then, as if everything else in the room has been swallowed up, her focus is suddenly sharpened. "But. Why are you giving this to me?" That question she cannot ignore. If Hancock did not like what was in the diary, why did he not destroy it? Did Constance truly write it? After all, this could just be a trap set by the admiralty. Another dissuasive tactic. She turns, half expecting Hancock and his medallioned stooges to burst through the door. Heart could well be in on it, too. She has no reason to trust him.

"It is only fair and right that you know what happened to your sister, Ms. Horton. Anyone deserves that, and what's written on these pages suggests that it was more than you, or even I, are being told."

"Look at the fingers wiggle. And not a grimace or a flinch from h—, from h—. Ah. Might somebody help me with this? A mop?"

"Mr. Heart," she addresses the clerk plainly, "you cannot expect me to simply accept that you would do such a thing for a stranger, for that is what we are to one another. I shall repeat the question. Why are you giving me this book?"

The clerk looks briefly taken aback. He brushes his fingers against the lapels of his jacket, his eyes swerving to the stage where an apprentice is hunched on all fours mopping up large pools of blood.

He sighs slowly through his nose.

"Hancock is a bully and a bigot."

Ah.

"Working with him is like having a manacle placed around one's neck and slowly tightened."

A simple case of vengeance. One-upmanship, even. She should have suspected.

"But what exists in the pages of this diary does not cast Sir Hancock in a positive light," he continues, gesturing towards her with a finger. "If it were revealed that he sent that ship into the Northwest Passage not, indeed, to search for Sir John Franklin, but to search for something else entirely, it would bring great shame on him and the admiralty. *That* is why he locked it away. But"—he leans back, crotch to the ceiling, impressed with himself—"I was able to get to it. To take it."

"If it would bring such shame, then why did Hancock keep it?" She *wants* it to be true. She so profoundly wants the words to be Constance's words. But she is a woman who must assess risk, make a plan. "Why did he not have it destroyed?"

"Leverage." He clasps thin fingers together. "Blackmail. To keep others in a bind. To protect himself."

Maude scoffs but she cannot deny she is intrigued. "Protect himself from what?"

"Exposure." Heart seems almost aggrieved to have to explain it further. "To preserve his role at the admiralty. There are far greater things at play here, Ms. Horton. As you'll see. Things that could be very damaging if revealed."

"Fetch my poodle!"

The surgeons are taking it in turns to suck on the remaining ether and the room is slowly fracturing into chaos.

"Someone on the ship, an ice master, Mance—you'll read about him in the very pages of that diary—was found dead just last week."

Maude considers it, shrugs. People die. Her sister died. Her parents died. Yet she is expected to continue living. Why should she care about this "Mance"—the death of a man she has never met?

"Mance is a big man. A beast. Obstinately healthy. Should have outlasted us all. Yet he was found slumped at a dockside tavern table, his face in a plate of cold mutton stew."

Maude stares at him. Blinks.

"I suspect foul play," says Heart.

"Richardson, your face is melting!"

"What do you mean, foul play?" Her patience is running out. She wants the link to her sister. She is here for Constance. She wants to read the diary.

"Poisoning, most likely," continues Heart. He doesn't even have to say it quietly; his words are smothered by the din of the frolicking men. "Something untraceable."

Carbolic acid, chloroform, arsenic trioxide—all untraceable, thinks Maude. Well, almost untraceable.

"Eeeeeeeeeeeeeeeeeh."

The men are giddy with the ether, hollering, singing, swaying. Others seem to be, if Maude's ears don't betray her, confessing their deepest, darkest, albeit incoherent, desires. She glances around at them, embarrassed by their louche behavior, their lack of control. She'd heard of the drug referred to as truth potion before but had never truly believed it.

She is still not satisfied with Heart's explanation though. "Why did you not just take the diary to Hancock's superior? Destroy him that way, if that is your intent?"

"Two reasons." Heart shifts on his elbows. "One, Hancock has no superior. He designed it that way. And two, I suspect it is foul play coming from *inside* the admiralty office. I suspect it goes further than Hancock."

"The police, then?"

He clasps pale hands together again.

"More than two reasons for that one. Many reasons." He gestures to the book below the table. "That diary alone is not enough, for a start. There are gaps that need filling. Answers required. Official documents needed."

"You could tell them what you know, tell them of the poisoning . . ."

Antimony. Potassium chlorate. Strychnine.

"Ms. Horton." He clears his throat. "I do not wish to offend your sensibilities, but men like me do not make it their habit to put themselves in the path of the police."

He casts an eye over his shoulder.

"They are not particularly friendly towards those who favor less . . . conventional pastimes."

Well Maude knows what that means, but still: why is he sharing such information with her? She is nothing to him.

"Look. Ms. Horton." He senses her reluctance. "What if I told you there was someone mentioned in this diary who I believe played a hand in your sister's death."

The world goes quiet.

"When you read it, I imagine you will draw the same conclusion."

"Who is it?" Every inch of her skin feels suddenly hot.

He leans in again. "A man named Edison Stowe. I believe he has links to this . . . conspiracy. Or cover-up. Or scheme, whatever it is."

"Where is he now?" She goes to lift the diary onto the table, she must know what it says about this man, this "Stowe."

"He is easily found." He pushes the book back down with a flat palm. "I need you to trail him."

"Mr. Heart." She is already shaking her head. "I am not capable of—"

"Ms. Horton. You have been blessed with something valuable: you are a woman." She frowns. The clerk has clearly never given any thought to what it is actually like to be a woman. "That, and your . . . social standing means you can get by unnoticed."

She waits.

"I don't think this man would react quite as well to being followed by me as he would to being followed by *you*." He opens two palms towards her, as if she is an item on display at an auction house.

He lowers his voice conspiratorially. "Wouldn't you like to know how Constance really died?"

She cannot speak, her mind is clogged. Heavy. But she will do anything to get to the truth. She knows that.

A body crashes into their table and folds slowly to the floor, then from its crumpled position, stiffens suddenly and howls like a banshee.

Heart leans closer. "In trailing this Stowe, in making his acquaintance, in encouraging him to confess to the circumstances of your sister's death, you could also provide *me* with more concrete information about Hancock's involvement." He smiles quickly. "That information could direct me towards any paper trail, any documents, any official agreements et cetera, et cetera that could be used against him."

Maude swallows. She cares little for Heart's petty pursuit of vengeance, but she can feel something new and indecipherable stir deep within her.

"If you need funds, I can provide you with funds."

"Thank you for the information, Mr. Heart. I shall consider it."

She knows, already, that she will do it.

He nods, not appearing completely gratified.

"I would ask that you do something for me in return," she adds.

He tilts his head.

"You said your brother was a surgeon?"

"That's right."

"I need the name of the surgeon on the *Makepeace*. He's likely the last person to have viewed Constance's body."

"Mr. Sedgewick, yes. He is mentioned in the diary."

Drat. That was easier than she thought. Has she shown her cards too early? She straightens her shoulders, makes another play. "Could your brother get a letter to him?"

"I'm sure he could try."

She feels that she is standing with her toes tipped over the edge of a very large cliff.

"And how might I find this man, this Edison Stowe?" She blinks away the vertigo.

"Read that diary and you'll be banging down his door, I assure you." Heart reaches into his pocket and pulls out a card.

On it, a picture of a skeleton, and an address.

The Journal of Jack Aldridge

●————————————————●

58.7°N, 3.2°W
Pentland Firth
15 May 1849

I WRITE THIS BY LANTERNLIGHT, tucked like a woodlouse
into my hammock in the dark belly of the *Makepeace*.
Rumpelstiltskin, the ship's cat, has wedged the small furnace
of his body into the space beneath my elbow. He is quite
content, purring idly as I scribble, the sleep noises of the
men filling the fo'c'sle around us from board to beam.

The *Makepeace* is a ship larger than any I have seen, and
she creaks and groans like a beast with cold, tired bones.
Above, she still has the smell of wood shavings and varnish
about her, the stench below decks, however, is enough to
make the eyes stream—burning whale oil, the filth of men,
mouldering clothes, and dank pails of urine cast about.

It's cramped down here, the space humming and ticking
with the intensity of men squashed in together. We lash up
our hammocks nightly and the tables for supper come down
from the ceiling on chains. There's little room to walk, save
for two narrow aisles which run along the hull at either side.
With less than six feet of headroom, the taller men exist in
perpetual hunched-over agony. Thankfully, I have no such
problem.

Even in daylight you'll find men slumbering down here—
those on night watch snatching rest or stokers spent from

feeding the coal-burner for hours. As a cabin boy, I've yet to
be assigned a night watch, but I'll soon prove to Despie and
the lieutenants that I can be trusted with the task.

There is no silence on this ship, even at night; men move
about at all hours, grumbling, singing, conversing. Mr. Penny,
the cook, seems himself to never sleep at all, baking biscuits
and stirring stews at his glowing stove well into the smallest
hours. I can hear him now, in the tiny galley next to the
fo'c'sle, mumbling shanties through the pipe stem clamped
forever between his teeth. It's a comfort to hear it. It reminds
me of Grandfather at his bench, and I can fancy I may not be
quite so far away from home after all.

If you were to push through the double doors and
climb the short man-ladder up to deck, you would see
that we are surrounded at present by the flinty waters of
the Pentland Firth. The air swarms with gulls, tossed like
white pebbles, their cries merging with the tinny whistle
of the wind. At night, the skies above us dim only slightly,
quick clouds veiling a bright fragmented moon, circled by
stars.

Our mission is to uncover the fate of Sir John Franklin,
as well as his two missing ships, and all 129 missing men.
I've been following Franklin's story for the past four years
now, ever since he first cast off his lines and set out for the
mysterious North Waters. I may not be this ship's intended
cabin boy, but I will make myself useful on this journey. I feel
most deeply that we will find the men alive, and their ships
quite intact—what glory that would bring! I can picture the
medal. Feel its cool weight already.

We'll be following Franklin's path, through Baffin Bay
and Lancaster Sound, towards King William Island,

where we'll commence our search proper, scouring the land and seas for cairns, messages and caches, any sign of life at all.

Captain Despie commands our ship with First Lieutenant Marshall below him. They are impressive leaders, both: forthright, unswerving in their focus, and immune to the sort of melancholy that occupies some of the other men on this ship.

The *High Regard* is led by Commander Forsyth and our ships will travel together into the Arctic as if held in place by string. The nearest white men, Despie says, are Hudson's Bay Company fur traders, some seven hundred miles away, across the bleakest, most unforgiving terrain on earth.

Despie knelt to splay a map onto the deck one morning. I strained on tiptoes to peer over the men's shoulders, the sting of salt and spindrift fresh on my cheeks. He traced out our route, running a finger over land and seas, until it reached the top of the map where the lines dissolved from their solid crispness into a yawning expanse of white.

Lady Jane Franklin has already proven herself to be indomitable in orchestrating the search for her husband and his men from back home in England. Although she is a seafarer too. A leader. Just like Jeanne Baret, disguised aboard the ship *L'Étoile*, or the guide Sacagawea, leading men through the uncharted lands of the American West! I know I have it within me to be like that. If I must appear as a man, at first, to prove it then let it be thus.

That's not to say I have not been fearful of my position. Indeed, I was quite paralyzed by the surety of discovery as soon as I set foot on this ship. As the rowboat sculled across the Thames towards the waiting brig two weeks ago, as I climbed the roped ladder up to deck and was shoved, by a barking first officer, down below to find my berth, I was certain it would be only minutes before my game was up and I'd be sent marching back to the docks. Surely they would take one look at me—my slim shoulders, the strawberry hue to my cheeks—and I would be ordered to gather my possessions and leave, head bowed in shame.

To my astonishment, it did not happen.

I had prepared well, I suppose, spending weeks considering how best I might disguise myself as a man. I studied the gentlemen that perused the shelves at the pharmacy, committing to memory their relaxed gait, the way they held themselves as a thing to be inspected and admired. From that first day on the *Makepeace*, I kept my chest lifted, my shoulders broad, and my legs wide. I made myself comfortable in my ship's clothing, thankful for the layers that such work at sea demands. On colder evenings, when the setting sun turned the sky the color of lavender heads, I'd see that, in that strange sort of twilight, all bodies look the same, even mine.

Now, I keep my chest bound daily with flannel salvaged from the purser's rags, and even when sweating with toil, I do not unbutton my sleeves or allow myself the relief of loosening the neck of my shirt. A funnel contraption, crudely fashioned from a length of tin, allows me to urinate standing as the other men do; and when I bleed, I will be sure to stash the soiled rags deep at the bottom of my sea chest.

So, I am careful, yes, yet I also take comfort in the knowledge that men care little about the body of a ship's boy. They care even less about the pitch of his voice on the rare occasions he might be induced, or allowed, to speak. I am

invisible to them. I am beneath them. Nothing. And so my
low station has become my saving grace.

My hands are changing by the day, growing blistered,
hard, and calloused. At night I hold them to my face and
inspect their grooves with awe, running my fingers over
every bit of hardened skin and every crack. My arms,
too, are becoming lean and taut, strengthening under the
weight of axes, ropes, and harnesses. The days pass with an
endless rotation of duties: holystoning the decks, shoveling,
hammering, always repairing something. Despie is a private
soul, and so once I've helped Cook with the bread and
cocoa for breakfast, assisted the captain with his toilet and
tipped away his shaving water, I'm left, largely, to my own
preoccupations and concerns. I try to make myself helpful
on deck, to show my quick learning, my acceptance of hard
toil. I so long to learn the compass, to know how to heave the
lead like the other men. I am drawn very much to the team
of nimble topmen who spend their days as high as the birds.
Led by Adams, a pensive man with a soft Irish brogue, they
work the highest rigging, topsail, and topgallant yards whether
day or night, in the highest seas, whatever the weather. I
am small, of course, and it didn't take much to prove my
agility to Adams. And so he allows me to assist, on occasion,
when one of the other men needs rest. That cobweb of lines
seemed impossible to navigate at first, but now I feel as
natural in the crow's nest, watching the ocean stretch around
me, as I do behind the till in Grandfather's shop.

———•———

Maude sits with the diary in her hands, spent, her restless foot
tapping a quick nervous beat on the floorboards.

Her room, this room that she shared with Constance, still rings with her sister's presence. Constance can be felt in the walls, the boards, the linen, in the small and neatly made bed, which she'd pretended was itself a tiny boat when she was a child. No one has slept in it since her sister left. No one has sat on it, even touched it. Maude won't allow it. If she looks closely, she can still see the shape of her sister's head sunk into the pillow, she can still pull away a single long, dark hair, left behind.

She can remember finding the letter the morning Constance left, the remains of her sister's braid—crudely severed with scissors—laid out neatly beside it on the counterpane. Maude's fingers had shaken as she'd opened the envelope. Within, Constance had explained how she had manufactured her plan, how she had stolen the place of someone else bound for that ship, the young Jack Aldridge's place, forging a letter from the admiralty to his family, explaining that his services were greatly appreciated but no longer necessary as the ship's company was full. There were apologies from her sister, of course, expressions of love, but the words had twirled around Maude's head, flighty, ungraspable.

She looks at the diary again. It still makes her head spin, to read Constance's words; some of them are hard to swallow.

I do not yet yearn for home.

Now, that line stung. Like being swiped by a shard of glass. She continues to read . . .

FOR IF YOU WERE TO stroll about this ship, you'd see it's just like London here. Everything in stark contrast: seamen forward, officers aft; us stuffed into our lamp-jaundiced space—just like the city's rookeries and slums—then the officers' Great Room to the stern, where they drink whisky and idly shuffle chess pieces about. Their spacious cabins are the Baker Streets, the gleaming Portman Squares, with their mahogany writing bureaus, shining inkwells, and washbasins.

These officers (handsome, clean, wealthy) fringed with gold like ambulant Christmas trees, walk fore to aft at a slow pace, hands clasped behind their backs as if strolling the corridors of a museum. It is as if they do not see us. The invisibles. Hurrying around them. Manning the yards. Sweating, toiling, trying.

As with any city, you'll find all stripes of men: noble men, ruined men, hardworking men, men hardened to all climates and all fatigues, men destined for great and noteworthy things, slovens and saints, squashed in together and sprinkled with salt like fish in a tin. I feel quite sure that there must be dangerous men here too. Whispers that pass between the plates at supper warn of men born bad. Men who've been sloughed into roughness by lives at sea. Men who've chased down whales in Nantucket, spearing them right through their blowholes, watching their blood shoot in crimson arcs across the sky.

But there are good men here too. On board is a surgeon, a Mr. Sedgewick. A man with bright, intelligent eyes, whose sick bay, tucked into the forepeak, is filled with the very bottles that line the shelves of the pharmacy. I find myself dwelling whenever I pass that door, inhaling the familiar herby odor of oregano oil and camphor. I so long to step inside, to scan his cabinets, to search for the distinctive crystal shapes of salicylic acid, the red resin of dragon's blood.

He caught me lurking, the other day, and I was most chastened. But he did not order me away. Instead, he smiled, his thick, black side-whiskers lifting, the light from the bulkhead lamp bouncing off the clean glass in his spectacles. I slipped away, however, too shy to speak, too sure that my curiosity would be taken for girlishness, and I'd be exposed.

It would take so very little for my secret to be uncovered here: an ill-timed slip of a button, a dropped rag, a snaking trail of suspicion. But I shall remain careful, private as a clam. I'll keep my gaze down, my comforter tight and my thoughts tilted inwards. This diary shall remain hidden, away from everyone's eyes but mine. I will keep myself safe, I will keep my position on this ship safe. I am Jack Aldridge, ship's boy, and I'm here to carry out this glorious mission.

———•————•———

The bond that is shared between sisters can be a cruel thing, Maude thinks as she closes the pages of the diary once more. Different to the love you read about in novels. Instead, it is a quiet love. An inevitability. A love that exists just as air exists. Just as the sky exists. The earth. A love that doesn't inspire poetry or songs but without which all else loses its meaning. With Constance gone, Maude had lost the very center of her earth. How cruel that such a thing exists. How cruel that it can be taken from her, just like that.

She had always felt a responsibility, had *welcomed* the responsibility, to care for Constance. She had placed Constance first, concerned herself only with Constance, prioritized Constance. To the detriment of herself, but she did not care. She could not exist if her sister did not exist, she was sure of that. After her parents died, caring was what she did. What did she have to offer anyone if not that?

Constance's wants were of adventure, a heady need for escape. Maude had seen her pore over stories of Lady Franklin. Seen her scour every broadside, every book, every public notice about the expedition. Her sister was always taken with sensation, with passion. She kept a stash of penny bloods under her bed, away from her grandfather's disapproving eyes. She inhaled their tales of murderous baronets, of pirates and shipwrecks, stories of women with knives, foreign princesses. Constance's life was filled with emotion and color, with one-woman plays performed for her patient sister and grandfather, with strange superstitions and fanciful rumor. "Don't ever walk over a trapdoor," she'd tell Maude with flashing, excitable eyes, "you'll fall through it into an underground lair, and you'll be robbed, killed, and your body sold to the doctors!" She had found impersonation easy. Here! It is Joan of Arc with her holy sword. Nay! It's Mary Anning, the fossil finder, arms laden with the heavy bones of her great lizards. Maude had never felt comfortable dressing in the clothes of another. She felt choked by the pretense. Throat stopped by truth.

Then, one day, Constance had simply left. The stories ceased and all that color had been sucked from their lives. Maude's first response, although she is ashamed to remember it now, had been fury. What selfishness from her sister, what reckless-ness, what sheer misguided folly to simply leave them here alone. How were they to cope? Maude had spent her life tying her sister close to her. Constance had carelessly snipped the bind. Maude had never felt so betrayed.

In the shop out front, the morning sun winks in through colored glass, casting gemstone shadows in the dust on the shelves. Maude had stayed up all night reading the diary. She knows every word of it now, has run her fingers over every single brush of ink, feverishly reading and rereading every single line. Blurry-eyed and parched, she had searched among her sister's words for some coded message, probing into any disguised name or hidden meaning.

But she hadn't needed to.

Heart was right. It was all quite clear.

She picks up the book again with aching hands and flicks steadily through the pages, the deep scores of her own pencil marks bold among her sister's words. The scores designate the same thing, underlined again and again. Ah. She has missed one; she reaches for the old, chewed pencil. With force she draws a line under the two words.

Edison Stowe, they read. *Edison Stowe. Edison Stowe. Edison Stowe.*

Chapter Four

Edison
OCTOBER 1850

The stairs down to Inchbold's shop creak like sheet ice underfoot. Edison descends slowly, bending to wiggle a rotting board with long fingers. He sucks his teeth. He'll have to fix it himself if he's to be lodging here a while. The man seems far too preoccupied with his specimens to entertain matters of safety.

Outside, London is already awake and streaming quickly past the shop window—a steady blur of suits, hats, cabs, and horses. Against it, the large gold lettering stands out. The words appear backwards when read from the inside.

MR. INCHBOLD'S BONES

The skeletons are sallow in the paltry morning light. Their bones fill the entire shop, some complicatedly assembled and stacked atop each other on buffed plinths, others positioned on the raised window platform to better display the allure of the animals. Edison hops off the final step and moves towards the cheetah, newly sourced from Tanganyika, procured by a professor whom Inchbold must have paid most handsomely for the service.

He crouches easily and assesses the assembled bones. The animal has been staged as if in motion. Two legs raised as if the skin simply scurried on ahead. He rises and scans the room for his own spoils: the bones of a ring seal suspended on chains from the ceiling; in the corner, a duo—a white Arctic fox mother with the delicate skeleton of her kit. He remembers them well. For a moment, he can still discern the ammoniacal reek of boiling viscera. He smiles, recalling the delicate beauty of sinew as it falls from bone.

A key rattles in the lock.

"Ah, he's alive." George Inchbold pushes in through the door, newspaper fastened under his arm. He tosses the key, without a glance, onto a polished silver plate, held in position by an imposing taxidermy bear. It stands on two large feet beside the doorway, the only animal in this shop to be blessed with fur. Edison had balked when he'd first seen the bear, "Frederick," muzzle pulled back exposing large yellow teeth. But customers, he soon observed, adored the bizarre curiosity, and whatever Inchbold arranged on that plate—business cards, advertising pamphlets, sweets—all disappeared in the beat of a bird's wing.

Inchbold's cap is low, casting his face, scored with the lines of middle age, in deep shadow, making him appear far more severe than he truly is. A dog trots in behind him, a lurcher, long limbs as quick as liquid, muzzle grizzled with wiry salt and pepper hairs.

"Livingstone." Inchbold calls the dog to heel, moving it gently from the skeleton of a juvenile chimpanzee. Mounted on its poles like that, Edison had always thought, made the ape look rather like the remains of a boy. Each skeleton in the shop has been sourced from Inchbold's curated network of collectors—friends from the Zoological Society bringing him hippopotamus skulls and the fragile carcasses of lemurs.

Colleagues returned from expeditions in the jungles of South America hoisting snakes double his length onto the counter, seeing what price they might get for the delicate bones inside.

When Edison returned from the Arctic in the summer, there had been vultures waiting for him in London. He had not one coin in his pocket to hold them off, but he did have something far more valuable than a handful of metal. He had an Arctic rarity, a legendary item that would have the collectors clamoring.

He had met Inchbold on several brief occasions in his lifetime. They had spoken at Society lectures, before Edison had been so unfairly ejected, shared an interest in the somewhat controversial work of Professor Owen. Neither man had lived up to their academic ambitions, and Edison could see that Inchbold carried the weight of that failure within him. They found, in one another, a kindred spirit; if one is not accepted in certain circles, he must seek out those who do recognize his talents.

Edison had heard that George Inchbold had a shop, and so with the sting of the Arctic still fresh on his skin, he waited patiently in line as other hopefuls touted their spoils at the till. They all came with "the rarest and most singular curiosity." But Inchbold batted them away. He was a man with specific tastes, a yearning for verisimilitude. He was not interested in falsifications—a monkey's arms fastened to the rib cage of an aardvark; the tiny head of a hummingbird passed off as a fairy's skull. He wanted surprise, he wanted rarity, and he wanted authenticity. Edison stepped forward and offered him all three.

"The tusk of the narwhal!" Inchbold had gasped when Edison had drawn the blanket away, revealing his treasure. "The sea unicorn. How did you get hold of this? Actually, forget that. How much do you want for it?"

"I want half of what you make on it," Edison bargained. "I want your full discretion, and I want that room." He gestured to the advert for lodgings affixed to the counter.

He could have sold the tusk quickly of course, paid back some of what he owed, even though it would likely have only made the tiniest of dents in his debts. Men of all tastes frequented the Society lectures: private anatomists; those in search of circus curiosities; men with singular interests, bulging cabinets, and wonder rooms. Lurking at its peripheries were those who favored the darker crevices of nature's body. The insatiable and the relentless, those who sought mutations, anomalies and aberrations. But Inchbold had been certain that waiting for exactly the right buyer would bring them even greater riches. He knew men who'd pay through the back teeth for such a specimen, they just had to wait for the right time.

Edison watches as the dog turns on its spot three times then makes for the corner of the room. Inchbold shrugs off his coat and hangs it carefully on the stand. Edison knows the man well enough now to sense that he has something to say. His stiff shoulders, his ever-wringing hands, give him away. Edison waits and, at length, the man turns, a deep line forged across the top of his nose. Here we go.

"They've been round here again."

Edison feels his throat constrict. Which one was it? Was it Him, as per their arrangement, or was it one of the other lackeys sniffing around?

"I can't keep making excuses for you. I shouldn't have to. Really." Inchbold says the last word with a jab of his finger, then he stuffs it back into its pocket.

Edison pictures the lean figure of the moneylender but finds the details in his mind blurred and unspecific. That's the danger, that lack. A normalcy that allows a person to become swallowed by the rest of London town. To look at Lucian Carter is to look upon a gentleman. Waistcoat and side-whiskers. Expensive buttons, black beaver hat, and shining shoes. But Carter is no gentleman. He is the puppet master of some of the most unforgiving men in London.

With a flicker of discomfort, Edison imagines timid Inchbold explaining to Carter's men that the person they seek is, yet again, unaccounted for. He imagines their vinegary faces. Inchbold's nervous hands twisting into fists.

Guilt curdles in his belly.

Inchbold hadn't had to be kind when Edison, hollow-cheeked and frostbitten, installed himself in the room above the shop. But he had done whatever he could to make him welcome in his home. Edison had gobbled up that kindness without thought—his mind still suspended in that vast, frozen wasteland. But once his thoughts had begun slowly to thaw, Edison attempted to make himself comfortable. He had arranged, first of all, for a small looking glass to be hung, and had asked Inchbold to clear some space in the long closet for his coats. When he'd opened it one morning, he had been alarmed to find an entire human skeleton impaled on a pole.

"Old doctor's specimen," Inchbold had muttered when Edison had probed him over supper. "No room in the shop. Throws things off." Edison had parted his lips and tipped a spoonful of bouillon down his throat, thinking of the skeleton's sunken eye sockets watching him.

Inchbold had sensed his pause, placed down his cutlery.

"I shall move him somewhere else," he promised. "Right away."

Edison runs his hands roughly through his curls.

"I can only apologize, George, really." He swallows dryly,

thinking of the debts. Thinking of the weight of them on his poor, tired shoulders. In the corner of the room, Livingstone stirs, lifts his nose to sniff the air. A flash of gray-brown darts across the floor, then dawdles a while near the toe bones of an aye-aye. Without pause, Edison crosses the room, raises his foot, and brings down his boot. The mouse succumbs with a piteous shriek, its body pulped into the boards.

"I will have the money for him, for you, soon. I just . . ." Edison raises his boot to inspect the bloodied sole. Tuts. "I need a little more time."

Inchbold's mouth hangs open and there's a long silence as Edison hops towards Livingstone and scrapes the remains of the rodent onto the floor beside the dog.

"Carter is not a good man," Inchbold warns once he has recovered his jaw.

Edison knows Carter is not a good man, he knows Carter would have him killed immediately, were it not for his own nimble thinking. "I have a show tonight," he counters.

"It will not end well if you keep him waiting much longer."

The sound of bones crunching drifts from Livingstone's corner.

"I'm sure it will be better attended than the last." Edison persists. "Anyway, any more offers on the tusk?"

Inchbold tuts. It's a question he has answered many times. Inchbold wants to wait for the Exhibition now, Edison knows that, although it would help get them both out of this bind if he just sold the damn thing. He had even offered, at one point, to sell the specimen to Inchbold outright; he would just take the money, move on, find somewhere else to live. But the man had refused; he seemed to like the power that shared ownership allowed him. It was as if he had Edison in a bind and was very happy about that indeed. With all the international interest the Exhibition would bring, Inchbold could strengthen his scientific standing too, put a collection of his bones together, command a higher price for everything. Edison also has a niggling suspicion that Inchbold is keeping the tusk in the shop to draw in more customers, to increase his chances of selling his more pedestrian items. But he *had* hoped that the small matter of Lucian Carter breathing down their necks might entice him to change his mind by now.

"Carter has killed before, you know." Inchbold moves across the shop floor. Livingstone's eyes follow. Inchbold bends and inspects the Indian bear, *Melursus ursinus*, a hairline crack running from the top of the skull to the right orbital socket.

"And I have to protect the animals." He says it like an apology.

Edison knows the tone means that he is off the hook for a little while longer. He allows his shoulders to relax.

"There are men who want their hands on these things," Inchbold says, gesturing around the shop, lowering his voice to a whisper. "*Bad men.*"

Edison makes a show of nodding in agreement.

"They're very valuable to the collectors. I'm taking a risk by letting you stay here."

"I will sort it. I assure you." Edison takes a bank note from his coat pocket and holds it out. "Please, take this small amount as a gesture of my intent to repay what is owed as promptly as possible."

Inchbold reluctantly takes the note, opening the till and tucking it safely inside a drawer with a rattle. The motion sets the tusk, suspended above the desk, swaying gently back and forth. Edison grits his teeth. He had expected Inchbold to refuse the money. He'll have to forego a cab to the show later.

"In fact," he says, recovering his resolve, "I'm quite sure I'll have cheering news on my return from the bank." He reaches for his hat and gives a farewell nod. He pushes open the door and allows himself a cautious glance back at Inchbold, but the man has already moved on, polishing the plinths with his thinning duster.

The streets are busy, even this early, and Edison is engulfed by the grimy sway of the city. Bodies brush past him at speed, smiting with shoulders, pummeling him back and forth like flotsam. He strains his neck in annoyance, chin jutted forward, then he draws a deep breath and joins the flow.

It took a while for Edison Stowe to become accustomed to the streets of London again. Because waking every morning to the clean waters of the Northwest Passage had been really rather different to this smog and smut. Icebergs the size of cathedrals had loomed crystalline on the horizon, fractured and serrated but powerful enough to crush the *Makepeace* into matchwood nonetheless. At sea, surrounded by so much ice, there was very little to smell in the air. In London, with so much blood and muck and shit, you needed plugs to prevent it all invading your nostrils.

When he reaches the bank, the clerk beckons him in with a perfunctory wave. Now, *this* place suits his tastes just perfectly. It smells like polish and expansive leather-topped desks: the pleasing fume of money. Edison sinks into it all like a bath. But fewer than two minutes later, he's back out the door. Head stooped, stinging with the gall of it.

"Not a suitable candidate for a loan."

For shame! Not a suitable candidate? If they do not consider *him* a suitable candidate for a loan, only the lord knows what exorable lice they are tossing their money at. He pushes away thoughts from "Before." Thoughts of the grand, heartless house he inherited from his mother when she died. How he'd filled those empty rooms with nights spent glugging warm brandy. How his hold on his money, his mother's money, had loosened over the years until it had fallen from his grasp entirely.

The ship was supposed to be an escape from everything. But now he was back right where he began.

He swallows, blinks. Something cold and heavy settles across his shoulders. If he cannot return what he owes, he knows Carter will stop at nothing to extract his penance. Edison's "solution" to hold him at bay, his secret agreement, is only a temporary stopgap. Something to buy him just a little more time. It won't hold forever. He thinks back to the moneylender's shining shopfront. Thought you might find Carter down a back alley? Pshaw! He prefers to gloat in plain sight while his cockroaches scuttle through the gutters of St. Giles's and Devil's Acre. Carter presents himself as a gentleman, and nobody would suspect a gentleman of charging such extortionate rates of interest. Nobody would suspect a gentleman of slicing off thumbs or branding the softest parts of the body with his own initials.

He's killed before. Whatever it takes to get what he's owed.

Hopeless, he allows his back to rest against a nearby wall. Beside him, a man with no hat scours the phlegm from his throat and launches a filmy green gob into the gutter. Louse. Edison turns away in disgust just as a large man barrels past and almost bowls him off his feet.

He feels a thread inside of him snap.

"What on earth can be so important that you must be there so quickly, *sir*?"

The man stops, half turns. He has an unfortunate look about him.

"The hanging." His tone implies incredulity at the questioning. "The hanging at Newgate." He turns and speeds off once more.

"Yes, of course," Edison mutters, although he had no knowledge of any hanging happening today.

For a moment, he straightens the sleeves of his coat, then, when enough time has passed, he takes off after the man at a trot. He trails the brute at a distance, passing cabs, dodging the steaming, fly-colonized mounds that hunker in the gutters. In his haste, at Cornhill, he crashes knee-first into a cage of rats for the pits. The impact sends the door swinging open and the rodents surge out onto the street like liquid. *There.* For just a second, he is back on the *Makepeace*, listening to the scrabble of the Norway rats in the orlop at night.

A shove in the ribs brings him back to the moment.

Bodies are streaming towards Old Bailey, the street that runs alongside Newgate Prison, and here and there he can see barriers have been erected to contain the thundering flow. He can hear the bluebottle murmur of the crowd, even from this distance. Soon, the impressive rise of the scaffold comes into focus. The tidy posts and crossbeam of the gallows set upon it, all painted a most ordinary dead black. Below the scaffold, and for as far as the eye can see, are humans, crammed in and seething, writhing, rippling like a bucket of putrefied meat. Humans have squashed themselves into every space imaginable, scrambling onto the rooftops, clinging to porticos and dangling from railings.

He is so distracted that he knocks, yet again, into someone.

"Oops, I do apologize." A dark-haired woman in a yellow dress flashes a pretty smile of apology. As their eyes meet, something strange crawls over him, something like ice, but she turns and pulls herself further into the crowd.

Edison follows her path for a while then, losing interest, moves his eyes upwards. From one window, he sees, a fashionable woman leans out with a pair of opera glasses held to her face. Moving her head from left to right she takes in every sordid detail of the fray. What must she see from her lofty vantage point? Hucksters, toffers, salesmen elbowing their way through the throng touting stewed eels, sheep's trotters, cockles, whatever they can proffer. Then children. The poor. The gentility. A swirling ocean of pot hats, mangy scalps, and bright ladies' bonnets.

The din is astounding—an untuned orchestra of leers. Edison, a powerless cog in the wheel now, turns back to the scaffold. All around it, drunks clamor to reach the gallows, beaten back by a phalanx of men with tricorns and pikes, their horses kicking up hoary plumes of dirt.

All this, he thinks, just to see one lowly criminal swing. Good grief.

A small boy sidles up to him.

"A learned gentleman like yourself deserves the inside story."

Edison does not shoo him.

"Just a penny for you, sir."

He takes the pamphlet and places a coin in the boy's palm, taking care to wipe his fingers on the fustian of his own corduroys. He eyes the paper. The crude woodcut displays the image of a body hanging from the gallows. Below, he presumes, is a portrait of the condemned: unremarkable, save for the fact that the man rests one foot on the dead-limp body of a maid. The expression the artist has gifted him is one of unfettered, elated triumph.

The Most Cruel and Inhuman Murder of Effie Strong, the title reads.

Edison scans the text—a story of a young domestic servant, sliced from ear to ear by her master after falling pregnant with his illegitimate child. Nothing too unusual.

His tongue finds the inside of his cheek. He rolls his shoulders, casting his gaze across the heaving crowd. Puppeteers shift dancing skeletons around their stages, holding their hats out for a shower of coins. Meat pies are sold, stuffed down throats. Boys selling last confessions fill their pockets with dirty, tinkling pennies.

This entire place is unabashedly dripping with money.

Perhaps it should surprise him that so many have been drawn to such a macabre spectacle. But murder was all you read about in the papers these days: the pipe maker who slaughtered his common-law wife, then cut her limbs from her body so he could more easily dispose of the corpse. The mad army sergeant who killed his two children with a razor, leaving their throats gashed in so terrible a manner as to show the vertebrae of their necks. And so it went—bodies pickled in barrels, husbands poisoned with arsenic. There was a microscopic focus on details that horrified him. At least it should do, shouldn't it? But people were always there, willing to read, willing to watch, willing to hear in just what manner exactly a throat had been slit.

A roar goes up from the crowd and Edison cranes his neck. A knot of uniformed bodies has appeared at Debtor's Door and is slowly untangling itself out into the street.

"Hats off, hats off."

The crowd caterwauls and blusters, clamoring to get the most favorable view of the prisoner. Edison spots what must be the Ordinary of Newgate, dressed in his full and gloomy canonicals. Then wardens, guards, and sheriffs in their bleak costumes too. On the scaffold, the hangman—broad, thick-set, and dressed in black—runs final tests on his equipment, with scant regard for the fact that he is in full view of the man he is about to hang.

"Move it."

"Doff your cap."

"Take off your hat so we can bloody see!"

Motion ripples across the crowd, the yells almost drowning out the sonorous groan of St. Sepulchre's bell.

Around him, Edison counts bare heads. Ten. Fifty. Two hundred. More. Something is building in his mind now, something hot and quick.

The first flickers of a match.

Edison Stowe has an idea.

The Journal of Jack Aldridge

69°N, 52°W
The Whale Fish Islands, Disko Bay, Greenland
2 July 1849

MEN DO NOT DECIDE THE DIRECTION in which a ship will sail. Nor are men at liberty to determine the speed at which it moves.

The ice decides.

There are men on the *Makepeace* with strange, surprising preoccupations—the young stoker's assistant, Baker, who is cultivating a cress farm in the bend of a warm galley pipe; Mansfield, the long-faced clerk in charge, who befuddles the men by speaking ornate Latin at dinner. Yet none are as mysterious to me as those whose job it is to converse with the ice. They are conductors atop the mainmast who maneuver their scopes with frostbitten fingers, translating the ice's wily, wordless orders. The way they speak among themselves sounds, to me, like singing. Not a melodic, choral hum, but something guttural, thick as a shanty. "Sludge ice," they murmur, "brash ice, drift ice," speaking to the staccato beat of a drum.

The ice master, however, the man in charge of navigating this entire frozen expanse, is a plain brute. Seaman Abel Mance. Rough as rocks and with eyes that have certainly never troubled themselves to smile. The men say he's spent his years working among walrus hunters in the north, guiding them through the narrowest leads in the ice, helming wooden boats, dripping with blood, through floes and drifts. He's a man of few words, I have judged. He takes his meals with the scientific officer, Stowe, who appears lofty and supercilious against the ice master's base brutality. It is not so uncommon for such bonds to be forged on a ship like this, though, especially when those of all stripes are hemmed in so close together. I watch them sometimes. One dirty, one clean: Mance in his stained canvas breeches; Stowe with the holy shine of an officer— polished calfskin boots and cutaway worsted coat, no marks. When I pass him in the companionway on my way to assist Mr. Penny in the galley, he smells always of pomade and antiseptic. Mance smells most detestably of crotch rot. Stowe picks at his food like a bird, while Mance tears into flesh in the manner of an old, starved dog.

I learn new things from the ice every day, as I gaze upon the ocean from my spot halfway up the rigging. The ice that streams down from the pole is not white, as I had expected it to be. Instead, it's a dazzling marbled blue on its underside. Or pewter, or on occasion as pink as the nose of a kitten. This whole landscape is alive! The bergs threaded with veins just like those you'll find in a living, breathing body. The skies are filled with life too: puffins, fulmars, eiders, snow geese, and gulls abound. There are whales now and then. Bowheads, the occasional pod of killers, barreling past the ship with dorsal fins rising taller than any man on the *Makepeace*. When the larger whales are sighted, breaking the waters with open mouths full of baleen, they mist the air with their breath, as if the ocean itself is exhaling.

Sometimes the whales are not even alive, as I learned

yesterday. We made our way through the entrance to the
Whale Fish Islands, and the men stood watch on the
starboard side, the air frigid, filled with the sharp whip-snap
of the halyards against the masts. The *Makepeace* moved
slowly, sails belly out, past an isthmus draped in fog.

As it went, the lookouts called down from the topmains.

"Westward, ho!" they called. "Westward, ho." As if it
were a song.

A rancid stench hit us like a wall.

It was as foul an odor as you could ever imagine. Some
men ducked below to escape it. Others, coaxed up on deck
by curiosity, wrapped their comforters tight around their
noses and scrambled up the ratlines for a better vantage. As
the ship inched past the beach, the fog began steadily to lift.
We craned our necks and strained our eyes, hands raised
against the liquid glare of the sun. The beach was shingly,
gray gravel sloping upwards, the land around it a ripple of
buckles and hillocks. Nearby, black cliffs were streaked with
the stark white droppings of murres.

When the mist cleared entirely, we could easily perceive
the source of the stench.

A large whale had beached itself on the gravel and died.
Its body was preposterously swollen. Black and stiff with
putrefaction. It must have been double its normal size,
I'd fancy, as if it had been inflated like the balloons the
aerialists use.

Gathered all around that huge dead whale were dozens of
white bears.

I could not believe my eyes. I've read about the Arctic
bears, the largest predator on this earth. One of the most
ferocious creatures you could ever encounter. I have read
about their power—how they can crush a man's rib cage and

sever his spine. But I've never read about them gathering to feed on the flesh of whales.

The bears were muscular, furred with dirty yellow, and pawing in a frenzy at the decaying meat. I fought the urge to cover my mouth. The animals were huffing and coughing, the astringent stink of them quite choking to the lungs. Their breath fogged the air, their teeth bared. It was as if a theater curtain had lifted to reveal the players all going at one another like cannibals.

When word got around, those who remained below emerged to gawp at the astonishing sight. The bears were not dissuaded by their audience. When they weren't pawing and tearing at blubber, they were swiping at one another, biting, rearing on their back legs to war the way of mythical things.

Someone passed round their glass, and just as I put it to my eye something cold washed across my whole body. I lowered the scope to see that the ice master, Mance, had appeared beside me. Side to side like this, my shoulders barely reached his waist. He had no comforter around his nose, he did not blink, did not wince as the bears flailed and roared. It did not faze him how they scattered blood and tissue and pulp around the beach, and I imagined how much death he must have seen on his walrus hunts. I heard lowered voices and glanced up—I could see that he was murmuring to someone. I stepped backwards and peered behind his bulk to find that the scientist, Stowe, was beside him now too. The two of them, their very presence, shifted something in the air. Their eyes were trained on the bears in front of them, oblivious to the gasps and retches of the other men. Stowe had balanced a Baker rifle at his thigh. It gleamed in the sun that pierced through the fog. But I was sure he could not be intending to shoot—not only would a gunshot cause chaos among the bears, who were already perilously close to our ship, but we have rations enough and these creatures were feasting on putrefying meat. Even if boiled bear was considered a delicacy, which it very much is not, we could not eat them.

But Stowe likes to shoot things. I've heard the rumors. He sees it as sport, the men say. He flenses his spoils, takes their bones to his cabin, and stashes them, intending to sell them back in England to his Society friends.

As the bears fought and feasted, I watched in surprise as he did indeed raise the rifle. My skin prickled as he squinted through the crosshairs. Despie would not like it. He would not like it one bit. He'd be angry at the slaughter. The risk.

Someone suggested he might like to put down his weapon.

The echo of the shot ricocheted off the cliffs.

What followed was an explosion. A volcano. Edison Stowe had missed.

Instead of the flesh of a bear, the bullet struck the swollen whale in the stomach. In an instant, it erupted and fell in a downpour of bloodied matter, carpeting the deck and those of us on it, in a most diabolical brown-red pulp. The bears fled, bounding from the carcass in fear. The men groaned. Spitting the filth from their mouths—some leaning over the gunwale to vomit.

I checked. Mance did not raise an eyebrow, and I watched as his tongue slid from his mouth to lick his filth-stained lips.

"I don't want a bear," Stowe chastised the men as if they were touched in the head. "I've no need for a bear. That's a sperm whale. That spermaceti is incredibly valuable."

I thought of the waxy substance inside the whale's skull. Stowe could have easily obliterated it with his shot, and we were lucky not to have had bears storming towards our ship.

He ordered that the ramp be lowered, then stomped off to the beach to retrieve his bounty.

So, I have learned another thing. That this is a ship filled with reckless men. Men at ease with placing themselves and others in danger to get exactly what they need. That much, I have learned.

Chapter Five

Edison

The turnout for the show that evening was abysmal. He knew it would be. No one is interested in the magic lantern any more. Not when Livery is charging half the price for his damned freak show next door, the hordes flocking in salivating droves to ogle the inked women and the sword swallowers. He'd only taken on the shows as a way to make money. Some might call it desperate, he preferred the term enterprising. Inchbold had a shabby lantern out the back of the shop, and being a man who could turn his hand to most things it had only taken Edison a bit of dusting to get it working again.

Livery's queues were already forming when Edison arrived at The World Turned Upside Down, the unwieldy lantern heavy under his arm. He had tried to ignore their obnoxious chatter, studying the globe out front of the tavern, watching it swing in the breeze at the edge of an old iron hook. On inspection, any patron, should any fancy peeling himself away from the giantesses, would see that this globe is quite remarkable—a lie, a ruse. The whole world in disguise. The southern shores of all its continents face downwards, with Spitzbergen and Nova Zembla languishing in the far Antarctic and Tierra Del Fuego on the latitude at which one would expect to find Labrador!

The globe always amuses him, appeals to his high wit. But he supposes such playful geography is lost on those who take women with webbed toes as entertainment.

He had pushed through the tavern door and nodded a greeting to Humphreys behind the bar, noticing with a dim beat of gratitude that the man had scrawled a few signs and affixed them hastily to the walls. A handful of attendees were gathered at the door to the back room and offered a paltry cheer as the bartender made his way over to unlock it.

Edison had made his preparations, eyeing the punters with distaste. No pedigree. Just some humdrum factory workers. He was sure to remove his hat immediately and hold it out. The shows commanded a two-shilling admittance, and he was not waiving that for anyone. One young mother had not had the coins and had therefore, regrettably, been ejected, along with her children, who had made such a dreadful din as they departed.

When all patrons were paid up and accounted for, and he was satisfied that his contraption was in order, he had made his way around the room extinguishing all the candles in their sconces. They left faint wisps in the air as he went. He kept one tallow lit at the table at the front of the room, then turned to address his audience.

"BEHOLD."

He swallowed a sigh.

"The most magnificent magic lantern show around."

Who was he kidding?

He had hoped volume might be an efficient substitute for enthusiasm, that the audience would not perceive how wearied he had become with such cheap theatricality. He did not have the strength to, yet again, explain why he could not honor refunds. Two shows a week had been thieving too much of his energy, the returns so paltry he'd barely made any dent in his debts. But, he told himself, he just had to get through this last one, then his new venture will be bringing him riches enough that he will never have to look at a damned lantern again.

With a tired flourish he had whisked away the cloth and exposed the equipment, the audience knowing full well that this was the point at which they were to commence their *oohs* and *aahs*. They'd fulfilled their role with aplomb. He'd struck the match and lit the whale oil, the thick reek of it rushing to every corner of the room to settle. With no slides in the lantern, the flame had thrown a simple circular light onto the sheet pinned across the back wall. He'd quickly polished the first, inserted it into the holder and the sheet had come alive.

ARCTIC EXPLORATIONS

The curved red letters each appeared as long as his arm against the fabric. They had been painted carefully onto the glass slide with transparent enamel, each feathered with white as if encrusted in ice. Below the words, a bewitching scene was projected—an ice maiden's frostscape of jagged bergs and towering white mountains, all ablaze with the incandescent light of the pole star. A familiar finger of ice slithered under Edison's collar, reminding him of the unyielding frozen north, calling him back to that unblemished white land as hard as stone and iron.

He squinted into the crowd, distracted momentarily by a flash of bright yellow. It was only there for a moment, caught in a kaleidoscope of lights from the back of the lantern, then it had gone, slipped out of the door and into the cold.

Edison blinked. Coughed himself back on track, turned to the projection.

Among the ridges and folds of the motionless sea, a ship was held in position. Ice hung in javelins off its every beam. On deck, tiny ant-like figures gazed onto unending Arctic wasteland.

"It's Franklin's ship!" One lad leapt from his bench. "I found it, I found it. Tell Lady Jane. Where's my reward? I'll be rich!" The audience chuckled and Edison quickly reached for the next two slides. He slotted them into the lantern and took the small levers in his fingers. With these, he could create a clever illusion of movement, making it seem as if the ship were sailing across a stormy sea. He glanced up, checking for the audience's reaction. The children in the front row appeared transfixed, although, to his annoyance, he could see two well-dressed men at the back of the room deep in conversation. They looked out of place there, among the rags and the sorrow. He sniffed and shoved in the next slide, throwing the shape of a large white whale onto the fabric. The audience murmured with delight. Children clambered onto their mothers' laps for a view of the leviathan.

"The beluga," he announced, remembering the shape the whales' bodies had made under water, how they would raise their heads above the surface and twist them side to side, just like an owl.

The next slide utilized a slipping mechanism, two sheets of rectangular glass within a small wooden frame. Painted on one was a man in his cold weather slops—heavy great coat, mittens, and Welsh wig hat. Beside him, on the ice, was a huge Arctic bear, its jaws open wide. On the other slide, the man was absent, so when Edison moved it in and out of the lantern, he seemed to disappear entirely, ravaged by the terrifying beast. A few audience members, with seemingly macabre inclinations, cackled in appreciation, clapped. A child buried his head into his mother's elbow and whimpered.

When the show was complete and Edison had sullenly packed up his contraption, he allowed his eyes to roam the faces of those scraping back their chairs and making for the door. What pity, these commoners who've never seen anything more riveting than a scabby bear in chains at Newmarket. He considered the smattering of shillings collected in the bottom of his hat, watched backs clad in mothballed shawls and shirts as they departed. These people were not going to get him the sort of money he needed to pay off his debts. His mind jolted back to the hanging that morning, the sheer *number* of those in the crowd, people for as far as the eye could see: faces groaning, howling, an ecstasy of morbid delight. He tossed the slide in his hand to the table, grabbed two coins from his hat and made his way to the chairs at the back of the room. The two men in their suits and hats were still absorbed in conversation.

"Gentleman," he greeted them. "If I may, just two seconds of your time."

The men turned together. Edison helped himself to the seat beside them.

"I hoped I might be able to canvas your opinion on a somewhat delicate matter." He took the coins from his pocket. "Research. A penny for your thoughts, if you will." The men grunted, one held out a palm for the coin.

"You a copper?" the man asked as he clamped his fingers tight around the money.

"Nothing like that. I assure you." Edison clasped his own hands together and looped them over one knee.

"A journalist?"

A pause. "Of sorts, I suppose. More of an academic. I'm preparing a paper."

He held the man's gaze.

A waxed moustache twitched in response.

"Tell me," Edison continued, "have you ever attended the hangings that take place in the city, in Old Bailey at Newgate?"

The man sucked in his cheeks.

"You trying to get a mark of my character?"

"I am . . . conducting a social experiment. Trying to prove my theory that even the most learned and well-to-do folk, like yourself"—he almost bowed—"are drawn to these events." Perhaps this sort of simpering might work. They looked the types. "I believe any man with a moral compass," Edison continued, "would be satisfied with seeing the most depraved criminals swing for their sins." The man watched him carefully. "How else are we to maintain a proper society without these events to warn of the consequences of crime?"

Edison saw the eyebrows of the other man jolt into life. His four-in-hand necktie crumpling as he leaned in.

"I have attended," he admitted. "Only the Mannings though. I don't know anyone who wasn't at the Mannings."

Edison nodded. Yes of course. *The Bermondsey Horror*, the papers had called it. The husband and wife had swung together outside Horsemonger Lane Gaol for the murder of Maria's lover, Patrick O'Connor. The papers spared few details of the crime, telling in lascivious prose how they'd shot and battered the man with a ripping chisel, salted him in quicklime, then buried him under the flagstones of their kitchen floor. Two and a half million broadsides had been printed. Some fifty thousand had turned out to watch the spectacle of their hanging.

"She had a black lace veil covering her features," the man muttered. "I saw it before Calcraft drew the nightcap over her head. Scarcely a hat was raised when that drop fell."

The other man leaned in to join them.

"I find it remarkably distasteful," he bit out, "to watch a person meet their death like that, before a baying crowd. No better than a bear in a pit." Edison nodded vigorously, briefly deterred. "Unless"—the man held one finger in the air, eyebrows quirked—"it is for the murder of a child." Edison and the moustached man grunted in assent. "In which case I'll be at the front of that crowd."

The men all nodded reverentially and then fell silent.

"Or," the man continued at a strangely high pitch after a while, "a murderess."

Grunts. More assents. "For I think we can all agree that there is nothing quite so depraved on this earth as a woman who kills."

The Journal of Jack Aldridge

69°N, 51°W
Alluttoq Island, Greenland
4 August 1849

I'VE BEEN CONSIDERING what it is to be a man. What
threads weave together to form the tapestry of who he
truly is.

Before this voyage, I had spent little time in the company
of men. Apart from Grandfather, of course. But now,
I live among them, privy daily to conversations usually
accompanied by pipe smoke and rounds of Bezique.

They ask me nothing of my life, of course, of my family, or
my wants. They are little concerned with stories from a ship's
boy, and for that I admit I am grateful. I would find it hard
to speak of family as "Jack." I'd long to tell them of those
I left behind, Constance's family—the way my sister has
pushed aside every thought of herself to care for me since
our parents died. How my grandfather hums tunelessly, just
like Mr. Penny, as he works at his bench. It can be lonely,
at times, to keep my stories to myself, listening to others'
tales of sweethearts and sisters, knowing I am safer sharing
none of my own, keeping them locked away—a secret. On
occasion, I'll meet the eyes of those close to me in age and
station—Baker, the stoker's assistant, or Hatton, the young
lad of fourteen who helps the carpenter with his work in the
hold. I glance quickly away when it happens, and I know

they must think me rude. But I cannot be drawn into such allegiances, not if I'm to remain disguised.

But freely, the other men talk.

Those of high standing enjoy very much, I have discovered, to speak of their achievements. Well-bred men. Well-educated men. Ex-public-school men simply love to tell stories of their own bravery. It feeds them like porridge.

Those men serving before the mast—many from the north of England, some Irish, Welsh, or Scot—look up to those in fine blue jackets and epaulettes, hoping one day to find themselves in their position. In return, those in blue jackets like to gloat to us boys and seamen of their adventures, of how they've traveled the world, to the colonies in Van Diemen's Land, to the most faraway Hudson's Bay outposts. They tell us stories of beautiful Cree women and whales that leap clean out of the water to capsize ships. They have each of them wrestled white bears with their own two fists, they have each bedded the daughters of the most noble chiefs, been to the finest balls you could ever imagine.

Women, or rather the love of a woman, and the act of "love" itself is the hardest worn topic by far. Clustered on sea chests or heaps of rope, accompanied by the sound of spoons scraping metal, the men speak through mouths of warm stew of their sweethearts back home. They tease one another about tavern whores or cuckoldom at the hands of their neighbors. I make the right noises, of course. Laugh at the correct moments, slap my knees. They are not to know my own familiarity with love, with heartbreak. They are not to know anything about me.

The men make a sport of lewdness, sharing ribald songs and crude carvings—a woman's naked form etched into whale tooth; figures in copulation hewn into wood discarded

by the carpenters. They speak of war also. Of families,
sometimes. There are men here whose sole desire it is to
keep themselves alive long enough to return to their marriage
engagements. Men whose children will be born and walking
by the time they're back at Woolwich.

When they disperse, descending the scuttle to bring
up stores, or heading above to tend to masts and rigging,
thoughts of love remain with me. And as I turn in to my
hammock at night, I push away the memories: a soft head
resting on my chest as we read together, a warm touch, rough
lips brushing mine, lean arms around me. I cannot have
those things, and so I am better off here, alone.

Chapter Six

Maude

She slams the door behind her and collapses against it. The room swims, bottles tilting on their sides, a smear of pharmacy equipment dragging across her vision.

The horror of it makes her clasp a palm to her mouth.

She had not expected to find it so difficult to hear him talk.

As she pushes herself forward, she staggers a little, catching the reflection of her dress in a large glass cabinet. She had selected it carefully. Put it to her chest in front of the mirror. Noticed how its bright color brought her blue eyes to life.

She shakes her head, pinches the bridge of her nose. Those images of the Arctic. The ship. The man's flourish as he stood silhouetted by lanternlight.

She is not accustomed to sneaking around, to evading detection. The unnaturalness of it depletes her and makes her head ache with fear. She can remember only one time that she has done such a thing—at Constance's behest, of course. They had slipped out, at night, without their grandfather's knowing. Maude had faltered, wanted to turn back, felt it was too dangerous to be doing such a thing alone in the dark. But Constance had laughed and dragged her forward by the arm. They'd ended up among a young crowd in an old, disused shop off Conduit Street. It had been turned into a theater. There were no playbills, no flocked velvet curtains, nothing so formal as that, but a rough stage had been erected at one end, and the remaining space filled with benches. Revellers were squeezed into every space, young men and women chattering with excitement, drinking, eating. The board above the stage displayed the name of the performance: *The Red Barn Murder*.

Against her better judgment, and against the part of her that wanted to take Constance by the collar and drag her out of such a gaff, Maude had become engrossed in the play on the stage. Automaton figures were made to move with wires attached to their hands and feet, telling the grisly story of Maria Marten, a young molecatcher's daughter, shot dead by her lover and buried in a sack in a Suffolk barn. Maude's jaw had slackened as a crimson handkerchief of blood flowered on Maria's chest as she died, and her dastardly killer hopped from foot to foot with a *he-he-he* of glee. But at that very moment, the entrance doors to the gaff had flown open behind Maude, and a stream of policemen had filed in. There was panic. The constables seized audience members by the shoulders, hauling them off the benches and dragging them down the aisles, out of the theater, and into the mouths of waiting wagons. The sisters had gripped their hands tightly together and pushed through the crowd, eventually managing to escape through a back door and out into the street where they ran and ran until their lungs felt scorched. Constance had arrived back at the pharmacy with a face alive with excitement. Maude had taken one look at it and slapped her for her recklessness, for putting them in such a position.

She had vowed never to take such a risk again. But now her sister was gone, and she could still feel the sting of that slap in her palm, still taste the guilt.

She was going to have to get used to doing things she was not supposed to do.

Edison Stowe had been easy to find, sequestered above a shop selling all manner of animal skeletons. Heart's card had led her there. *Rare curiosities*, it read. *Fine skeletons, no fakes (no mermaids)*. A strange place to hide, Maude had thought as she assessed the antelope skulls that peered out from the window glass. The shopfront was spotless, shining bright and as clean as a dragonfly's wings.

It was emblazoned with large, gold lettering.

MR. INCHBOLD'S BONES

She could not summon the nerve to go in and so had watched the man for days, observing his behaviors at a distance. She knew the details of his appearance from Constance's diary. Fair hair, cold eyes, slim build but rangy, strong. She waited for him as he descended the stairs each morning, listening for the bell as he pushed his way out of the shop door. She had been surprised, at first, at his outward innocuousness. His limbs long and slender in worsted trousers and day coat, his hair lightly curled and parted severely to one side. He left the shop at the same time every morning, just after the bells of St James's had tolled eight, so it was easy to become accustomed to his tedious patterns of living—the routes he took along the streets, the way his face slackened when he thought no one was watching. Sometimes she stayed and watched Mr. Inchbold and his specimens. He took great care over the bones, she observed, handling them as delicately as a child would a lamb. He showed great patience for the smaller creatures in particular, spending hours inspecting monkeys and fragile, strange-looking cats. The larger ones—the sturdy bears impressive on their hind legs; the mighty tiger positioned in the act of stalking its prey in the jungle—he approached with a sort of quiet reverence.

Most often though, Maude followed Edison Stowe through the streets. He walked with an insouciant bounce in his step, straight as a rifle, his body propelled forwards by his prominent pointed nose. He wore clothes favored by the dandies, black frock coats with rounded edges and high necks, fawn trousers, and preposterous cravats. When Heart told her of his suspicions, Maude had not been sure quite who she had expected to find. But it was certainly not a man who looked like every privileged bore in London.

His nonchalance angered her most. She trailed him carefully down alleys cast in patchwork shadow. She tracked him around courtyard hovels strung with laundry. As she walked, the dirt surrendered with a squelch under her old, unpolished boots. But he moved far more comfortably than she did through the streets. That was, of course, because he looked as if he owned them.

At first, she had dulled her looks with lifeless mantles, simple cloth coats, and old, unfashionable bonnets. This allowed her to become forgettable on the occasions she was required to take a cab to pursue him. But apart from a brief visit to the Society, where he appeared to be denied admittance, and a morning trailing him all the way to the docks, just to wait as he spent hours inside a warehouse, he had had no other appointments and would simply walk around the city, pushing the hours away with his calfskin shoes, returning only at the end of the day as women emerged from the rookeries like night-singing birds.

This morning, after two weeks of tracking him, she had found, with a strange feeling, that she finally wanted him to notice her. It was as if she were ready to hold a finger to that flame. And so she had selected a gown the color of churned butter, one that had belonged to her mother, one that gave her the look of a lady of higher standing than her own. She had trailed him as delicately as she could to the bank, from which he emerged with a face cast over with storm clouds. Then she followed as he took off at pace down the busy thoroughfare. When they had come upon the hanging at Newgate, after a bout of running that she was sure would ruin the dress entirely, she had tied herself close to his trail, at one point so dangerously close that he had knocked his shoulders straight into hers. Their eyes had met, and she had felt it like a strike to the skull, his ice-shard gaze, and in its palest blue: the faintest flicker of recognition.

She had drawn quickly away, burning with dual flames of heat and frost, allowing herself to be swallowed by the crowd, but careful never to lose sight of Edison Stowe. She could have returned to the pharmacy, then, gathered her resolve, left the confrontation for another day. But she found she needed more; her pursuit of the man had become like a drug to her system. So, when evening fell, she did not return to her grandfather and his crammed, dusty shelves. Instead, she cleaved once more to Stowe's meandering trail, hovering in the shadows, ignoring her hunger and the bitter, winter air as he led her, unknowingly, into the audience of his magic lantern show.

The unease was thick in that unfamiliar room, yet her curiosity, her need to know more, had kept her yoked to the bench, hunched down as far as she could to avoid detection. But as soon as the ship had sprung to life, emblazoned as high as a hansom cab across the sheet, she had felt her fortitude desert her.

"BEHOLD," the man had bellowed, and she had flinched so

violently the gentleman beside her had cast an alarmed glance her way. Stowe continued, doling out empty theatrics to the seats, and she had squirmed under the torture of his voice. She kept her gaze to her lap. She could not look at that ship without imagining Constance's life aboard it. She could not bear to see that ice and picture her body trapped beneath.

And so she had fled, all the way back across London to the pharmacy, pounding the city's dark streets, filled with anger and fear and chagrin at her own lack of courage. She did not have him yet, but she would get him. She just had to find the right time.

The floorboards creak as she makes her way to her bedroom. Peering into the dispensing room she finds her grandfather asleep in his chair, the dwindling light from a chamberstick trailing its fingers across his old, slack features.

It is a position she has found him in many times since they learned of Constance's death. It is as if, Maude has often thought, he cannot allow himself the comfort of a bed if his granddaughter is not permitted to rest in her own.

When she reaches her room she collapses, exhausted, onto the bed. The sheets feel oddly warm. She moves a hand under the counterpane and her fingers hit something hard and hot. She smiles. Her grandfather has placed a warming pan between the sheets so that she does not catch a cold. Guilt pricks at her sternum. She has not been truthful with him these past couple of weeks. She has not yet told him about Constance's diary or her daily pursuits of Stowe. She knows that when she does, he will try to stop her. He has already lost one of them; he will not readily allow his only remaining granddaughter to place herself in the path of a dangerous man.

She tells herself that he will know the truth, eventually. But for as long as he remains content with her excuses—believing that she is spending her time in the newspaper archives, researching the crew of the *Makepeace*; that she is taking some air in the nearest park, foraging for herbs and ingredients just as she and Constance used to do together—she will do this alone. She just needs time. She just needs courage enough to step foot through that shop door and confront Edison Stowe.

The Journal of Jack Aldridge

———————●————————————●———————

70.5°N, 55°W
Qeqertarsuatsiaq Island, Greenland
15 August 1849

IT HAS BEEN THREE MONTHS since I first set foot on the *Makepeace*. Still my secret remains undiscovered.

The crew have found an easy familiarity with one another. I am merely a face in the crowd, a boy among a muster of men. The acceptance, to have had them fooled for this long, brings me sly satisfaction.

Mr. Penny has taken me under his wing now, eyeing the jut of my shoulder blades and the hollows in my cheeks as I assist him in the galley. He slips me biscuits, lime juice, or extra portions of Poor John when no one's looking. I am lucky he is not more suspicious. He has no idea that I stash this book behind his huge glowing stove every evening, that I pull back the loose plank of wood and tuck my secrets away, from everyone on this ship.

The landscape around us is shifting now. Barren islands eventually morphed into sheer black cliffs, which have dropped away to reveal fields of vast impenetrable soil. There's a drudgery to the earth, a bleakness that leaves my mind open to dangerous thoughts—nostalgia snakes in, thoughts of home tap softly at the porthole windows to be admitted.

But I have found something to distract me.

I have written previously of the surgeon, Sedgewick, of how I would linger outside his door, hoping for a glimpse of his chosen medicines. One day, a few weeks back, as I sniffed the air in the companionway, attempting to discern if it was bergamot or cannabis he was using for his sleeping tinctures, I heard the rush of a door sliding open and there stood Sedgewick himself, arms folded, leaning against the doorjamb with a curious smile about his face. I froze. He was almost a foot taller than I am, at a guess. He wore shirtsleeves, waistcoat, cravat, and apron. He looked the part, but I did not want to show him how he impressed me. I did not want him to know how desperate I was to see inside.

"It's chamomile," he said. "I add it to the laudanum for the men who cannot sleep." He removed his spectacles, polished them on his shirtsleeves. The ship lurched.

He is a handsome man, Sedgewick. I'm sure that would be the first thing any woman would notice. Mr. Penny says his mother was a Cree woman from one of the outposts. She died when Sedgewick was a young child and he was taken in by a passing medical man, buffeted around the Arctic wilds, taught the vagaries of the surgical craft under the light of the full, cold moon.

But while he might be handsome, I was far more preoccupied with what resided in his cabin—and that, I could not hide. I peered over his shoulder at the bottles on his shelves. Again, he caught me looking.

"I thought it might have been bergamot." I prayed he would not find the suggestion an affront.

He raised an eyebrow, slotting the spectacles back over his ears. "You know plants?"

I paused then. Unsure whether to speak the truth. "I know

some. My grandfather is a chemist." It was a risk. But I
wanted to see inside the sick bay.

He considered it. His eyes running over my face as if
performing calculations. What must he have seen? My wide-
set eyes, my thin boyish lips, my dark eyebrows. I clenched at
the scrutiny.

"I've just finished up," he said, at length. "You are quite
welcome to have a look inside."

The room was spartan and glorious. A single lamp hung from
the crossbeam, illuminating a surgeon's bed beneath it. Two
candles guttered on a table drawn against the hull, the wall
cabinets crammed with flasks, powders and pots. Open shelves
held objects with which I am familiar: camphor, arsenical
soap, gauze, pillboxes, and sealing wax; and those with which
I am not: curved needles, cupping instruments, forceps, and
what looked to be turnscrews. The room was clouded in a
thick, chemical reek, but notes of iron clawed through, the
unmistakable stink of blood. I stepped across to the cabinet
and glanced tentatively at the surgeon. He nodded his
permission, and I began slowly to pick up the stoppered glass
bottles in turn and inspect them. Laudanum, opium pills, blue
vitriol, calomel. I recognized the shortened Latin from similar
labels in the pharmacy—*SYR* to denote syrups or sugar water
mixture; liniments designated by *LIN* and so on. The toxic
solutions were easily identifiable by their green glass bottles. I
knew, also, by the quantity of Epsom salts and castor oil that
the bowels on this ship must be as slow-moving as the ice.

And so it began. Sedgewick asked Despie if he might train
me as a sort of apprentice. His intended assistant never
boarded at Woolwich, so he had been sharing one with

Blacklock from *High Regard*. Despie, more interested in the movement of the early ice than the preoccupations of his lowly cabin boy, agreed.

Society, I am aware, finds it difficult to conceive of an arrangement between a man and a woman that is neither romantic nor carnal. But such things do exist, and Sedgewick and I have struck up an odd sort of friendship (although, I do have to remind myself sometimes that he does not know my true identity, thinking me instead a young, eager boy of fifteen). It might seem improper to others that he converses so freely with me, but in truth, I believe he is flattered by my curiosity, and fancy he finds it freeing to discuss the particulars of his craft without judgment or challenge.

As a ship's boy, I have no presence. It matters not if he tells me his worries or his far-fetched hypotheses. He is at liberty to test his theories about debility, to explain to an interested audience why he disagrees so vehemently with the fashionable thinkings of phrenology. He sees in me, I believe, an eager pupil and even allows me to assist him in his minor surgeries (only if Despie is distracted). We've been busy these past weeks, with fingers trapped between railings, toes crushed by falling chisels, skin torn from palms. We've been preoccupied with bronchitis, stomach complaints, abrasions, avulsions, and suppurating boils. Sometimes I watch him and remember how M and I would observe Grandfather at work when we were children. Leaning our small bodies over the countertop as he weighed and sifted and grinded and pulped.

Just as Grandfather never did, Sedgewick does not shy from grisly details. It gratifies me to be considered robust enough to hear, in lurid detail, about the helmsman who lost an eye while using a scope up on deck. To be regaled with the perils of frostbite and in exactly what manner it ruptures cells to claim fingers and toes with ease. He speaks freely of how men will have their beards ripped from their skin when the temperatures fall. How he'll have to amputate ears as the flaps of the men's wet Welsh wig hats freeze to them and kill the tissue.

I am grateful for how he treats me. I am grateful that he considers me as much of a man as any on this ship. For he is not to know any different and I shall not tell him so. I will do nothing to put my position here at risk.

Chapter Seven

Edison

"M s. Swan is ready to receive you."

The old woman, atrophy in motion, begins her slow journey up the staircase. Edison follows, impatiently studying the walls. They are papered in a sumptuous print. It looks like exotic fruits—strawberries, mangoes, and ripe persimmon—dripping with juice. Yet, on closer inspection it refracts into the shape of bodies, reclined in postures of ecstasy, conjoined in deeds of lust.

He coughs.

Halfway up the stairs the woman pauses and wordlessly holds out a wizened palm behind her. He deposits the remaining coins from the lantern show into its folds. The woman's fingers snap shut.

Oh, how he wishes he were rich. He *deserves* to be rich. How can it not be so? A man of quality, of skill, of intelligence, should not feel so troubled to part with coin. He was once what the society women would call "well off." He straightens his shoulders.

But no, that did not stick.

No matter: what he lacks in coin he makes up for in

ingenuity. He knew a solution would arrive eventually and here it has presented itself like a pig ripe for sticking.

It merely needs some fine tuning.

"In there." The old woman gestures nowhere, but Edison knows which door he needs. He knocks, pushes it open.

The room is abrasively red. Scarlet curtains are hung on all sides and at its center a large rococo bed flaunts itself atop a crimson Persian rug. There is something claustrophobic about this room. It has always felt, to him, disconcertingly womb-like.

"Edison, dear." The woman has already begun to unlace her bodice. "Are you keeping well?"

"Adelaide," he nods, appraising the dusky ribbons at her back. "That won't be necessary." He strides past her and takes a seat on the chaise by the dresser. The air smells of shoe polish and ambergris.

She pauses, shakes her head, then laces it all back up, moving to the dresser to take out a slim cigar. She offers one to him. He declines.

"I want to speak to you about something." He folds his hands together and rests them on his knee.

"You want to *speak*? Very well." Adelaide strikes a Vesta and holds it in front of the cigar, sucking deeply as the tip burns firefly bright.

He reaches for a stool, drags it into position in front of the chaise. Taps it. "Sit."

She does, fixing him with opaline eyes as she takes another drag.

"What do you want to talk about, Edison?" The smoke she billows out is as harsh and bitter as aniseed.

Adelaide Swan is the most intelligent woman Edison has ever met. No one else of her sex can hold a conversation about books, about politics, about philosophy. She has not quite the intellect to rival a man, of course, but if there is anyone who might provide an astute and informed opinion on his business plans, then it is this clever little strumpet.

"Tell me," he says. "Have you much experience with train travel?"

"Trains?" She juts out her bottom lip like an actress. "Instead of unlacing my bodice you came here to speak of trains. Well, I'm horribly offended." She grins and puffs out a perfect ring of smoke.

"You must have been escorted on train journeys by other . . . clients." He knows she has; Adelaide Swan has welcomed some of London's finest minds between her thighs.

She rises and moves to the mirror on the dresser, bends, inspecting her face—feline, beautiful, but beginning to line. She reaches for a small gold container and raises it to her lips, reapplying her rouge in a vermillion gash.

"You must have witnessed many events that way. Many spectacles." He widens his eyes at the word.

"I suppose I have," she concedes, blotting her lips with a square of silk and taking a seat back on the stool. "Prize fights, arboretum balls, pleasure gardens, things like that."

"And these excursion trains," Edison continues, growing slowly more animated. "The ones Cook packs out with thousands. Is it just . . ." He pauses, unsure of which words to use, given the woman's standing. "Is it just the *lower* classes"—he whispers it—"that partake in these cheap trips?"

Adelaide considers. "I would say not. I've seen all sorts."

"They share a carriage?"

"Yes, unless first is specifically hired for the purpose. Not much room though." She half turns on her stool. "What's this all about?"

He mulls it over. Thomas Cook was adroit in his business,

chaperoning crowds from London to Sheffield, Bradford, York, and Shields. Steaming them to Birmingham to observe precious metals in production, to the Isle of Man for those desirous of a short, brisk sail. He'd already seen posters, placards, and handbills advertising the agent's tours to the Great Exhibition next year. But what if the excursion crowds wanted *more* of a spectacle? What if they desired something *truly* unique?

A critic might accuse him of impulsivity. It would not be a lazy accusation; it had been leveled at him before, he supposes. Impulsiveness had led him to failure more than once. Impulsiveness had cost him his home, it had cost him much, much more than that. Returning to London from the Arctic, shunned by family, penniless, hoodwinked, homeless. He supposes that is a consequence of impulsivity. But what is life if not loaded with risk?

This will not be the easiest, nor the quickest, nor the safest way to make his money. But he could raise a hundred chickens, sell golden eggs for a year, and get nowhere near the amount that this enterprise promises to bring in.

It is a gamble, but gambling is what he's used to. If you wanted to win big, you had to play big and by God, Edison Stowe must be owed his big payout soon.

The timing is right—England is gripped in a fervor. *Punch* is printing article upon article about this so-called Murder Mania. It has London clamoring after news of slit throats and bludgeoned skulls like Billingsgate fishwives after the last crate of eels. Tales of murder are the mainstay at London's finest theaters, just as they are in the fit-ups and the peepshows favored by traveling showmen, toured around local fairs. It is like listening to the rain while you are all tucked up inside by the fire, is it not? People want their proximity to crime, to death, they want to *feel* it, without having to deal with its messy consequences.

There is money to be made, that's for sure, and nobody is doing *this*.

So, he tells Adelaide Swan of his plan. And when he is done, he sits and waits, fingers clenching at his knee.

She appears to carefully consider what she has heard, rubbing her fingertips together as if trying to feel her way through the concept. The woman is not a fool. She must be able to see the money that this could bring in.

"*Catch-em alive-o!*" The cries of a fly-trap seller saunter in through the window.

Edison swallows. He feels a wire tightening slowly round his chest. It will work. It *will* work. She must agree that it will work.

"I have heard of such a thing," she eventually nods. "There was an excursion train some years ago that ran from Wadebridge to see the Lightfoot Brothers swing at Bodmin. Over a thousand people if I'm not wrong. I know girls who went. Train stopped on the tracks just below the walls of the gaol to watch the whole thing." A puff of smoke.

He nods vigorously. So, it *can* be done.

"How are you going to arrange such a thing, Edison? Thousands of people. Have you the money? The means?"

He bristles at the slight, pauses for a moment, but no apology comes.

"I don't need thousands." He unfolds his legs. "Just a select few. A very *wealthy* select few. My tours will command more interest from the right characters and, yes, more money, if they are private, bespoke, tailored. Like a fine suit." He glances dubiously at his own coat, worn around the buttons.

"Do you not think it somewhat distasteful, though?" She takes a puff on her cigar.

He is surprised at this. Adelaide Swan may be an intelligent whore, but she is still just that: a whore. What does she know of taste?

"Many celebrities have attended hangings," he responds coolly. "They don't appear to find it distasteful."

"Who?" Puff, puff.

"Thackeray, Byron, Dickens . . ."

"Dickens reviled the scene!"

"Ah, but he was there, was he not?"

She rolls her eyes.

"Melville paid half a crown for a spot on the roof overlooking the drop when the Mannings swung."

She watches him dubiously.

"There is business to be had here, money to be made." He thinks briefly of Carter, of clean severed toes, of ears hacked from heads, plopped into buckets. "Regardless, these hangings, these *spectacles* are not so different to what tourists have been clamoring after for centuries."

"What on earth do you mean?"

Wonderful. He *really* has her attention now. "Well"—he leans forward on the chaise—"what of the spectators who traveled long distances to watch death as a sport at the gladiatorial games in the Colosseum? During which, I might add, criminals were also executed, as part of the entertainment."

"Two thousand years ago! That's hardly the same, E—"

"What of Waterloo, one of the most visited locations in the world? The nobility watched on from the surrounding hilltops as the battle was fought." He cannot quite remember if this is true, but he is caught in a rush of passion so continues. "Did they balk at the blood? Nay. They were more concerned with the quality of the picnic food!"

She cannot help but grin.

"People of all stripes are drawn to the dark and the macabre, from the factory worker to the senior clerk. We are only human."

Adelaide sighs, returns to her mirror.

"Execution hospitality. I'll be at the forefront. Ushering in the progress."

"*Execution hospi*— Well, now I really have heard everything." She is concealed now behind a cloud of face powder.

"You know of The Magpie and Stump?" Edison asks.

Everyone in her game knows the busy public house at Old Bailey, opposite Newgate Prison.

"I passed it earlier and saw a poster advertising their package. For a fee, patrons can stay overnight, enjoy a breakfast, and then obtain a privileged view of the hangings. From their very own bedroom window!"

She appears to have lost the strength to argue.

"Think about it." His fingertips crackle with promise. He rises from the chaise to place his hands on Adelaide's shoulders. He turns her to face the mirror so he can speak directly to her reflection.

"Adelaide Swan, answer me this: what is travel if not a form of voyeurism? Think of how many noble young European gentlemen have spent their Tours scratching their names into the excavated walls of Pompeii."

"Why are we now talking about Pompeii?" she almost shrieks.

"A scene of tragedy and suffering and death. Much visited. And what"—he pauses to lend gravitas to his words—"is death if not the heritage that all of us share?"

She frowns. Sighs again. Turns to inspect her nose in profile.

He leans in closer. "Travel and spectacle." The words quietly simmer. "Combine the two and you have something quite remarkable."

She clasps his fingers at her shoulder, briefly. He takes it as encouragement and not as a sign that he should remove them.

"It will be an excursion company. EDISON STOWE LIMITED. Stowe's Limited Tours. Edison's Adventures. No, that's terrible . . ."

The sound of horses' hooves clatters in through the open window.

"Just like Cook's." He speaks so quickly now the words have the consistency of spilt liquid. "I shall escort travelers around the country to witness the executions of some of its most desultory, ignoble characters! Guests will appreciate my background, of course. Being guided by a seasoned explorer."

Adelaide yawns.

"We shall travel by train. Spend a night, perhaps two, in the country's finest cities. Observe the *spectacle* of the executions and then return in comfort to London."

And he will be rich.

He feels his stomach lurch as if he is running too fast down a hill. This is good. He knows it's good.

"Not like the cheap trips designed to cater to the masses. But pleasure trips, for the discerning traveler. Extended tours. All arrangements put in place by myself."

And he will be rich.

His heart roars.

"Frankly, I don't see how it's any different to hiring a steam packet and offering a trip to a regatta." How *is* it different? He is simply filling a gap. Plugging a hole. He is an entrepreneur supplying a product. If he does not do it, someone else will, and he has no intention of being bested.

"It is a most unique business idea, Edison," Adelaide demurs. "I'm sure if anyone can pull it off, you can."

"Yes!" He claps once.

Then he pauses, brow creased, fist to his lips as he ponders.

"If I commissioned handbills, would you leave them in this room for your clients to browse?" He'll ask Inchbold if he can leave some with Frederick the bear at the entrance to the shop.

Adelaide rises from her stool, taking Edison's hat from the end of the bed and holding it out to him. Now that, he knows, is a signal for him to leave.

"Of course, Edison," she agrees. "Whatever you need. I am at your service."

He bows in mock gratitude and takes the hat.

"But just one thing," she calls as he reaches for the door. "You are to give me ten percent of the profits."

The Journal of Jack Aldridge

———•———•———

69°N, 53°W
Disko Island, Greenland
22 August 1849

BACK HOME IN LONDON, I spent years picturing what
might be found in the Arctic. I knew to expect strange and
remarkable beasts; I'd seen white bears on pots of hair grease,
plump seals in the slides of a magic lantern show. But there
are animals here of which I could have never conceived,
those I would not have imagined it possible to exist.

Sedgewick has designs on spotting a sea unicorn. A
narwhal, he tells me, is its true name, but I have never heard
of such a thing—a whale with the mottled body of a corpse
and a tusk thicker than a lamp post and taller than a man?
The Esquimaux track the creatures through cracks in the ice,
snare them, sharpen their tusks with their flintstones, use
them as tools for hunting.

The walruses, too, are most extraordinary, huge mounds
of flesh that huddle together on their haul-outs, sending
puffs of air through boot-brush whiskers. Approaching a herd
of walruses in a small whaling boat is not for the faint of
heart—Johnson, the boatswain, says he's seen one pull a man
from his dinghy and savage him half to death before. The
creatures have a habit of sliding in one great ugly lump into
the water as we pass. The weight of their bodies causes such
a swell, it can be hard to keep a boat upright. And as the

water boils with them, we hear their strange noises—guttural bellows, belches, and splutters and, on occasion, a sad and haunting sort of chime. Like the wind trickling through ivory beads. Sometimes I allow myself the romantic notion that the creatures know who we are. That they know what we are doing here, that they are singing us on our way.

I continue to keep myself busy, assisting Sedgewick, seeing to Despie's needs or working with Mr. Penny in the small confines of the galley. If I keep my head down and concern myself only with toil, I can imagine we are the only people who exist on this earth, alone in this white wilderness under clouds of pink, purple, and blue. But I confess I have started to dream of those faces I am trying to forget. I'll wake in a fog of confusion and alarm each morning. I'll sit up in my hammock and my heart will sink a little heavier in my chest at being reminded that I am alone.

I have come to breathe as the ship breathes, to sway as the ship sways. I feel as if I am existing inside the rib cage of something enormous and alive. As if I have been swallowed whole. As if I might never get out.

We're at the largest of the Whale Fish Islands now, and the men are busy taking magnetic observations and arranging repairs to the ships.

Despie gathers all of us, with all our differences, together each evening, the men clutching cigarettes and rubbing their hands together to keep warm as he talks. The officers and Royal Navy lieutenants are briefed separately, under skylights with cut glasses of brandy and polished telescopes. But for us, crammed together in our undershirts and corduroys, as the ship around us creaks and sways, these differences can make themselves loudly known. Most pronounced, perhaps, is the difference in manner: some rock on their heels, impatient and strung as tight as fiddle strings, others lounge on casks and chests, their ambivalence wafting outwards from their skin. The younger boys can seem awkward, indifferent, or else overly eager, biddable. Those older in age have a looseness to them, as if what holds them together has been tugged apart by the passing years.

Every time we are all gathered, I find myself considering our bodies. The organs and the bones that exist inside this cold weather clothing. The differences between their bodies and mine.

Sedgewick knows these bodies best of all. He examines them, heals them, stitches them, applies salves and balms to their weather-beaten skin. He knows best of all whose knees are crumbling with the cold, whose teeth are soft and prone to pain, who is showing signs of debility, of weakness.

What power he has.

But it's not just bodies he knows. We speak often of the workings of the sailors' minds. He talks of new theories, of how illness might perhaps show itself through a body's behaviors as well as its wounds. Well, I was raised to believe in bodily matters, taught that flesh, blood, and bone—and the bruises, burns, breaks, and infections that blight them— are of chief concern when it comes to health. But Sedgewick has an alternative way of thinking, quite novel, maintaining that a man can present with a healthy body while being quite unwell in his mind. He has books which, I understand, are considered quite contentious in his circles. I picked one up the other day and found little within its pages I could understand. But it intrigued me—the idea that someone can deviate from a natural state of mind while maintaining an outwardly healthy intellect; that there are certain disordered conditions of the brain that mean a person can harbor morbid perversions and unnatural impulses while appearing quite normal.

Of course, tales of madness are not hard to come by here in the Arctic—stories of men sent the way of lunatics by debility, men who become lost in their own loneliness and desperation. Never to find their way back. There are many, we are told, who leave their minds in the Arctic north, returning irrevocably changed, empty behind the eyes, ruined, hollowed out, and unsavable. Perhaps, I have realized, it is not the bears or the ice that we should fear. Perhaps, instead, it is what takes place inside our minds that is the greatest danger.

Chapter Eight

Edison

When he returns to his room, enlivened by his conversation with Adelaide, he checks his reflection in the glass. He expects to find the sort of glow gifted upon one's countenance when one knows one is about to come into a *lot* of money. Instead, he looks withered. Wrung out. He always does these days. The Arctic has sucked the life out of him entirely.

He makes his way to the dresser, *The Times* still open on one of Cook's adverts. A tour of a ceramics factory. Riveting. Where is the blood, Mr. Cook? Where is the thrill?

He retrieves a sheet of notepaper from the bureau, on it the logo he had begun sketching—a steam train encircled by the tight weave of a hangman's noose. The name of his company: *Edison Stowe's Moral Compass Tours* will get biggest billing. He'd thought of it on the walk home (again, he could not waste money on a cab). It has everything he wants. Adventure. Order. The inevitable punishment of crime. His impending fortune. But as he ponders it, an image arrives. Unwanted, as they often are, of his mother's possessions being carried out of the house by bailiffs. In his mind's eye, an armoire is being passed slowly over his head. It blocks out the sun, makes him squint. He is on his back, slumped halfway down the steps outside his mother's house, *his* house. Vomit caked into the creases of his neck. The men step easily over him as they strip the house of everything, the settees and the rugs and the rosewood tables—a pretty little procession passing over his head, reminding him of everything he has lost.

It had been a slow decline, at first. Just a little flutter here and there. He was a man on the town, a bachelor! Living alone with money to spare. Then the here and there became every week, then every night, then, out of necessity more than anything else, every morning and afternoon. The quality of the billiard halls and of the company he kept slowly dwindled, until he was slithering through back alleys and low haunts to fritter his money away. He began borrowing from characters who levied inconceivable margins of interest on the funds that they lent. Then he borrowed more, then more, then just a *touch* more. Then, of course, came the time when he had nothing left at all. Desolation.

He will not end up the same way again. Penniless. Homeless. A man of gentility forced to beg for help. In gulfs of debt. When it had happened, he'd gone to the only place he could think of, the only relative that he knew existed, since his father had left them without a forwarding address. Not that he really knew this relative, of course, he was just a name in his memory, words uttered by his mother's cruel lips before she died. An uncle, she had said, in the Queen's admiralty. Quite powerful too. And like most powerful men, when his nephew turned up on his doorstep, he took great pains to show him abhorrence and disdain. No, he would not grant Edison money. No, he was not interested in offering a loan.

But. There *was* a job Edison could do for him.

"Join this ship," he said. "Just a little ride out to the Northwest Passage and back."

Edison had frowned. He knew the Passage, of course, and had read newspaper articles about Sir John Franklin, even attended lectures on the subject at the Society before he was ignominiously ejected. But had he actually paid attention? These things were far more often about who you were sat next to than what was being said on the stage.

"We can pass you off as a scientific officer. Doesn't really mean anything. No one will be interested enough to bother you," his uncle said.

Edison winced but had found himself nodding. Science he could do, of course. He had always harbored scientific ambitions, had always assessed things for their constituent parts, the workings beneath the skin. The pulp. The blood. His keen mind was well suited to science, and lord knows he had put in his hours at the Society. He cannot be blamed if they had shunned him. He cannot be blamed if the world had conspired against him to squander any academic success he might have had. This was an escape. No moneylender was going to get to him on a ship, regardless of how many thumbs they'd sliced off in the past.

"Collect some algae, sketch some jellyfish, and bring something back for me. Something important."

When more specifics had been revealed, Edison had fought to keep his countenance calm. He did not want his uncle thinking he was in awe of him.

"What's in it for me?" he had braved.

His uncle had pressed his tongue against his cheek. "What's in it for *you*?" He laughed bitterly. "Salvation at this point, I should think."

He will not feel that way again. He will not reduce himself to begging. He will be conducting tours for the wealthy, and he will remind the world that it is among the wealthy and the great that he belongs.

He loosens his cravat. He needs a bath after the whore-house. He should never have touched the furniture. "Hattie!" He strides to the doorway to call out to Inchbold's housemaid. "I need bathwater!" After a lazy while, a shuffling musters itself in one of the rooms. He hears the maid make her way to work the fire and noisily fill the buckets. Eventually, preceded by clanks and rattles like a ghoul from one of Dickens's tales, she arrives, a delicate-featured young woman with hair the color of field mice in a coil at the base of her skull. What a false image. While her appearance is ordered, Hattie's actions are noth-ing of the sort. Since she presented herself at the bone shop offering her services as a housemaid—a proposition to which Inchbold seems to have acquiesced out of fear of offense more than anything—Edison has found himself needled by the girl's clumsiness, her lack of detail when folding bedsheets, her wanton tendency to knock trinkets off the sideboard as she dusts. He's mentioned her ineptitude to Inchbold more than once, lowering his voice over dinner to report a smashed mantel clock or a vase gone undusted. But the man seems to care little; Edison is certain this is because he simply enjoys having someone else in the house.

In Edison's chamber, Hattie struggles with the buckets, spilling pools of water onto the floorboards, shifting a handle to the crook of her elbow to push damp hairs from her forehead.

"Just give me the damned things," Edison snaps, tugging the buckets off her arms and placing them next to the tub. As he bends to do so he notices something on the tin. It makes the muscles in his jaw flex. Aha. He summons the maid back from the doorway.

"Have you an explanation for this?" He unlaces his cravat

fully with jerking tugs, then gestures to the tub. It demands a bit of squinting to see it, but there is the faintest smear of something, that's for sure.

"I scrubbed it for half an hour, sir," the maid pleads, "specially after last time. It's clean as anything, that tub. I'm sure of it."

"If it's clean then it won't trouble you to lick it."

The maid blinks back at him, nostrils widening. "Sir."

"If the tub is as clean as you say it is"—he pauses to allow the maid to keep up—"then you will happily lick it, to demonstrate the fact."

The maid's eyes dart around his face. He keeps his features passive. She must learn.

He nods towards the floor, and the maid reluctantly takes up her skirts and kneels until her head is at the side of the tub.

"Lick," he orders. But the maid does not move. "Lick it."

As she leans forwards her shoulders begin ever so slightly to quake, and Edison bends to watch as a pink sliver of tongue slides out from her mouth. Her eyes moisten as she moves her hands to grip the sides of the tub, white finger bones showing themselves through the skin.

He leans closer, and closer, until his breath must be hot in her ear then—"Yeow!"

Pain seizes his left buttock, and he leaps upright, twisting to find that the lurcher, Livingstone, has its jaws firmly fastened to his backside.

"Get away!" He strikes the dog hard on the nose and it backs off with a pathetic whimper. As it retreats, it licks its muzzle with a long, dry tongue. He straightens his trousers, the skin on his buttock throbbing. Hattie gathers herself and bolts from the room, leaving him alone to do her job, the job of a *maid*, not a man. Edison tuts, sucks in his cheeks, picks up one of the steaming buckets, and begins, slowly, resentfully, to fill the bath.

The Journal of Jack Aldridge

70°N, 68°W
Clyde River, Baffin Island
8 September 1849

WE'VE BEEN TRAPPING ARCTIC FOXES. Despie had the
idea. He ordered the blacksmith to fashion several small
copper collars that could be easily fastened around the
animals' necks. On them, he stamped the last position of our
ships and the locations of the depots we've been laying along
the way. We have a message for Franklin and his men. "We
are here," it says, "we are ready to help."

The traps were set a few days ago and yesterday a party
(I among their company) was sent to retrieve the ready
messengers. Baker, the young stoker's assistant, had been
assigned to the group too and we tried our best to conceal
our excitement at being allowed off the ship. I chose not to
think of myself as a woman alone, away from the safety of
the *Makepeace*. I was Jack now, I was safe in his clothing,
and this was a responsibility I had earned.

As we set out, clouds were coiled tightly on the horizon,
the sky awash with the pink and blue of dirty paint water. The
air was bitter, the early moon white and shining. Beyond the
dreariness of the scree shoreline, the wind fingered the tips of
the shrubs on the hillside.

We made our way from the gangplank as one up the beach.
The first of the wooden traps was located easily. Much to our

disappointment, its door was still wide open and its insides empty. The second, the third, and fourth similarly yielded nothing, although a ptarmigan had somehow found its way into one and was pecking around aimlessly inside. It flapped and fussed as we grabbed it. The purser, Harris, wanted to wring its neck and take it back for Cook's pot. None of us disagreed. Our bellies rumbled.

With little hope we approached the final trap, but as we did, we heard a wailing sound. It was coming from inside. The door was down.

Inside, was a fox kit. Not white as you might expect but gray instead. It had been injured, its front right leg hanging limply. We sighed. No use for our purposes.

"Another for the pot," announced the purser and bent to retrieve the animal.

"Wait!"

We all turned.

It had come from Mansfield, the clerk, a keen water-colorist, who had campaigned for a place in the party in the hopes that the landscapes might inspire his sketches.

Some of the men frowned, began to grumble, protest. But it was clear that others were less ready to allow the animal to be killed.

"It's very small," continued Mansfield. "Not much to eat."

The fox had been silenced by fear, and quaked in the corner of the trap, its pale, doleful eyes turned upwards.

"Perhaps Sedgewick can salvage its leg," I offered. "He could bind it until it heals, then we can send it out with a collar."

There was a pause as the shrill wind whipped around our comforters. Then eventually the men began, one by one, to nod. We would likely be admonished by other hungry men, but we decided to take it back to the ship alive.

As we approached we drew the attention of those on deck, shuffling closer until we were just a few yards from the *Makepeace's* hull. I held the fox in my arms. It had wriggled in distress at first but was too exhausted to put up much of a fight. They must have thought it strange to see us approach with a gray ball of fur among our party, and as we went to make up the ramp, the fox opened its eyes and shivered.

Then, something happened. Something came to us on the wind. A noise. Something eerie and inhuman. It was quiet at first and we could barely make it out above the men's chatter up on deck. Then it came louder. An unusual call. Not like a rooster, nor the bark of a dog, nor the shriek of a gull. But something approximating all three at the same time. It sent a chill through every one of my vertebrae.

We turned our heads and I could sense the fear rippling through the men. Suspicion is strong in seamen, I have learned; they believe in all manner of things—hexes, ghosts, Jonahs, faeries.

Then we saw her trot towards us. The mother fox. Head thrust back, calling out to her missing young.

The men did not know what to do. They panicked, talking over one other, voices mingling so that I could only hear taut snatches of conversation.

"Ah, hell, what shall we do with her?" They asked.

"Don't tell Cook, he'll definitely want her for Sunday supper. She's bigger. More meat to go round!"

The kit grew agitated again in my arms. The mother fox wailed and barked. Its cry, so full of grief, was getting to the men.

They continued to debate.

"Just grab her. That's a gift that is," someone shouted from above. "Fresh meat that we haven't had to hunt."

I wanted it all to stop, suggested that we let the kit go, let the mother fox take it back with her.

I was ignored.

"Just grab her by the—"

The sentence was never finished. The crack of a bullet rang out across the ice and the kit jerked wildly in my arms.

I turned to see the mother fox slumped to the ground. I could not help but gasp, the cold air searing my lungs.

Everyone's voices sounded far away after that.

"Jesus Christ, you could have had my ankle off!"

Someone asked who the hell was firing bullets at the land party.

We lifted our heads. On deck, Edison Stowe stood with his rifle over the rail. He pulled it away from his eye and straightened his back. I knew what he was going to say before he said it:

"The bones are mine."

I took the kit to Sedgewick later that evening. He promised to bind the leg as best he could but wasn't confident the animal would survive. I held the poor creature in place as he fitted a small splint against its foot. I waited for a while, watching in silence, then asked the question that had been troubling me.

I asked him if Edison Stowe was quite well in the head.

When I first boarded this ship, it was my belief, my assumption, that Abel Mance was the most dangerous man in this muster. But, as I soon realized, men like that are ten a penny up here. Their brutality is uninteresting. It's chiseled into them by their environment.

As he bent to inspect the bandages, I told him that I had been troubled by Stowe's behaviors. Stowe looks like a gentleman, that's for sure. A passing glance would assess him as officer class, someone respectable, successful, proud. But I have observed twice now just how easily the man finds it to kill. It does not trouble him to shoot at a whale or a bear. Nor to slaughter a mother fox that is crying out for its young.

There's a coldness that comes with such slaughter. A precision. I had assumed that this was a result of his position, his training—he is a man of science, is he not? Biology—life, death—is as straightforward a concept for him as it is for a surgeon.

But now I am not so sure.

Sedgewick, who had been watching me intently as I spoke, set down the bandages and gave a grim nod.

"I have seen it," he admitted, "and I fear he may be capable of worse."

Chapter Nine

Maude

November 1850

The crowds of Central Station churn like fish in a barrel, emitting a din that reaches all the way to the wide, arched ceiling. Bodies busy past, heads bowed, the clank of metal and the shriek of steam flattening the cold air.

On the platform, Maude waits. She has forgotten to wear gloves and her fingers worry the dry cuticles at her thumbs. She feels as if she is in the wrong body entirely. As if the wrong Horton sister is standing on the platform waiting to board a train. She shakes her head, admonishes herself for her lack of courage. If the situation were reversed, Constance would not be worried. Constance would do whatever it took to get answers. She would not bat an eyelid at any obstacle that stood before her. But Maude has always been so meek compared to Constance, so dull, so uninteresting. She has wondered, on occasion, when she is feeling so very low, whether her grandfather might lament the fact that the more interesting sister had to die. It cannot be just, can it? How can someone with so much life in them be no longer alive? It is as if, Maude considers, the brightest flames burn out the quickest.

The train before her is sleek, painted the same rich green as the bottles in the pharmacy. Porters fuss about with luggage and men in sooty waistcoats and shirtsleeves scramble up ladders to the sate the boiler. The steel contracts as it drinks, the locomotive releasing a long, satisfied hiss. Train travel feels aspirational to Maude. Expensive. Too expensive for someone like her. But of course, she is not the one footing the bill here. Heart has seen to that.

It had taken some convincing for her grandfather to allow her on this journey. She had not told him the truth, of course, and it had startled Maude to find that she was becoming more accustomed to deception.

A cousin had written to enquire as to whether, in light of the tragedy, Maude might find it pleasurable to escape the crush of London for a weekend in the country. At least, that's what Henry had been led to believe. And that was not so absurdly far from the truth, was it? At least, in the broadest concept of the word. There might, after all, be some countryside to be enjoyed on this journey.

She places her portmanteau, the leather stiff with underuse, on the platform and flexes an aching wrist, trying to ignore the nerves that flutter hotly at her chest. She is not accustomed to carrying luggage. Not because she is used to having someone carry it for her, but because she has never really had any cause to travel.

Her grandfather had demanded to escort her here, to see her on her way. But as they left the shop, Maude had been careful to turn her elbow just so and send a bottle crashing to the floor.

Mercury.

A careful cleanup and appropriate disposal of the waste was needed. Her grandfather would have to stay behind. What a pity. Maude reassured him she was quite certain she could manage at the station alone.

When Maude had first begun her pursuit for answers, she

had not expected it to lead her somewhere like this. But when the opportunity to finally meet Edison Stowe had presented itself, it had been impossible to resist. It arose when she, at last, found the courage to step inside Mr. Inchbold's bone shop. She had waited across the street, quietly hidden as usual, until Stowe had left for his morning's meanderings. Once she was quite sure he would not return, she hurried to the door and stepped inside.

There were far more skeletons than she had anticipated. The shop was simply stuffed with them, stacked to the ceiling, specimens stretching all the way to the storage room out back. The bones clung together to resemble strange, unfamiliar creatures: an animal that appeared like a small horse but with a longer neck and a skull like that of a dog; something low and armored, with a thin, protruding nose and a shell of cartilage on its back, knuckles grazing the floor like an ape's. Her eye was caught by a large, hexagonal case and she stepped across to it. Inside, a five-meter-long python sat coiled like an enormous chain necklace. The skeleton was almost entirely backbone, with hundreds of delicate hair-like ribs running from its tip to its tail. Astonishing.

"Can I help you at all, ma'am?" The shopkeeper stood at the till, cleaning what appeared to be a femur. Above his head, a sharp tusk whorled with ridges hung like a polished musket on display.

"I was just . . . I wanted to . . ." She felt her face redden. "I wondered. Might you be so kind as to tell me the time?"

The man smiled, turned to look at the wall clock over his shoulder.

"Twenty past the hour of eight, ma'am."

"Thank you," she stammered and turned. "Thank you kindly." The flush on her neck deepened. She should have asked him about Stowe, the thought had tapped at her shoulder as she made her way out. She should have asked after his nature, asked if he'd told any stories about an accident that occurred on the *Makepeace*. Instead, all strength had deserted her, and she'd chosen to flee. That was, until she almost barreled into a bear on its hind legs beside the door.

"Oops. I do apologize." She had paused and rolled her eyes at herself. Only *she* would apologize to a stuffed animal. *Find some courage, Maude!* But then she'd noticed the silver plate that it held in its paws, and the stack of handbills upon it. She picked one up. An illustration of a steam train was encircled by a noose. *Edison Stowe's Moral Compass Tours*, the words read. She glanced quickly back at Inchbold, still busy caressing the thigh bone, then clenched the paper in her fist and pushed her way back out onto the busy street.

On the platform, the guard blasts his whistle. The train is veiled in steam now, and Maude knows that she must board. She bends to retrieve her portmanteau and makes towards the carriage doors, but as she goes, the clasp of the bag springs open and its insides burst out, flinging themselves across the platform. Drat. Maude casts her eyes around frantically. She gathers the items, stuffing them quickly back in the case—a plum-colored dress, a book, several small glass bottles.

The whistle shrieks again and once she has retrieved everything, she fixes the clasps firmly together, taking off at a run, hoping it is not a driver's way to depart when he can see a woman hurrying towards him on the platform. She is almost at the carriage when she feels a firm hand seize her shoulder.

Disappointment floods her veins.

It is her grandfather. She knows it. He must have arrived

late and will be wondering why she is running towards this particular train. He will be trying to stop her.

But as she turns, she sees that it is not her grandfather at all. It is the guard. With an impatient scowl, he holds out a strange, hard necklace.

"Ma'am, you dropped this, but you really do need to board the train now, we're already running late."

She snatches the cord from him, holds it behind her back. Then remembers her manners. "Thank you."

She cannot believe she almost left it.

Shoving the necklace back into her bag, she rushes along the platform and pulls her way up into the carriage. The guard leaps up behind her, pulling the door to a close.

She wonders for a moment, as she regains her breath, if this task is beyond her. Her sister was always the forthright one, the one to take risks, the one who would see a door cracked open, push it wide and step wholeheartedly in. Maude did not take risks. That was not her way.

But she has not truly been herself lately, has she?

She needs to find answers to her questions. And those answers are seated in this very train carriage.

The Journal of Jack Aldridge

•————————•

70°N, 68°W
Clyde River, Baffin Island
18 September 1849

THE FOX KIT DIED and the weather is turning, revolving
into a cold so bitter you can still see your breath in the air
when you go down below. Everything is damp—the blankets,
our clothing, Rumpelstiltskin even. Ice sheaths the beams
and bulkheads. The skylights are rimed with snow. Still, it's
sixty degrees warmer than out on deck, and as your toes thaw
when you descend the man ladder it feels as if they're being
set about by needles.

The enormity of the task at hand weighs heavily on the
men. Each day we sail deeper into this place of infernal ice
and snow, this bleak and inhospitable land, and our resolve
suffers another fracture.

I sometimes find myself wondering at night, when the
air glows with the deepest, darkest blue, and the glimmer
of lamplight bounces off the dead-black water, just what
Franklin's party is doing right now. Whether *Erebus* and
Terror are simply frozen in somewhere further north, ships
lodged firm in the ice like marrow in bones. I wonder
whether they wait for us, pray for our arrival. Or if they've
been sunk by something malevolent. And sometimes, when
the air is thickest with night, I allow my mind to question
whether those sounds we hear aren't the pipes creaking and

the ice groaning, but the water-drowned bodies of Franklin and his men knocking against the bottom of our ship.

I am becoming more convinced, too, that there are those on board who do not share our goal of finding Franklin.

Since my conversation with Sedgewick, I have been watching Edison Stowe. Closely.

He has singular ways about him. He appears constantly to clean himself, always demanding more ice water be heated so that he can scrub at his skin until it is red and raw and hot. As I eat, elbow to elbow with the other boys, I observe his eating habits too. Mr. Penny detests him, for he makes a nuisance of himself whenever any meal is served.

"Where's this meat from?" he'll bark as something brown is slopped onto his plate. "Have these potatoes been scrubbed?"

Every time, the cook raises his eyes to the deck beams.

"I'll spare you the breath, Stowe," he hisses. "It's all from a bloody tin."

Each dinnertime he withdraws to sit alone, away from the rest of the men. I've rarely seen him utter more than two words to anyone but the ice master, Mance. Most avoid him entirely, passing him in the companionway as one might a discarded shoe. Even Rumpelstiltskin shows no interest, and I'm quite sure that cat would cozy up to a hammock of bloodhounds.

Stowe is never roused, as the other men are, when Despie speaks to us of Franklin, when our captain gathers us together, pipe clenched between his teeth, to remind us how we serve our queen and country. He looks, if anything, bored by the prospect. He seems to care not one jot that we are here to search for a naval hero, that we are here to become heroes ourselves.

*

I took the greatest risk of all today. I decided to trail Stowe to his cabin.

I thought perhaps I might catch a glimpse of what he keeps in there. Sedgewick would relish such observations. I just had to make myself invisible.

The cramped dark wood hovel of his cabin gave off a similar sulfurous reek to Sedgewick's sick bay. The door was closed but, once I'd checked for others in the companionway, I crouched and found that I could see through the gaps in the slats. I peered in and saw Stowe, his back to me, examining his shelves. The lamplight flickered, illuminating the sharp contours of his face. His fair hair glowed a pellucid gold. It gave him the appearance of a ghoul.

Tucked all around the built-in bunk were jars, all the stores for his specimens, labeled and numbered, filled with liquids the color of bloodied water. There were things floating: small eels, crustaceans, and plants, the algaed, globular masses I'd seen him haul in from the ship's trailing nets. I had not seen a looking glass in any other cabin but Despie's, yet Stowe seemed to have affixed one to the bulkhead, its yellowing glass reflecting clustered stacks of scalpels and lancets. As I squinted further into the cabin, an itchy sensation came upon my flesh. It was clear that Stowe was stockpiling the bones of all the animals the men had shot—what must have been rabbits lay in piles of disassembled ribs; ptarmigan skulls trapped in a jar like pickled eggs. In the shadows, small and indiscernible shapes cowered, hunched and embalmed.

I held my breath and bent to look even closer through the slats, but to my alarm another figure stepped across the doorway. My lungs sucked in a sharp breath. He must have been right in the corner of the cabin, out of sight before. But I recognized those crumpled shirtsleeves and braces, the unshaven beard, the long, unkempt hair. Mance's shoulders took up most of the space inside.

Slowly, silently, I stepped back in my crouched position so that they would not see me through the slats.

Still, I listened.

"He's a wily sod, but persistent. Typical whaler." Mance's voice was deep and gruff, filtering thickly out into the companionway. "Did Hancock give him a date?"

I glanced down towards the officers' quarters, to check that no one was coming.

"He'll wait, won't he? He knows we're on our way? Besides, it's not as if he's going anywhere." Stowe's timbre, hushed and wary, had less gravitas than the ice master's boom.

"Aye, he'll wait. Greed lends men great patience. How much we talking? What did Hancock promise?"

I leaned in closer to the slats to better hear them, but as I went my boot skidded out beneath me. I caught myself just before I tumbled, but to keep myself upright I'd grasped the wooden slats of the door. I let go as if they'd burnt me.

Mance was on me in a flash.

He had pulled open the door and was looming like an ice mountain above. Behind him, Stowe glared. I rose to my feet, swallowed, certain they could hear my heart thundering.

"Jellyfish!" I stammered. Reaching for something, anything that would explain my presence. "Green jellyfish, glowing, like the aurora. I saw them off the port bow. Thought it might interest you, Mr. Stowe."

Well, you could have smashed the air in that companionway with a hammer. The men glared, unmoving, jaws tight, eyes never leaving my face. They were wondering, I was sure, how much I had heard. Who I might tell. Whether I, a simple ship's boy, was a threat to them.

After a while, Mance must have deduced that I was not. Just a pest. An inconvenience but nothing more than that.

"Only dogs wait at doorways, boy." Mance pushed past me. I watched as he disappeared down the tunnel, reaching for his pipe as he went.

"Am I to find jellyfish in the waters if I go above?" Stowe's eyes were wolf-like.

I nodded. Tamping down the terror.

"Jellyfish," I said again, in little more than a whisper.

He turned, reached behind him for a notebook, then raised a hand and shooed me away like the dog I was.

Chapter Ten

Edison

Edison is irked, as Edison so very often is. The lack of air in the carriage is stifling, and what little there is has a distinct miasmic quality to it.

He'd passed airy third class on the way to his seat, and on seeing its open roof and Stonehenge excursionists packed like sardines onto the benches, he'd found himself envying how they would soon feel the fresh breeze on their cheeks.

This is just one carriage. Small, cramped and hemmed in. Two rows of seats facing one another, eight in total. Putting him uncomfortably close to the guests on his tour.

He blinks at the empty seat beside him—a line of dirt has accumulated in the folds of the upholstery.

He *can't* move to third, he does not belong in third. Anyone would discern with half a glance that he does not belong in third. Regardless, he'd already spent half his profits booking out this damned carriage, so he was very well going to sit in it.

He allows his eyes to roam the assembled group, a motley sort, all of whom had answered his advertisement in *The Times*. To his left, at the window, is a well-to-do man in an egregiously expensive-looking coat. He had barely raised a smile when Edison had introduced himself.

"Jameson," he said.

Edison had handed him a small black ribbon. "So it's clear we're traveling as a group," he had explained. "I thought the black rather apt." The man glared at it in his hands as if he had tossed him a snake.

To Edison's right, an elderly woman takes the empty seat and eagerly fixes her own black ribbon to her chest. She has the appearance of a splendidly groomed toad, her brown eyes quick and flighty, her gloves fine silk, her long hair pinned with expensive jewels. She smells quite overwhelmingly, Edison realizes, of wealth. Not the iron muddiness of coins, but the crispness of paper money sprung from the mint.

The woman leans across the gap to the seat opposite and slaps her husband's hand. He releases his grasp on his newspaper and takes the ribbon she holds out to him, glances at it before pocketing it and returning to his reading.

"Daphne Westbury," the old woman announces to the two people sitting to her husband's right—a plain woman in traveling twill, about twenty-three years of age, and a tall gentleman at the window, opposite Jameson, far too old to be her husband. "Lady Daphne Westbury," she repeats. The guests smile politely.

"Hollis," the tall man replies with a tip of his hat.

That's a man with strong bones, Edison thinks, picturing solid femurs and a rib cage like a barrel. It calls to mind Frederick, the bear dumbwaiter in Inchbold's shop.

"And this is my wife, Charlotte."

Wife! Good gracious.

The younger woman nods a staid greeting from beneath her bonnet.

"Lady Westbury will be an asset to us," Edison announces to the group. "There's very little she does not know about the judicial process, about capital punishment and suchlike." He attempts a laissez-faire gesture with his hand. "Was it more than fifty you said you'd observed, Lady Westbury?"

"Fifty-four. One for every year of my age." She dips her head as if acknowledging some kind compliment. Fifty-four? Edison is not sure who she thinks she is kidding.

"She's already spotted Calcraft in second class," he adds. "Bag and all."

"Calcraft?" The plain woman, the wife, asks in a soft, curious voice.

"The hangman?" Lady Westbury poses it as a question. "You are from London, are you not? You are not familiar with Calcraft?"

"Charlotte chooses not to engage with the newspapers." Her husband answers on her behalf. "She's an artist, aren't you dear? A talented sculptor."

Mr. Westbury scoffs and noisily turns the pages of his paper.

"William Calcraft is the busiest executioner in the country," Lady Westbury explains. "He's seen to almost all of London's most detestable characters."

"I expect many of them will have crossed your path, Mr. Hollis," Edison adds. "Or at least their likenesses? If I remember your occupation correctly."

Lady Westbury raises a silver eyebrow.

Hollis nods. "I'm a wax worker at Tussaud's," he explains to the rest of the group. "We have many of them in the Separate Room." He coughs. "Immortalized."

Edison pictures the cordoned-off dungeon at Tussaud's, with its death masks, its spectral gloom, its wax figures of England's most notorious criminals. Too appalling for unchaperoned female sensibilities like Lady Westbury's, although something tells him she would not be trifled by such horrors.

"Bishop and Williams?" She waits and duly receives a nod from Hollis.

"They killed a child." She leans in closer to Charlotte. "A young boy, sold his corpse to the anatomists."

Edison is sure to grunt in distaste.

"James Greenacre," she posits confidently. "The Edgeware Road Murderer. I believe the police liberated his fiancée's head from Regent's Canal, but you must have cast his own in wax?"

Charlotte Hollis's hand goes to her mouth.

"You'll all know the Mannings." A low murmur rumbles around the carriage. "They're certainly in the Separate Room." She pauses briefly to adjust the huge ruby at her throat. "One murder makes a villain, a million a hero," she continues in the manner of someone who is proving a point. "Calcraft did a fine job that day. Although he's not always so skilful."

"The bag, though? What does he keep in the bag, do you think?" Frank Hollis asks. "I've always wondered."

"Tackle," Lady Westbury answers. "Pinioning straps et cetera, et cetera."

There is a brief silence and the shrill guard's whistle sounds on the platform.

"Why would he be traveling to Salisbury if he's a London hangman?"

Edison watches Charlotte as she says it. There is something in her eyes, something probing, something sharp. 'Tis a pity the rest of her is so dull to look at.

"Proficient hangmen are required to travel to assize towns now and again to carry out their duties. It's a skill, you understand. They get paid quite handsomely for the task too."

"What makes him so skilful?" Charlotte asks.

The dullard has a lot of questions.

Mr. Westbury flips down his newspaper and peers over the top through his spectacles. "His victims take an inordinately long time to die."

Charlotte Hollis is still holding salts to her nose when the woman enters the carriage. Her arrival shifts every molecule in the space. She pauses, framed by the carriage door, checking her ticket to ensure she is in the right place. Edison feels the air around him crackle. He moves his hand to the back of his neck, certain he can feel cold fingers trailing down the skin.

The woman is beautiful. Her beauty the sort that hooks the eyes and holds them close. Even from his seat, he can observe the fullness of her cheeks, the intensity of her pale blue eyes, her hair smooth with the gloss of polished jet. Her lips, he decides, are as delicately pink as the inside of a whelk.

He tries to stand to greet her, but his legs feel heavy. Most unusual. He is not the type to be rendered speechless by beauty. But this woman. *This* woman. Her beauty has such power to it. Like Helen of Troy. Nay—the seductress Salome!

Perhaps he is getting a bit carried away.

But there is something about her. Something flighty. Something in the faint crinkles next to her eyes, the way her jaw tightens ever so slightly as she smiles. Is it the actress Sarah Siddons, the likeness?

"Welcome," he finally manages to stand, charmed to see a flush of pink on her pretty cheeks. "This must be the last member of our party."

He notices that Charlotte Hollis will not meet the woman's eye, the corners of her mouth remaining stubbornly flat as she folds her handkerchief and tucks it back into her coat sleeve. Envy, he supposes. It must be galling to one so unremarkable to be presented with everything one is not.

Mr. Westbury chuckles quietly and shakes out his paper.

"What's your name, dear?" Mrs. Westbury gestures to the spare seat next to her, at the window.

The woman sits, and deposits her small traveling bag into the recess.

She looks up and around at the assembled passengers.

"It's nice to meet you all," she says blinking once, twice. "I'm Maude."

The Journal of Jack Aldridge

•———————————•

70°N, 71°W
Sillem Island, Baffin Bay
25 September 1849

S hale upon shale, sleet upon sleet. I have lost a part of myself to the weather now.

I was on watch yesterday as nautical twilight fell with its glowing, gloomy navy blue. The wind shrieked around our heads. The sleet billowed so thick it obscured the lamps of the other men on duty. The boatswain, Johnson, came to relieve me, made four times larger than his actual size by his swaddling.

I told him I felt that my very skeleton would shatter.

"Aye," he said. "Cold bones. That's what you'll get out here. Cold bones, cold blood, cold bastard soul."

I trudged to the ladderway, stamping my feet to keep the stubborn blood from freezing in its veins. As I went, I felt an odd pressure building inside my head. I could not place the feeling, but in this cold, I am surprised every day by a new pain. I heard a strange sound, like the shell of an egg cracking. Then: an explosion within my skull, and I felt a hard object shoot to the back of my throat. I retched, then opened my mouth to spit out the remains.

It was a molar tooth, cracked in two by the freezing temperatures, pale as old milk in my mittened palm. I moved my tongue to the gap it had left in my jaw. Soft, wet, and lonely.

I do not quite know what compelled me to do so, but once off watch I asked the carpenter's assistant if he had something that might drill a hole through the pieces of tooth, then I threaded them onto a length of cord and tied it around my neck. Two halves of a whole, I thought. Like two sisters, or lovers.

I told Sedgewick what I heard down in Stowe's cabin, that he and Mance were discussing something secret. I am quite sure they have a dark plan afoot and was certain he would think so too. He frowned and pushed me for details, and I tried to recount them. The name, I eventually recalled: Hancock.

"But there is no man on the *Makepeace* with that name," I said. "Perhaps on *High Regard*?"

He rasped his hands over his beard. "The only Hancock I know is . . ." His voice trailed off like steam.

I waited.

"The only Hancock I know of is Sir Horatio Hancock," he said.

"Of the admiralty?" I continued. I had come across him during my research before boarding the *Makepeace*.

"He's one of the most powerful men in the admiralty office." He appeared to consider it. "They must be speaking of someone else. It is not an uncommon name."

"I'm not sure that they were," I replied. The passion was hot in my blood as I remembered the strange feeling in that cabin.

"Trade with the whalers is commonplace. It is almost certainly that," he said.

I knew it was not my place to do so—Sedgewick is my superior, my mentor, a guide—but I had to disagree. I felt that by not saying something I might be putting us, putting the whole ship, in danger.

I assured him it was more than the usual trade with the whalers.

I have read stories, accounts, of mutinies on ships like this. Of attempts to overthrow a captain, to change the path of a voyage for personal gain. And I have found myself, at night, unable to shake the image of Stowe's face from my mind. Two parts that do not belong together: a mouth that performs as it should—speaking, eating, twisting itself into a horrid, unnatural smile—but eyes that do not change with it. Harsh as fractured glass. Impenetrable.

"Stowe is a scientist, not a pirate," Sedgewick scoffed.

"But you said yourself he's not . . . normal."

"Being of unsound mind does not make you a mutineer. Besides, Mance might have a chance through sheer strength, but mutineers need allies—Stowe could never influence a crew."

"What if it's something else then?" I wanted to keep pushing for an answer. I felt it like an ache. "What if this Hancock is involved? What if it's something greater than just what takes place on this ship?"

He eyed me through his spectacles, and I was sure he felt that I had turned mad myself, then. I had become the sort of person he might read about in his books.

I said it anyway. "They could be planning to sink the *Makepeace.*"

He seemed so taken aback that, momentarily, his face simply did not move. He opened his mouth, grasping, seeming to find no words before shutting it again. I knew it was a stretch. But I explained to him, carefully, that I had read about such a thing before in *The Times*. A ship purposefully sunk for the underwriter's insurance.

He scoffed again. But I could tell he was considering it.

"What would a scientist and a seaman have to gain from sinking an admiralty ship?" he argued. "And Hancock? There is likely no man on this earth who wants our expedition to end in success more than him. The admiralty's reputation is at stake. He will be considered a hero if Franklin is found. He'll be glorified, admired, furnished with more medals than would fit on his chest. He would not conspire with two lowly hands to dunk a navy vessel. It's not possible."

He urged me to calm myself after that. Said my thoughts were running away with me. But something has grasped hold inside and it will not let go.

Mr. Penny says I am distracted, as we shuffle around one another in the galley. I burnt the biscuits the other day and the men admonished me, tapping the scorched, hard hexagons against the tabletop.

But regardless, each night as I lie, restless, in my hammock, I consider the ways in which the *Makepeace* might be sunk. I have learned to think beyond natural causes— a storm could splinter the ship but cannot be mustered by human hands. A fire blazing its way through the ship, however, could destroy us all. A boiler explosion would cause chaos and injury, flood us into a watery grave. But it is the ice, I have concluded, that can be wielded as a weapon out here. And Mance is the man on board who knows that ice best of all. It is he who will know how best to use it for his darkest purposes. The scenario ends, in my mind's eye, with bodies strewn about the water; bloated corpses bobbing like seals, men screaming, flailing, so much death all around. The fear has etched harsh lines across my forehead, the lack of sleep leaving purple smears under my eyes. But I cannot rest, I must find a way to convince Sedgewick of the danger that confronts us. I must find a way to uncover the truth.

Chapter Eleven

Maude

The countryside tugs by in a blur. Fields, valleys, and hamlets smear like paint across a canvas. But Maude cares little for the scenery. She only has eyes for Edison Stowe.

What had she imagined she might do when she finally met him? When she could look into his eyes, search for any scrap of truth about what really happened on that ship? It is almost impossible for her to remain in her seat; the act of sitting excruciating. She takes the fabric of her skirt in her hands, runs it between her fingers, then picks at the bitten cuticles of her thumbnails instead. Every fiber of her aches to stand and demand, in front of this strange audience, that the truth be told. But however much she wants to rail and holler, she knows that is not the way to get the truth from those who do not want it heard.

She had been remembering lately a game that she and Constance used to play in the pharmacy when they were children. Taking two frilled tablecloths, they would drape them over their heads in the manner of bridal veils. With great care, they'd use the stool to help one another up to the mixing bench, their chins barely peering over the top, four wide eyes floating above the counter. There, they'd set about creating their poisons. In mortars, they'd mix whatever odds and ends they thought Henry wouldn't miss, some crushed catmint here, a pinch of bentonite clay there, a few pounded Dover's powder tablets retrieved from one of the old jars out back. They'd grind it all together, teeth gritted in concentration. Once their mixtures were finely milled, they'd clutch their bowls to their chests and discuss exactly how they would administer their poisons and to whom. Mr. Brackett from across the street who they'd seen on multiple occasions kicking the cats? The frequent customer with a long gray moustache, carefully waxed, who, when he thought they weren't looking, pinched the skin on his wife's arm until her eyes watered?

Constance favored the arsenic approach—a small quantity tipped into their dinner every night, slowly increasing the dose until the body regresses into seizures and shock. Maude had always preferred something quicker: cyanide injected directly into the blood. The game always ended in giggles, or when their grandfather stormed in demanding to know why his jars had been upturned and his table was a mess. They'd keep their lips sealed but he had an answer for that. "You two are telling lies. I've got some truth serum out the back, I'll make you talk. Just you wait!" The girls would squeal with delight and their grandfather would tickle them until they laughed so hard they felt their chests would burst.

That's exactly what Maude had remembered at The Two Lungs as she watched the surgeons puffing on ether. Chemicals can loosen lips. She knew that. And what did she have access to if not chemicals?

She had been trailing Stowe for long enough and now it was time to make him talk. Truth serum, of course, was the stuff of her grandfather's whimsy. But she had all manner of other drugs. Ether, she had considered first. A colorless liquid that could be slipped into a drink. The effects were not long-lasting, only about fifteen minutes or so, but long enough and only a small dose was needed for intoxication. But the solution was not particularly soluble, and the smell was distinctive. She'd be caught. Laudanum? Perhaps, if she could administer a large enough quantity. Laudanum added to chloroform would be better, tip in some mercury and he'll be singing like a church bell. She has stronger options in her portmanteau, nostrums that entice men to hallucinate, become disembodied from their own consciousness and reveal their inner desires. Mescal, peyote, nitrous oxide. She is not yet sure if she has it in her, but she has to make him trust her first, has to get close to him, get him on his own. Then she'll see what makes him give up his secrets.

She makes a show of watching the view from the window as the other guests converse. She must concede, at least, that it's a pleasant escape from the noise and tumult of London. Here and there: a church, a school, an inn. Above a stretched strip of green, a puff of tiny black birds lifts and falls like seeds. Basingstoke is rather pretty. The town lies stretched out in a hollow, bathed in the golden light of early morning. The driver slows as they pass the Gothic remains of the ruined chapel, then picks up speed again, plunging them through woodland and cloaking the carriages in shade. There is something else she is going to have to overcome on this trip. She had tried not to think too much of the hangings yet. But given Lady Westbury's enthusiasm—the woman had not stopped talking of gallows and pinioning methods since Maude took her seat—she is going to have to become accustomed to such proclivities and subjects. But the brutality of it? The horror? How can society arrive at a position where it believes that the only solution for wickedness and suffering is to enact exactly that on others?

She swallows suddenly. Her ears have become very hot. That is not what she is doing, is it? No, she just wants answers and is using the tools at her disposal to help her find them. No one has to get hurt.

She looks away from the window and finds that Stowe is watching her. He seems alarmed to have been caught and glances quickly away.

Being this close to him makes her heart feel cold. She knows his character by now, has read thousands of words attesting to his strangeness, his lack of integrity, his dark obsessions. But being able to *see* him, perceive his every blond eyelash, the faint hardening of the skin across his cheeks, it is disarming.

The others must all wonder why she is here. She has already caught Lady Westbury side-eyeing her simple frock and lack of jewels. She can tell the woman is desperate to ask questions, but Maude has kept her gaze firmly out the window and her lips resolutely shut. She does not trust herself yet to talk. They must think her a working woman, surely. Unchaperoned on such a tawdry train journey. But it is not in her interests to correct them right now.

When they reach Winchester, Frank Hollis disembarks briefly as the train is watered. Maude considers a stretch but by the time she moves the guards are badgering the passengers back into the cramped carriages. Hollis returns, cheeks plummy from the cold, with a newspaper in hand. Maude watches as he draws a paperknife from his pocket and slices open the pages, shaking them out wide, revealing the headline.

FRANKLIN, it booms. *STILL MISSING*.

She leans in closer.

A £20,000 reward is to be given by Her Majesty's Government, to any party or parties, of any country who shall render efficient assistance to the crews of the Discovery ships under the command of Sir John Franklin.

Maude feels the knot in her stomach tie itself even tighter. She thinks of Constance's obsessions, a mind that felt trapped by London, by the expectations of what it was to be a woman. As a young girl, her sister was occupied by tales of adventure, feverishly tearing through stories of balloon expeditions, trips by canoe into mystical rivers, journeys to the depths of the rainforest to collect rare medicinal plants. They were uncommon, but it was the stories of women adventurers she relished most of all. To Constance, these women had everything she wanted: freedom, adventure, a chance to scrawl their names in the history books. Maude had always wondered if it were strange that she herself felt quite so content in her grandfather's pharmacy. She had never courted, had never felt the need to do so, not when she had the companionship of her sister and her grandfather. And she could not marry. She could not leave them; they needed her. But sometimes she envied her sister for her purpose, her ambition. And the fact that she *did* leave. Constance had not assumed it her duty as a woman, as a sister, to stay. Should Maude be striving for more? Sometimes she thought perhaps she should. But that's just another way in which Maude has weighed her own attributes and found them wanting. Constance would not be having these doubts if the situation were reversed. She wishes, right now, that she had half her sister's resolve. She wishes so very much that she were with her on this train.

SALISBURY

Chapter Twelve

Maude

Every costermonger in Salisbury must have had an ear out for the approaching train. By the time Maude and the group have disembarked and been swept onto the street with the eager Stonehenge excursionists, they are arranged in their gauntlet, hollering, coaxing, touting.

What's on offer, Maude discerns, is of varying quality. On one side, pretty fruit sellers proffer baskets stacked with spit-polished apples. Some have trays hung by straps around their necks, oranges showing only the slightest dappling of mold. Less fragrant are the men selling trotters and flaccid animal parts, categorized ostensibly by their varyingly insipid shades of gray. Above them, the sun is up in earnest, gilding the water meadows with the amber glow of ale.

As Maude negotiates the concourse, Edison draws level with her. There is a change in the temperature of the air as he passes, she is sure of it. As if he has brought his own waft of the Arctic back with him. She watches his shoulders as he strides onwards, and as he stops and they slacken in awe, and the magnificent spire of Salisbury Cathedral heaves into view.

Edison arranges three cabs—the men and women will

travel separately to Fisherton Anger Gaol for the hanging. As he barters with the drivers, Maude refamiliarizes herself with the body she has spent the past few weeks following. He is not broad, but his limbs are lean and taut, a show of animal strength. All sinew. His legs are long, his arms robust enough. But he does not look like a man accustomed to violence, to digression.

He gestures to the women—Maude, the unassuming Charlotte Hollis, and the far from unassuming Lady Westbury—and they make their way towards the hansom. It will be a squeeze with the three of them, but it will have to do. She goes to climb in. Edison watches her as she moves, she realizes. His eyes quick and intent. She hopes he cannot see the shadow of her sister beneath her skin.

When they arrive at the gibbet, a crowd has already collected, paltry compared to the gaudy London spectacles, but in number enough to churn up a low and pulsing grumble. The air smells of hard dirt and freshly baked gingerbread. Maude is nervous for what's to come.

Onlookers huddle atop their carts. One man has even brought a stepladder with him from which to observe the morning's proceedings. There is a hideous intimacy to the occasion; with no scaffold, the crowd is so close they will be able to sense every twitch of the condemned. They will hear every muttered word, every fearful breath, every last wet rattle of the lungs. She swallows drily.

Pie men slip easily through the crowd selling penny sandwiches, sweetmeats, and tarts to those whose hunger is stoked by the sight of the gibbet.

A broadside is thrust into Maude's hands.

THE MOST SANGUINARY MURDER AND MUTILATION OF NANCY BIRD, AGED 15, BY HER FATHER PERCIVAL BIRD, AGED 45, AT DEVIZES, WILTSHIRE.

His committal and confession. With a copy of the letter.
Also, the full particulars of the poisoning in Essex

She lowers it. A father. A daughter. She can recall her own father's appearance only in glimpses now, details lit by ever-dwindling candlelight. Her mother's, too, she struggles to recall in focus. A soft, grainy picture of a wide smile, safe hands, kind eyes. She remembers visiting the site of their graves, can still recall the cobweb pattern of the lichen creeping up the side of the headstones. She imagines now a narrow grave dug beside them for her sister, pictures peering down into the hole to find a coffin, open and empty. There is no body, they were never given anything to bury, her sister kept hostage from them all in death. She imagines clawing at that earth, railing at the sky, the soil cool in her hands as she wails, wild with the emptiness, the unjustness of it all, the horror.

A piercing laugh spears across the crowd and Maude's head whips up. The rest of the group have gathered around a small exhibit nearby. As she nears, she sees a large wire cage, which occupies nearly half of a handbarrow. The rest of the cart has been boarded over to create a stage for unusual performers. She steps closer. In the cage is a clutch of underfed animals—two cats, half a dozen mice, and a handful of canaries. She watches as the exhibitor furnishes the cats with tiny boxing gloves and entices them to spar. It's an unconvincing act, but the onlookers chuckle with delight. Next, the mice are encouraged to walk a thread-like tightrope, balancing poles fixed to their backs. Men sniff in approval, women in brown aprons titter. Then, the canaries are coaxed into position. With a pop one bird fires a tiny cannon with its beak. Another, affecting itself to have been killed, permits itself to be placed in a coffin and towed away on a miniature hearse. The bird offers no sign of life until the carriage stops, when it suddenly revives itself and hops to its feet. Meanwhile, the avian murderer is taken for retribution. Its head is placed in a small noose, suspended from a gibbet, which another bird tightens by pulling with its beak. Once the bird has "swung', the showman bends to retrieve the poor creature. He displays it to the crowd, very much alive, its wings flapping wildly. Then he pulls the cap from his head and offers it around for coins.

A loud bell signals the start to more sober proceedings. The clouds take this as their cue to release fat droplets of rain, which sit like grim pearls on felt hat brims and the black-painted crossbeams of the gibbet.

A cart rattles down the track towards the waiting crowd, flanked by constables on horseback. As the cart nears, Maude's eyes cling to the prisoner inside. He wears a white shirt over his clothes and sits, slumped like a discarded sack against the side of the cart. It is by virtue of this positioning that, merci-fully, he will not see Calcraft, enveloped in a long brown coat like a bat in its wings, pulling on the rope to test its strength.

As the guard hauls the condemned out of the cart, Maude catches, out of the corner of her eye, Mr. Jameson—so far, the quietest member of their group, besides her—reach into his coat and pull out a wedge of handbills.

"Shame on you!"

Alarmed, Maude swivels to see who he might be shouting at.

"Shame," he booms. "Shame. Shame."

The bell maintains its atonal tolling too.

Jameson continues his solitary protest as the guard carries

the man, who has quite lost the use of his legs, up to the gibbet. He continues as the chaplain leads the crowd in the first of the solemn psalms.

"Wicked," Jameson hisses. A man in a stained cap turns to him in annoyance.

"Wicked." He says it again as the psalms swell around him. A few men jeer. Someone hurls a half-eaten pie in his direction.

"Look at yourselves," he bellows, gesturing to the bemused crowd. "No sorrow, no salutary terror, no abhorrence."

Maude is not entirely sure what's happening, but she knows she likes it. Edison's face has gone quite white, its pallor matched only by the cadaverousness of the man about to be hanged.

A man in farmer's clothing takes a handbill from Jameson's pile then pleads with him to be quiet. *"There's a show going on. Give the hangman some respect."*

"This is not a deterrent," Jameson continues without pause. "This is not a means of repentance or reform. This is vile, ribald entertainment. This is MURDER."

Maude glances at the pamphlet clutched in her hands. A father. A murderer. Taking the life of his own daughter.

Jameson turns to holler at the gibbet now. "Calcraft! Swine! Have you no sanctity? Are you not fallible yourself? Will you insist on meeting sin with sin?"

Jameson continues his spirited protest for a while, but halfway through the second psalm he is hoisted off his feet by two large men who each take an arm and drag him out of earshot.

Atop the cart, the prisoner waits with the rope loose around his neck. It is tied to the top of the gibbet, which is not particularly high, and Maude can see him assessing the drop, as if calculating how long it might take for him to die. Her throat goes liquid. She hopes, for his sake, the man's death is quick.

After a lull, the chaplain calls for any family members to offer their final goodbyes. A crooked-backed man, a brother perhaps, slowly climbs the steps. He cups the man's face in his hand and offers a few hushed words, sacred to the two of them.

When it happens, she does not watch as Calcraft covers the man's face with his hood. Nor as he lashes the horses that draw the cart, which slips from under his feet to seal his fate. She does not watch the man drop. Instead, she seeks out the brother, who stands with his hat clasped to his chest a small distance away. When a few minutes have passed, and the crowd has begun to thin, the brother goes to the body and squeezes the dead man's boot, for just a second. Maude feels it then, that thunderclap of grief. She sees her sister's feet, inanimate, buried under several feet of snow. Unyielding, horrifying snow. Did they let Constance keep her boots on as she was buried? Is she cold out there? Are her bones cold? Is she scared, in that wide Arctic wasteland?

The Journal of Jack Aldridge

———•————————————•———

72°N, 77°W
30 September 1849
Pond Inlet, Baffin Bay

SOMETHING HAS CHANGED. I must put a record to paper,
even though it afears me to do so.

We met with the whalers in Baffin Bay. A few days ago,
two late Scotch schooners from the summer fleet passed
us to the south on their way home, flags high and a fair,
bright wind behind them. The schooners had all manner
of equipment splayed out across their deck, bomb guns,
lances, harpoons, all the tools pertaining to a whaling outfit,
but which made the ships look more like men-o'-war easing
by. They cast reflections on the water as they went, and I
couldn't help but picture their insides—stacks of whalebone,
barrels of blubber. A ship stuffed full of death.

We came across three more brigs at anchor farther along
the coast, and as we nosed into the harbor to join them,
we saw something that we haven't seen for a long while:
habitation. After so long accompanied by nothing but ice
and sea and the same dreary, wind-beaten crew, it felt
implausible, fantastical almost, that there could be other men
alive on this earth.

The landscape was bitterly cold yet brilliant with sunshine,
spiky with structures made from wood that looked to be
dwellings or stores. Nearby, a circle of tents was covered with

animal skins. As I squinted into the sun it appeared as if their beams were made of bones, but bones larger than any I have ever seen. More like the ribs of a leviathan, or some felled giant stripped of its flesh.

I shimmied up the rigging for a clearer vantage.

As soon as I was up there, I heard my name being called.

Sedgewick was peering up at me.

"Come and see this."

I scrambled down, followed the line of his gaze and then froze in my spot.

Women had begun to board our ship.

I'd only ever seen pictures of the Esquimaux in books before. But here they were in their skin parkas and their fur pants—a dozen of them carrying items to trade.

These women were the first of my own sex I had seen in months. I had to consider that they might take one look at me and see me for what I truly am. Something unspoken could pass between us should we touch hands or share a nervous smile. Something indecipherable could unite us, we women in a wild landscape with whalers and lonely seamen.

I had imagined, many times, what might happen should my secret be laid bare. Unwelcome sequences had played out in my mind's eye as I stoned the deck or kept watch in the crow's nest. None were favorable. All were dangerous. I could be banished to the hold, kept in bondage down below, separated from the men for my own protection or theirs. I could be tossed overboard by those superstitious enough to believe that a woman brings bad luck to a ship and not vice versa. I could be threatened with violence, exposed to torture, to the unrelenting needs of men. Each of the sequences was more terrifying than the last. But this felt the closest I had come to tasting the reality of any.

And so I hid myself, watching from a distance as the men went to inspect the goods on offer. Dried codfish, caribou skins, walrus tusk knives, rubbery bales of seals. Some of the women had brought children with them and the purser, Harris, a man with boundless energy, merrily chased them round the deck, the children shrieking with delight.

It was an easy camaraderie and eventually the men disappeared below, returning with plenty of goods of their own to barter with, clasp knives and steel needles, files, beads, and tobacco. But it was their shining gilt buttons, carved with the Royal Arms, that the women coveted most of all.

Sedgewick served as translator, being the only man on either ship who could speak a stilted version of the women's language. Stowe was on him like a hawk, badgering the surgeon, again and again, to ask them questions. Sedgewick patiently translated, but the women shook their heads and moved on. Stowe retreated, muttering to himself as he went below, leaving the hatchway to the stepladder open.

The women's arrival assuaged the boredom that comes with so long at sea. It had everyone in high spirits, yet it had planted something caustic in my stomach.

I picked my way past them, skirting the deck, keeping as far from the women as I could. For the men, these women were a distraction, a means of acquiring goods. A titillation, even. To me, they posed nothing but danger.

Then, to my horror, one of the women lifted her head and her eyes sought me out. I felt them on me, shrunk as I was against the gunwale near the hatch to below decks. Slowly, she tilted her head, and her keen eyes probed my face. She smiled, and in that moment, it felt as if I had swallowed a musket ball. I swayed a little. The woman detached herself from her child and made her way towards me. I knew I had to move quickly; I knew she could see my secret. After all, it takes one woman to know another.

I made for the hatchway doors, keeping my eyes fixed on her as I leaned backwards, unthinkingly, to open them.

Of course, they were already open.

The horizon tipped upwards as I tumbled into the darkness, crashing down the steps, heavy and fast, coming to a heap at the bottom. The pain was hot and immediate. There was no breath left in my body. I groaned and clamped a hand to my mouth.

I could not draw attention to myself.

Tears came as I moved my hand into the back of my shirt and felt under the flannel bind. The skin was tender. Hot to the touch. I was sure I had broken my ribs.

Then, a face appeared in the hatchway above.

I moved a hand across my face to hide.

Sedgewick.

He descended, bending without pause to inspect my injuries.

I tried to push him away. To insist that I was fine.

He lifted me and wordlessly carried me to the sick bay.

Never have I felt so exposed and so vulnerable. Sedgewick clearly had not sensed my apprehension, and set about arranging his jars, waiting politely for me to remove my clothing for examination.

I remained fully dressed.

When he bent to listen to my heart, I could see every line on his face. I could see the threads of silver in his hair.

He stood again and fixed me in the eye.

"Shirt," he ordered. He said it oddly, like a challenge.

I did not move. Sedgewick did not move either.

I realized then that he knew.

I went as slowly as I could, my clumsy fingers dithering over the buttons. The air was so cold it turned my skin to gooseflesh. Sedgewick turned away to polish his stethoscope. A small kindness. When the buttons were undone, he came to sit again on the stool in front of me.

"Turn to show me your back." He sounded almost regretful. "I must assess if anything is broken."

I did as he asked, and he took the back of my shirt in his hand and lifted. Almost as soon as it lifted, it dropped. He must have seen the bind.

He was about to send for Despie, I knew it.

"I need to check your rib for a fracture. For that I will need you to remove the shirt." Then, after a pause, "I'm sorry."

Trembling, I pulled my right arm from its sleeve and slid off the shirt. I turned my shoulder and Sedgewick moved closer, bending to lift the bottom of the bind.

For a moment, I stopped breathing.

He pressed his fingers gently into my back.

"Are you going to tell Despie?" The words came out as a whisper.

"It's not broken." He replaced the flannel and moved away as if he had not heard me. "But the bruising will be painful. I'll give you some arnica."

I pulled the shirt back and began to fasten the buttons, watching as he moved to his cabinet to assemble a poultice.

"Will you tell Despie?" I asked again. Louder. I had to know my fate.

He paused, sighed, then turned. Met my eye. "No."

The relief was profound.

But his answer puzzled me. Why would he not tell Despie? Any other man on this ship would tell Despie.

"Are you not surprised?" It was a risk to ask, but I could not help it.

He raised his eyebrows.

"Aldridge, I don't know any other ship's boys who can read, let alone tell blue vitriol from lapis lazuli. I was quite aware that you were not who you were trying to convince us you were."

My mouth fell open. He had known all this time.

"You're not angry?" The question felt needy. Girlish. I scrambled to rectify. "Knowing could be dangerous for you."

He regarded me as if assessing my state of mind. Then he said very slowly, in the manner of someone explaining bad news to someone slow of wit, "I'm afraid the one in danger here is you, not me." He wiped his hands on a cloth. "To reveal your truth to Despie, and in turn to the other men, would be fatal. Again, for you. In case that wasn't clear."

He saw me crumple, came to sit beside me.

"I assume you've heard the stories about my mother?"

I nodded. I had heard the rumors.

"It's true, mostly. She was taken by force. Defiled. Battered. By men at a Company outpost." The muscles in his jaw twitched. "I know what happens when men are cut off from the world. I know what happens when they find a woman among them."

He rose from the stool, and I heard him open a drawer. "Take this."

I turned to see that he had his arm outstretched. An item, shiny as a halfpenny, sat in his palm. I leaned closer, expecting to see a spoon for a tincture, arnica for the bruising, even a charm for protection, good luck.

It was none of those things. It was a knife.

Chapter Thirteen

Edison

He draws all members of the group together. This is damage control; he cannot let Jameson's words get to them. Oily swine.

In the melee, Lady Westbury excuses herself, then returns some minutes later with a length of cord draped around her neck. Beside her, her husband tuts loudly.

"What is it?" Charlotte asks.

Mr. Westbury releases an aggrieved sigh. "It's nonsense, is what it is." His wife is already shaking her head.

"It most certainly is not nonsense." She fingers the cord. "The hangman's rope has curative powers for all manner of ailments. And with your chest"—she waggles a rubied finger at her husband—"you'd be wise to try it."

Good. At least his most lucrative customer has not been dissuaded by Jameson's ridiculous protests. He considers the cord around her neck. Nothing but shrewd entrepreneurialism. He had heard claims about such behaviors—grasping a dead man's hand to cure goiters, rubbing a gallows splinter on one's gums as a treatment for toothache et cetera et cetera. He had never heard anything about the curative properties of a hangman's rope. He makes a note to investigate further later. All beliefs could be monetized, no matter how misguided.

"Bound round the head for headaches." Lady Westbury takes it from her neck and proffers it to Ms. Horton, who declines with a blink of distaste.

"Oh, come on, it's hardly as gruesome as what Sanson carried. He'd have sold you skulls, fingerbones, pieces of hair. This is merely a textile, but . . ." She points firmly at her husband again. "A single strand can ward off fits and fevers."

Lady Westbury does not blink when they pass an emaciated man some yards down the road selling what *he* promises is the real hangman's rope. Nor when they stride by a second, then a third. At the fourth, she raises her hands to the frayed material and wraps its length once more around her neck.

The lodgings, at least, are a success. Such age; such history. He turns to see Lady Westbury inspecting the portico.

"Could we have not gone with The Red Lion?" She eyes the Tudor timber.

"Look." He gestures to the skirting sign: *Noted House for Wines and Spirits.* "Now that is a witty double entendre; the proprietor tells a marvelous ghost story. Come."

He counts the group in through the low doorway: the Hollises, the reluctant Westburys, Jameson—who returned sheepishly as they left Fisherton Anger Gaol, requesting a lift back into town—and finally Ms. Horton. Maude.

Since she'd stepped into that train cabin, Edison has found himself quite consumed with thoughts of the woman, wondering where she has come from, why she is here alone, considering with a scientific eye, of course, what she might look like on the inside. He finds he wants to hold her skull in his hand. Touch that skin, bright like a pearl, stroke her cheek, feel his way down to the sharp point of her chin. He wonders, when he allows himself, what her skeleton might look like. How it would compare to the specimens in Inchbold's shop. Delicate, he decides. Like the bewitching bones of a bird.

The inn is cramped on the inside. But it is impossible, Edison hopes, to deny its charm. The walls have been blackened by pipe smoke but the floor at least, a monochromatic checkerboard of tiles, has been given the once over with a mop. A ready fire arcs and crackles in the hearth and a sign above the bar announces LIVE EELS. To its left, a small set of stairs leads to a raised dining level where men toss back porter and turn dripping bones of beef in their fists.

"Rooms are up top." The landlord, vigorously polishing tankards below the eel sign, raises a finger to the ceiling. His head is perfectly framed by an enormous set of antlers mounted on the wall behind him.

"I'll help you ladies with your bags." He opens the hatch and strides out from behind the bar, bending to grasp their luggage in his fists.

"On you go, ahead," he orders. Mrs. Hollis and Ms. Horton begin nimbly to ascend the stairs. Edison hangs back, he might allow himself a tot of whisky before dinner. He watches their figures as they climb and is intrigued to see that Maude's traveling bag has fallen open. There must be a problem with the clasp. As the landlord heaves it to the crook of his elbow, something falls out and lands in the shadow of an overhanging step. The barman does not notice, nor does Maude above him, and they continue up the dark, winding staircase to the sleeping quarters. Edison allows his gaze to quickly roam the room. Mr. Westbury has his head in a newspaper next to the fire, Jameson is busy inspecting the eels, and Lady Westbury has engaged Frank Hollis and another unsuspecting soul in conversation. Unobserved, Edison strides over and snatches the item from the shadow.

He opens his palm, recoils.

At first, he thinks it might be scrimshaw and his mind goes immediately back to the ship; to men hunched over, tongues pressed into the hollows of their cheeks, whittling scenes of adventure, pornography, or natural history into sperm whale teeth. But this is not scrimshaw, nor is it the toe bones of elk that he'd seen the Esquimaux wear as jewelery. This is something quite different entirely.

He moves his hand closer to his eyes to inspect it again and as the details of it become clearer, his curiosity grows.

It is a tooth. Yes. Two halves of a molar. Cracked apart and strung together on a small length of string. As if it might be worn as a necklace, like Lady Westbury's thread of noose. He inspects the two shards once more, takes the cord between his thumb and forefinger, rubs it. What an unnatural trinket; why would a woman like Maude Horton carry such a thing?

Unless.

His stomach briefly warms. It crosses his mind that his measure of Maude Horton might be entirely incorrect. She is a woman, alone, on a tour that some might, narrow-mindedly, consider macabre. Perhaps he has underestimated her. Perhaps, instead of being saintly, innocent, fragile as a wren, she is drawn instead to the shades of darkness from which others shy away. Perhaps it is *aberration* that has enticed Maude Horton here. Perhaps, he allows himself to imagine, her story is just like his. Perhaps, in Maude Horton, he has found someone who might indulge his inclinations.

Against his urge to pocket the necklace, he calls her name. Climbs quickly to the top of the stairs and holds it out to her.

As he does, their eyes meet, and he finds a look he knows well. It brings about a muggy sort of pleasure. It is a look, he knows, of terror.

*

Once, when Edison was a boy, he fashioned a gift for his father. His father had not yet left them, at least not permanently, and when he returned from his research trips, or late nights at Society lectures reeking of gin and cigars, he would bring back precious gifts for Edison—an embalmed goliath beetle; the knife-sharp talon of a cassowary bird; the fragile, crushable skull of a rare ghost bat. His parents would often argue long into the night. She'd accuse him of drinking too much; he'd accuse her of spending all their money on fripperies, and their raised voices and crashes would travel up the stairs to Edison's room. In the morning, Edison's mother would cover her face with her hand so he could not see the bruises and cuts. But he knew his father did not mean it. Not really. He knew his mother had riled him unnecessarily, he knew he *had* to make him stay.

And so he had snuck out of the house to find a gift that was beautiful enough to keep his father here with them. He'd scoured the gutters for anything eye-catching, ogled rubbish heaps and even climbed a couple of trees, but it was not the right season for birds' eggs. Finally, he came across his treasure in a carton out the back of the grocer's shop. A mother cat and her three kittens had clearly crawled into the carton before succumbing to the cold. They were stiff in there, perfectly preserved in death. Beautiful. His father would be utterly fascinated.

He carried the carton back to his room and tucked it carefully in the corner. How best to present his gift to his father?

Should he clean the animals' fur? Place them atop a plinth of sorts? He thought of the bat skull his father had given him, the way he'd spoken in awe of the delicate bones, how animated he'd always become when talking about skeletons. So, Edison decided to strip the cats of their flesh and present the bones, in situ, to his father. That was bound to impress him. It took a while to peel the skin off the carcasses with the kitchen knife, to scoop out the organs and the viscera, to dump it all in a box to be dealt with later. When he'd finished, he could not have been prouder. His face was smeared with blood, his room was an appalling mess, but he did not care. He knew his father would be delighted to see just how hard Edison had worked. That he was going to be a scientist too.

His parents arrived back at the house together and as he heard them climbing the stairs, he could barely contain his excitement. He knew his small exhibit would garner a reaction, but he had not expected the one he got. His mother began to scream. The horror clear in her voice. His father stood with his head in his hands, slouched against the doorjamb as his mother shrieked at the bloodied cat skeletons arranged on the bed.

"You did this!" She wheeled on his father, jabbing a shaking finger towards his face. "You turned him into this. Look what you've done. He's a monster!"

His father laughed, then held up his hands as if admitting defeat.

"Get out," she ordered. "Get out."

And so he did. Edison never saw him again.

*

The group assembles again at dinner, the tavern is growing busier by the minute, gentlemen traders and hagglers pushing through the doors with the bruised-vegetable stink of the market nearby. The crowd grows in surliness too, as the sky outside darkens like a dying candle. With only a small amount of reshuffling, the Moral Compass tourists have fitted themselves around one table. Although maintaining as much propriety as they can: the women are seated on one side and the men on the other. Edison was cautious not to place himself directly opposite Ms. Horton, but instead diagonally to her right. This makes it easier for him to watch her.

Dinner is plentiful, although everything, including the garden peas, is jellied in fat. He prods at the food with the tines of his fork. Turning the pale chop and inspecting it, before raising it to his reluctant lips to chew. His mind goes to flensing. The art of butchering a seal. He recalls the routine—turning the corpse over, cutting round the hind flipper then slashing it open from the neck to the genitals. He'd push his knife into the space between the meat and the blubber, working carefully to cut and prise away the outer layers. It was a delicate act, and one he'd perfected. There was a satisfaction to the way a hook went into skin, how the body could be dragged along the ice to leave a bold, crimson message: I was here.

Lady Westbury is a graceless eater; Charlotte Hollis, in comparison, is mouse-like and neat. Edison fancies he can see every bone in her hand working beneath her skin. She is insular, he observes, a stark contrast to her husband, who is engaged in a loud but not unfriendly argument with Mr. Jameson, who had nowhere else to eat.

They discuss tomorrow's plans, a trip to the cathedral then a period of rest before the evening's soirée at Wilton House. He had noticed Maude's comely face flush at the mention of the party. She had cleared her throat and apologized: she had not brought anything suitable to wear to such an occasion, she'd have to decline. Frank Hollis made a conciliatory grunt, but at his side his wife could not mask her triumph. He had told Ms. Horton, had he not, about the dance at Wilton? All included in the tour.

"I'm sure I've got something that will fit you, dear." Lady Westbury scrapes back her chair. "Come, let us have a rummage now."

Charlotte announces that she will turn in too.

"Mr. Hollis," Edison asks as she rises. "A drop of whisky before bed? I'd love to pick your brains about Tussaud's."

"You'll hear her walking the corridors up there, but don't worry. She's friendly enough." Last orders have cleared the taproom, leaving dregs of bodies slumped across the tables. A few indefatigable strumpets pick their way through the waste, like birds after worms, hoping to coax some poor unfortunate back to consciousness.

The landlord has joined Edison, Hollis, Jameson, and Mr. Westbury, and has brought his lantern with him too. He has placed it, absolutely intentionally, under his chin so that the shadows are sucked into every crevice of his skull.

"She's the lady ghost but we have a coupla gentlemun too. One of them a dreadful pervert." He raises his eyebrows at Edison. "And we've a cat ghost, Eurydice, and the spirit of a small child. He likes to giggle in yur ear while you're tucked up in bed. *Don't* be drawn by it."

"What wonderful stories, thank you, Cecil." Edison takes his clasped hands from his knee and taps the table. He glances at the gentlemen's faces to find a triptych of exhaustion, boredom, and terror.

"I'm sure we shall sleep soundly regardless of any otherworldly companions." Frank Hollis raises his eyes to the staircase with the air of a man about to grasp his musket and head out to Waterloo.

The corridor is bitter, and the floorboards mewl as Edison makes his way to his room. He loosens his cravat and pushes open the door, revealing a bare space furnished with simple bedstead and a small side table. Not London standards, but nothing worse than he's suffered before. As he steps in and goes to lock the door behind him, a sound comes from out in the hallway. Like the tinkle of child's laughter. Surely not.

He puts an ear to the door. Waits. Then shakes his head, chastising himself for allowing the man's tall tales to find their way under his skin. His shoulders soften until, once more, it comes. The soft cluck of a child's giggle. He leaps away from the door and crosses straight to the dresser to pour a large measure of whisky from the carafe. He downs it in burning gulps. When the glass is finished, and the roaring sound in his ears has subsided, he is calm enough to take in the room, noticing, with annoyance, that no one has come to re-stoke the fire. He throws on a log and gives it a resentful jab with the poker, cursing when he realizes it's left a trail of black soot across his palm.

Outside, the rain begins to fall, each droplet like the tap of a finger against the window. He rolls his shoulders, the vertebrae in his neck uncoiling, then shrugs off his coat, places it on the peg at the back of the door and lets out an exhausted groan. Removing his shoes, he tucks them neatly into a corner, then moves his fingers to the collar of his shirt as a scream rips through the air.

The Journal of Jack Aldridge

72°N, 77°W
Pond Inlet, Baffin Bay
2 October 1849

I KNEW THEY WERE UP TO SOMETHING. I knew it. Stowe, and Mance. I knew I had overheard something important in that cabin.

I am safe in my hammock for now, but all around me the shadows loom and darken. What I have just seen has unstrung my nerves and cast them loose. My fingers shake as I write. But write I must. For I am starting to believe the things we record, the things we write, the things I put to paper in this very diary, might be seen by other eyes some day. Eyes of those who have had to secure our rescue or, worse, retrieve our possessions, our bodies, once our souls are gone.

We were invited to dine with the whalers. I should start there.

The invitation gave me pause. I knew I wasn't the only one to fear the whalers. We were all wary of their roughness; we'd heard stories of brutality and baseness, of blood. It was not hard to imagine them looking upon me with hunger, taking advantage if they found me—small, weaker than the other men—alone.

The afternoon was dreary, the leaden sky swirling with mist. We disembarked the *Makepeace* at four bells and trudged our way in a line across the gravel. As we neared the large mess hut we passed two whalers, drenched in blood, hard at work inside the mouth of a bowhead. The fish was laid out, long as a schooner, a stepladder shape hacked into its flesh. Its head had split apart so its jaws gaped horribly open. Blood had seeped from its corpse to stain the ice a gaudy crimson. Nearby, a pack of dogs strained on long metal chains.

In the near distance we could see more men at work, balanced on boards spread across huge iron try pots. With paddles they stirred bubbling liquid. Around them, clouds of nickel smoke spiralled into the air.

Some of our men held sleeves to their noses. Others watched with a morbid fascination as the men toiled. With curved knives and clean movements, the whalers cut away the lower part of the bowhead's jaw, then they bent to lift its huge pink tongue, muttering as if discussing how best to remove it.

Then, something even more obtuse: one of the men glanced up at our passing party and froze, a look of recognition taking a hold of his weather-lined face. I followed his gaze back to our group and saw that he had locked eyes with the ice master, Mance, who appeared, in turn, to nod and lower his eyes, before continuing his silent path towards the warmth of the hut. As he went, head stooped, I turned to watch as the whaler shifted his small body up and out of the animal, setting a path to follow us, to follow Mance, into the shelter.

Inside, the space was dark and filled with smoke. A fire hissed at its center and dozens of men congregated at makeshift tables. In the corner, a limp American flag hung from a rusting stake. Furs were strewn all around. We hovered at the door, unsure of whether our presence was welcome. I felt my shoulders widen and my nose tip up. Assuming my actor's posture, just as I had that first morning on the *Makepeace*.

"Ah, the Brits are here." A man rose from an upturned barrel and clapped his large hands. From his dress I deduced that this must be Captain Ellis, head of the whaling fleet, although there were no shining epaulettes on his threadbare jacket. He was tall and sturdy, and if not large enough to be called imposing, he emanated the sort of easy authority you find in men with unflinching strength of mind. With a large, fixed smile, he moved across the hut towards us and opened his palms in greeting.

"Ignore this miserable horde." He had an unplaceable accent. "The cold's got to them. Or is it the blood?" His teeth flashed white. "Make yourselves comfortable. Stanford! Get the men a drink."

The whalers afforded us a cursory glance, eyeing the officers' jackets with amusement. Some grunted, and eventually a man in a stained waistcoat detached himself and went to fetch us rum and water.

We took our seats, filling the shadows, cross-legged on furs, grateful for the comfort but unsure of how to make conversation with the Yanks. I tried to ignore my rising sense of unease. What if they ferreted out my female scent? Would they tear me to pieces like their dogs chained up outside? I assessed the weapons that easily littered the hut—the rusty blubber knives, the staves, the hatchets, and the pistols. The air carried an acrid tang: the reek of unwashed souls who've locked themselves away from society.

At one point the door behind us opened, letting in a blast of freezing air, and the whaler who'd locked eyes with Mance

stepped in, shirt still soaked in blood. He was slight and
short for a whaler but had the sort of grizzled features hewn
by experience. I turned to check for Mance's reaction. He
blinked twice quickly, glanced at Stowe, then moved his eyes
to his boots.

The evening sped on and as the men became more lubricated
the chatter thickened. A filthy-aproned cook produced a pot
of meat for dinner, and we all tucked in. Sitting awkwardly
slumped for so long was causing my bruised ribs to burn,
so I sipped at the rum to try and dull the pain, thinking of
the arnica I had stashed in my sea chest back on board.
The whalers, I could see, were a motley mix: white men,
black men, and even Esquimaux. I shared my surprise with
Sedgewick quietly. He told me the best whaling harpooners
he had ever met were Esquimaux.

Despie refilled his pipe in a loop and engaged Captain
Ellis in polite conversation. From what I could hear, they
spoke of Jamaica, from whence Ellis hailed—which explained
the accent—and around which Despie had sailed extensively.
Then their talk turned to Nantucket, the whaling season, the
search for Franklin. The rest of us listened in for a while,
warming numbed fingers by the fire. But I was distracted,
intrigued by the man who so clearly had recognized Mance.
I wondered if he could be the one he and Stowe were
discussing in the cabin. The whaler with whom they and
Hancock had an arrangement.

As Despie and Ellis traded tales of plundering pirates,
I saw, out of the side of my vision, two figures stand and
move to the door. I knew immediately who it would be. My
nerves fizzed under my skin. I was seated too close to Despie
to follow; I could not draw attention to myself, nor reveal

my suspicions to Stowe and Mance. So I remained seated, agonizingly inert, as they left the hut and, after a while, as the whaler followed wordlessly after them.

Hours later, back on the ship, the men were quick into their hammocks, doused in drink and fatigued by a night of card playing. I had no time for rest; I was due on middle watch, so I pulled on my woolen outer coat and went reluctantly above into the cold. The rain had cleared, and the night sky was alive with the green glow of the aurora. My tongue filled the empty space left by my shattered tooth as I considered what it was that I had witnessed at the camp. I was frustrated that I hadn't been able to slip out. I hadn't actually seen anything. I had no evidence. But I felt deep in the marrow of my bones that something was not right.

All proceeded as normal until a short time after five bells, when I noticed a hunched figure scuttling down the gangway. I was alarmed. I had not seen anyone come above from the man ladder. But I watched as they tiptoed, drenched in viridescent light, away from the ship and into the shadows of the settlement.

I could not tell who it was, at first, swaddled in so much cold weather gear.

I had my suspicions, of course.

I considered, momentarily, whether it was appropriate to leave my watch. But if Mance and Stowe were planning something that would put this expedition in danger, I had to know what it was. Only then would I be able to do something to stop it.

I left the ship.

On the gangway I felt exposed under the aurora's bright blaze. It gifted the landscape a preternatural glow, illuminating the very things I wanted to hide: my body, my mission.

Still, I stalked onto the gravel, my breath held, the landscape ringing with silence as I reached the first buildings of the settlement. A blur of white lurched suddenly towards me. I almost leapt out of my skin, squeezing my eyes tight against it. Then, a clink of chains. I opened one eye. Two. A dog snapped at my ankles.

I hushed it, shuffling backwards into the shadows of a hut. As I went, I saw a tall, vague figure pass to my left.

I paused for a moment, my whole body stiff with fear then, at a distance, I began to follow the figure through the settlement.

I watched as it rounded the side of a large tent and came to the entrance of a makeshift store. Dozens of barrels sat beneath a four-post structure, covered with a roughshod tarpaulin roof. I watched as the figure stopped, scuffed its feet as if to keep itself warm, then checked its surroundings.

He was waiting for something. Or someone.

Then, he turned his face right to me. I cowered into the shadows, but the unrelenting light of the aurora fell across his face. Sharp features, pale eyes, prominent vulpine nose.

Stowe.

Before I had time to react, someone rounded the side of the store and joined him. Even from my position in the gloom, I could see from his short stature, his basic clothing, that it was the whaler from earlier. The men exchanged a few inaudible words, before the whaler moved off to examine the barrels. He ran his hands over each until they rested on one. He tipped it onto its side and began rolling it slowly, very carefully, towards the scientist.

I was baffled. What need did Edison Stowe have for whale oil? And why would he do this in the dead of night?

Stowe seemed to be asking questions about the barrel and its contents, glancing furtively around the settlement.

After a moment, the whaler held out his palm. Expecting money, I presumed, or tobacco, whatever had been agreed upon for the trade.

Stowe regarded the man's hand for one cold second, then abruptly, and without warning, his own palms sprang up to encircle the whaler's neck. I was blindsided at first, unable to process what I was seeing. Then, when the reality dawned, my blood felt as if it were crystallizing in my veins. I heard an awful sound as the whaler tried to cry out, as he wheeled his arms, the breath dragging from his crushed throat with a horrid gurgle. He was fighting for his life, but he could not get close to Stowe's body, the scientist being far taller, far stronger than he. I watched, horrified, dread flattening my whole body into the shadows as under the light of the aurora the whites of the whaler's eyes widened. I watched as it dawned on him that he was about to die. The realization seemed only to strengthen Stowe's resolve and he tightened his grip, arms shaking with effort. The whites of those eyes turned red and Edison Stowe finally succeeded in choking the life out of the whaler.

I should have called out.

I should have gone over there, interrupted him. Begged him to stop. Something. Anything. I am beyond ashamed to say that I did not do that.

I did not call out. I did not intervene.

I ran as fast as I could.

Driven by the terror and barely registering the immense

ache in my ribs, I ran all the way back to the *Makepeace*, legs stumbling through thick snow. I bolted up the gangway and skidded back to my position on watch. It was only when I had thrust myself up against the gunwale, panting hard and with a screaming, horrifying sound in my skull, that I noticed someone watching me from the top of the ladderway. I turned. Frantic. Heart wanting to burst out through my throat. Before I could see who it was, they had disappeared down below.

I know that sleep will not come for me tonight. I cannot allow it to. Sedgewick's knife is tucked into the waistband of my under trousers. My ears are alert to every creak of the boards. My nerves coiled tight, ready for any breath that warms my ear in the middle of the night, any fingers that creep beneath my collar. There will be no rest for me now, not ever, not now I know what Edison Stowe is capable of, not now I know that someone observed me returning from the camp.

I am full of regret. Chastened by my own foolishness, the recklessness of it all. To think that I could come here, among brutal men, to live as they live, to hide my true nature, to be at ease with such risk. Those were the fantasies of a child. A girl. Only now I have lived it do I realize how so very wrong I was.

But I must protect myself. I must protect Sedgewick, Mr. Penny, those on this ship who are innocent, who know nothing of this barbarity. I must protect the *Makepeace* and *High Regard*. I must return home to those who love me. I must stay alive.

Chapter Fourteen

Edison

His eyes dart back to the door. The tail-end of the scream rings around his room like the chime of a struck fork. His gaze hovers on the handle. If he were of a different disposition, he might expect that handle to rattle, he might expect the door to creak slowly open so that the "ghost" of the wailing woman could sidle its way into his chamber.

But Edison Stowe is not a superstitious man. He entertains tales of ghosts and spirits only when they allow him to charge a higher rate for his accommodations. He is aware that common folk can become rapt with phantasmagorical ideas. Claptrap, of course. Trite, foolish nonsense! But if such things fill his pockets? So be it. Bring on the ghouls.

A crash erupts from out in the hallway. Then other sounds: the slamming of a door, raised voices, footsteps pummeling the stairs.

He goes to his door again. More muffled voices come from somewhere nearby.

He grasps the handle, twists, and pulls it open a crack. The smell finds him immediately. Harsh and acrid, with the faintest hint of the medicinal.

Something is burning.

He steps out into the hallway, swinging his head from left to right. A few candles, burnt down to puddles, throw off a weak, jaundiced light. Although none of them appears to be the source of the smoke that fills every inch of the corridor. Moving further, he sees that, a few rooms away, a door has been propped half open. From it, plumes of thick gray smoke spiral and twist into the hallway.

He runs towards it. Whose room is that? He cannot recall. But whoever's it is, he cannot afford to lose a tour member. And he will damn well not be paying any damages to the owner of this tavern.

He reaches the room and pulls the door open wider. The heat slams into him and he raises his arms against it. Inside, he sees, through a blanket of smoke, flames lick with tremendous ferocity up the window curtains. In front of them, Ms. Horton, still in her day dress, swats frantically at the fire with a blanket. She must have been the source of the scream.

Those curtains look expensive.

Edison strides towards the bed, still neatly made, and tugs off the coverlet. He folds it in half, slings it over a shoulder, and joins Ms. Horton in front of the flames.

"How on earth . . ." he splutters as he swings the coverlet back and forth. The flames dwindle temporarily before returning with renewed verve. Ms. Horton has stepped back and covers her eyes with a forearm. "Did you topple a chamberstick?" He swings the coverlet again. They seem only to be making things worse.

"It fell." Maude coughs and steps forwards to take a swing. "Yes, it fell."

Edison's eyes flick quickly around the room, landing on the chamberstick on the bedside table, quite upright.

"I found one."

Edison turns to see Charlotte Hollis has entered the room, she is breathless and clasps a large bucket of water in her arms. She pauses, briefly, when she sees him. Then, she rushes towards the flames and hurls the water across the curtains.

The flames retreat with a mournful hiss.

"One more should do it," says Charlotte, and Edison catches the women sharing a glance—but before he can question it, she has left, and he hears the thud of her footsteps on the stairs.

"Good heavens!" He does not have to turn to see that Lady Westbury has blessed them with her presence, no doubt roused from slumber by the threat that she might miss something to gossip about at breakfast. She joins them, strange attendees at the aftermath of an inferno. The lady's silk nightgown looks as expensive as her jewels. Green and yellow, shining somehow through the smoke like a beetle's armored wings.

"Good lord." Frank Hollis steps in behind her.

Christ. What a farce.

"I thought I could smell smoke, let me fetch some water, hold on."

"Your wife is seeing to that." Edison beats once more with the coverlet, but it's an unnecessary action. He appraises the damage to the dimity. How is he going to talk his way out of this one? He will have to demand, with regret of course, that Ms. Horton pays for the damages from her own pocket.

Lady Westbury coughs and gasps dramatically, although the smoke is already retreating.

"Let's get you back to your room." Frank Hollis offers an elbow and the two totter out the door. As Edison turns back to assess the damage once more, he sees that Ms. Horton has stepped away and is quietly clearing something from the sideboard. She glances quickly over her shoulder, sweeping the contents into a drawer. Mrs. Hollis returns, placing the bucket on the floor when she realizes the crisis has been quite overcome.

"I shall bid you ladies a good night, then." Edison nods, ignoring the strange feeling in his stomach, and steps back out into the hallway.

Back in his room, Edison has questions. He pours himself another glass from the carafe. Did Charlotte Hollis not wake her husband when she first smelt smoke? She must have more to her than he previously thought if she is willing to run straight towards a fire without the assistance of a man. And Ms. Horton herself. What had she been so quick to hide from him? What had she swept into the drawer of that sideboard? Perhaps the source of the fire itself (for he knows it was not the chamberstick).

He considers returning to her room, demanding to know what exactly had caused the fire. Perhaps for an official report? But that would have all the subtlety of a sledgehammer. He needs something cannier. He allows his mind to drift, then, to the softness of her skin. That ripe mouth. Those eyes. That strange, unsettled feeling when those eyes meet his. He is interrupted by a knock on his door and knows, with a frisson of surety, that it is her.

It is not. It is Lady Westbury.

Her message is brisk.

"I will recompense the landlord for the damage to the curtains. Do not trouble Ms. Horton for that." Her eyes, not rheumy like those you might expect from someone so haggard by age, but bright and sharp as a needle, search the room behind him. Divested of her jewels and bonnet she looks frail, even though she is plump. She has spurs in the bones at her wrist, he notices, long phalanges and sharp clavicles that look altogether too easy to snap.

"Very well, Lady Westbury. I will make arrangements in the morning." He goes to close the door.

"It was a cry for help, I'm quite sure of it." Lady Westbury has seized the side of the door and pushes it open again.

He pauses. He wants her gone, but anything concerning Ms. Horton's state of mind intrigues him.

"It will not surprise you, I'm sure, to know that I prize knowledge above almost anything else." Edison resists the urge to scoff. Knowledge. That's what the Lady calls her cheap gossip, is it? "You will understand that prior to taking this trip I saw fit to conduct my own research into my fellow attendees," Lady Westbury continues. "I like to know what I am going to be faced with." Edison swallows thickly. He is in equal parts intrigued and alarmed. Has she researched his own background too? "If you'd done the same, you'd have known that Jameson is an ardent and vocal opponent of capital punishment." Yes. Granted. All right. That would have saved him a lot of embarrassment. "You'd also have known that Ms. Horton is not long bereaved," she adds. "And death makes us do strange things. She should not have to bear the financial burden of actions brought about by despair."

"Of course." He nods briskly, as if he had known that all along. But he did not know Maude Horton was bereaved. Is she a widow? She was not in weeds, nor a cap, nor anything else that might suggest she was in mourning.

"The death of a loved one can have a most unnatural effect," says Lady Westbury.

A candle flickers over her shoulder as it releases its wax.

"I trust you will treat her with care, Mr. Stowe."

The woman smiles and the dwindling candlelight buries

itself in the folds of her wrinkles. "When she is in your charge, on this tour, I trust that you will do what you can to keep her safe."

The impertinence. Such brazen disrespect. How *dare* this crone tell him how to run his tours.

"You have my word, Lady Westbury."

He pushes the door firmly shut and turns the key in the lock.

The Journal of Jack Aldridge

——————•——————

74°N, 84°W
Lancaster Sound, Northwest Passage
4 October 1849

MAUDE. My situation has become far graver since I last wrote in this diary. I wonder if these words might end up in your hands. If they do, know this: I am sorry. I am sorry that I came here. I am sorry that I left you. And I am sorry that I never told you enough how grateful I am to have had you as my sister. I never deserved it, but you always put me first. I took that kindness, and I betrayed it by abandoning you.

It happened like this: I needed to tell Sedgewick what I had witnessed at the settlement. Despie told us at six bells the next morning that Ellis had come to him to report that one of his whalers had died. He'd consumed too much alcohol and fallen asleep among the whale oil barrels where he froze to death. I, of course, knew that this is not what had occurred.

I needed to tell the surgeon that he was right about Stowe's disordered mind. That he was not like the other men on this ship. That we had a killer among us.

After Despie's briefing, I went straight to the sick bay, only to be told that Sedgewick had left. In that moment, I felt all color drain from my face. How could he be gone? The assistant's words had barely registered as I battled to retain my composure before him. Sedgewick had been called over to *High Regard,* he said, to aid with an amputation. He would stay there while the ships sailed for Lancaster Sound.

And so off we went, leaving the whalers and what I had witnessed behind. And there I was: left on a ship with a man who kills and with no one to tell.

I considered over the next few hours if I could simply forget what I had seen. Stowe, as best to my knowledge, had not seen me at the settlement. Only the figure on the stepladder did. That could have been any seaman returning from watch, but given his size I had my horrible suspicions as to who it was.

My mind would not rest. I had questions that demanded answers. Why did Edison Stowe kill the whaler? What was in that barrel of oil? Is our ship in danger?

So I went looking for the barrel.

The orlop is where the rats gather, where icicles cling to the crevices in the timber. I wagered that once he'd completed his deed, the scientist had rolled the barrel back to the ship and stashed it deep in the orlop. It was too large to be kept in his cabin and, regardless, would not have made it through the narrow doorway.

I descended first to the unheated hold deck, where the iron water tanks and the coal provisions sat in murky bilge water. Then I lifted the hatch to lower myself another six feet to a place filled with darkness and slush, where my breath froze like suspended crystals in the air.

I made my way through the gloom. The bitter chill made my bruised ribs ache. I felt unwelcome, as if I had stumbled into the lair of something evil, and so I quickly surveyed the provisions to see if I could find where Stowe had stashed his barrel. I had not wanted to risk bringing a lamp, and so

it took a while for my eyes to adjust. With such little sight,
I flinched at every contraction of wood and moan of metal.
At first, I could not find what I was looking for, dizzied by
the silhouettes of hogsheads, casks of salt meat, and lumpen
coal sacks. I blundered through it all, clumsily searching for
the evidence I needed. Then something snagged my eye.
Something stashed to starboard, out of the way of the other
provisions, covered in rough cloth. My breath faltered and
the orlop rang with the silence of a sepulchre. I drew a deep
breath, made my way over and began to pull away the cloth.

Footsteps.

I leapt away, scrambling to find somewhere to hide.
With horror, I realized that the voices were growing closer,
preceded by the vague glow of a lamp. Just as two figures
entered the space, I tucked my body awkwardly behind a
stack of tins, ignoring the pain that set my still-tender ribs
alight.

The men moved through the provisions in silence at
first. Then a low voice struck through the darkness. I
recognized it immediately.

"Just one barrel?" Mance's gruff brogue was unmistakable.

"It's heavy." Stowe responded. "Took me an age to roll it
back."

"Give me that."

I risked peering out just as Stowe handed Mance a
wrench. I watched, hidden, as they worked to prize the barrel
open, then Mance reached down into its guts and withdrew
an arm soaked in oil. In his hand, he held a dark and solid
object, like a large rock, rough around the edges.

"How much have we got in here?"

"He didn't say, but Hancock must be expecting a fair
amount for that money. Unless he just wants it as proof."

That name again: Hancock. So, this was a trade, but of what? And why had Edison Stowe killed a man to obtain it?

"They don't look much like rubies to me," Mance muttered.

"Well, of course they don't." Stowe's tone was supercilious but not altogether convincing. "They haven't been cut or cleaned. The Esquimaux do not have the tools or the skills, nor the whalers. I'm sure we'll get these back and they'll be shined up nicely."

Rubies. Gemstones. My eyes widened in the dark. There had been rumors, I'd read stories about treasures in the mountains of Greenland. Some believed there to be whole islands made of gems in the frozen north. But we all knew about Frobisher's "gold", his embarrassing black ore. How all twelve hundred tons of it were revealed to be worthless. Could there really be rubies hidden here?

"Did he vouch for them? The whaler." Mance dipped his arm in and retrieved another clod of oil-soaked rock. "How do we know he'll keep his trap shut?"

A quick, unnatural sound came from Stowe. It set the hairs on the back of my neck rising.

"He won't be saying anything to anyone."

"He's not . . ." Mance was slow, but Stowe appeared to relish the creeping pause. "He didn't . . . He's not that sod that froze to death . . . ? Is he?"

Stowe's laugh was a strange, high-pitched bark. "Who am I to correct them? If Ellis says he froze to death, he froze to death."

Mance shook his head slowly, but eventually I could see a reluctant smile splitting his face. "Hancock didn't order a murder, Stowe. He ordered a trade. He wants proof of the gems." He said it in the way that a parent might admonish a child.

"No," Stowe conceded, his voice stretching out as he reached in for another rock to inspect. "But this way we get paid what we actually deserve. Hancock never has to know the money wasn't handed over."

My head was dizzy. My breath trapped in my chest by my clumsy position behind the tins, my ribs screaming out for the relief of movement. But I had to stay still. I had found myself witness to a murder, to smuggling, to plans orchestrated, if Sedgewick was correct, by a member of the admiralty itself. I could not reveal myself to Mance and Stowe. I would certainly be killed. But the pain felt as if I had been kicked in the back by a horse. I could only move an inch to relieve it, that would have to be enough. But an inch was all it took to send the tins flying. The tower collapsed with a roar that shook the entire orlop. The men's heads whipped round.

"Weasel!" Stowe yelled as Mance seized my shoulders and hauled me against a coil of rope. The pain was blistering now, but fear had cast my body in a caul of ice. "Pestilential spy. Who sent you here? Despie?" The vapor of his breath coiled slowly in the lamplight.

My mouth gaped. I knew not what to do. What could I say? To reveal what I knew, what I saw, what I'd heard? Or to lie? To beg for mercy.

"I know you," he spat. "You were the one lurking outside my cabin speaking horseshit about jellyfish. What's your name?" Stowe's harsh eyes flashed in the half-light. How foolish I'd been to stash Sedgewick's knife away in my hammock this morning.

"I'm just the cabin boy." I stammered. "I'm no one. I don't mean any trouble."

I could see, as I spoke, the recognition come upon Mance's face too. His eyes, red and venous, slowly narrowed.

"I saw you," he spat, holding a thick, pipe-blackened finger inches from my face. It made me think of Grandfather, of how his fingers were always stained orange from the turmeric.

"He was there. Last night." He turned to Stowe. "On deck. Must have seen you coming back." He shook his head. "He's seen too much."

I knew what that meant.

"He'll tell." Mance hissed to Stowe, my shirt still seized in his fist. My back twisted and spasmed in agony. "If you tell, I'll slice you open like a seal, hook my finger into your intestines, and pull them out while you're still breathing."

"I won't." It was a whisper, but I wanted to scream it. To beg. To convince them I'd keep their secret. Whatever I had to do to keep myself alive.

"People saw us down here," I said. "They'll know."

Mance loosened his grip in response, and without half a breath I twisted away from them and sprinted out of the orlop, clattering up the stairs, towards air, towards men, towards safety.

They did not follow. They stayed below, no doubt snuffing out all signs of their smuggling, their crime.

I could not go to Despie, I was just a ship's boy. I was powerless. Sedgewick was still on *High Regard*.

I had no one.

So, I sit now, folded into the darkest corner of the galley, surrounded by crumbs and oil smears, watching the rats sniffing the air and retreating with distaste.

I cannot return to my hammock to sleep, for if I did, I am certain I would not draw breath in the morning. I will stay awake tonight, I will endure the pain, I will keep watch for any glint of knife. I will keep myself hidden, for now and until Sedgewick returns. He will know what to do. He will know how to protect me, protect us, protect the ship. I just have to hold on until then. Maude, I just have to survive a few more days. And I will. For you, and for Grandfather. I am living for you now, and I will return. I assure you. But God grant me safety until then.

Chapter Fifteen

Maude

Reflections can be dangerous things, Maude has come to realize. A shop window can be an affront. The mirrored door of a wardrobe an incontestable assault. To study herself for too long in a looking glass is a risk she simply cannot take. For in a reflection, Maude so very often finds Constance.

The oyster brocade feels unnatural around her waist. She smooths her palm over her stomach, adjusts the bertha, and fixes a strand of loose hair. She glances again at the face in the carriage window. She eyes it warily: pale, powdered skin; dark hair, smoothed down, parted in the middle, and curled into ringlets.

Maude had sometimes been told she was beautiful. Even when it wasn't spoken, she could feel it in the weight of men's gazes. She could sense it in the shift of the air when women turned their husbands from her.

In the pharmacy, she'd had visitors. Young men who made a show of coming in to browse the pomade, but who would glance over their shoulders at her as she worked. Most meant no harm, she knew, and could never muster the courage to engage her in conversation, reddening if she accidentally met their eye. Coughing, making for the door. But it made her fists clench, sometimes, to be observed as intently as a bug under glass. There was one visitor, however, she had looked forward to each week. Andrew Hale, the butcher's son. Tall, with freckles across his nose and a smile as warm as toast. He was always so polite as he collected his father's medicines. He would say nice things to Maude. Ask her about her week, offer an observation about the weather. She'd always felt a little thrill when the bell announced a customer and it was Andrew Hale who stepped, beaming, through the door. Then Constance had gone and ruined it all.

"I told Andrew Hale he should ask Grandfather if you might accompany him on a stroll this weekend."

Maude had frozen in position by the counter as Constance grinned, desperately hoping she had misheard her sister's words.

"Whyever would you do that?" she had asked, trying to keep her voice level.

"He's such a nice boy. So polite, just like his father. I'm sorry, I thought you enjoyed his company. It would do you good to get out."

She had breathed in deeply through her nose. Tried to calm her racing heart. Her toes clenching in her boots. "I do not need my *sister* to facilitate such engagements for me." Maude had trembled as she bit out the words. "In fact, I do not need you to make any arrangements on my behalf at all."

She could see the confusion on Constance's face, felt a twist of guilt in her stomach. But how could she explain to her sister that entertaining anything of the sort, that even the prospect of leaving her sister and their grandfather alone in the pharmacy to start a new life with someone else was the most terrifying, impossible thing she could imagine?

She had refused Andrew's invitation and although he continued to collect his father's medicine, his smile was never as warm as it once was, and he never again mentioned the weather.

She had been surprised to learn, after Constance's disappearance, that her sister had not shared the same views when it came to courting.

The news came in the form of a letter, about three weeks after Constance had left for the Arctic. It had dropped through the letterbox in the pharmacy one morning; Maude had been alerted by the unfamiliar rattle of the brass flap. The Hortons did not receive many letters. Their grandfather had only recently had the letterbox installed. So, Maude had been intrigued enough to rush over to the doormat. As she bent to pick up the letter, she saw it was her sister's name— *C Horton*—on the front of the envelope.

She had considered leaving it unopened. She could keep it safe there, in the pharmacy, until her sister returned. But what if it was something pressing? What if the letter contained information that she or her grandfather needed to know about Constance's voyage? Eventually, Maude had torn the seal open, surprised to find a formal notice had been slipped inside.

LONDON DISTRICT POST OFFICE, the notice was headed.

> *The enclosed has been opened by the proper Officer, and is returned to you for the reason assigned thereon.*

Maude scanned the single page.

> *Postage of a letter from one part of Town to another, both being within the delivery of the General Post-Office, is Two pence; and to and from the parts beyond that delivery Three pence. Letters for the Three-pence post are*

frequently by mistake put into the General Post, by which
they are unavoidably delayed or returned.

Maude blinked. Constance must have tried to send a letter
before she left and made a mistake with her postage. She
imagined her sister carefully affixing two Penny Black stamps
to an envelope. Dropping a letter in the post box. Had she been
trying to send something to Surrey or Kent? If so, she must not
have included the extra Penny postage.

Maude had frowned. Wracked her brain. She had not known
that her sister had any cause to send a letter before she left.
So, with curiosity and trepidation she had pulled the returned
letter out of the envelope and quickly unfolded it.

My love,

The words made her heart stop in her chest.

Do not be sad that I am gone.

Maude's mouth had dropped open, and she'd swung round to
see if her grandfather was watching. The bench was empty. He
must have been out the back. She continued, hurriedly, to read.

Do not trouble yourself with anger. Do not shed a single,
salty tear.
   Because I will leave part of myself behind when I board
the Makepeace *tomorrow. My heart will still be there with*
you in Richmond, and it beats, and it beats, consumed
with love for every inch of you.
   Can you feel its pulse, my love? Feel it in your bones,
your soul, in every groove in your palm.

If you ever feel alone, wait for it and it will come.

Know that I will think of you always. When I rise from my hammock in the morning and as my feet hit the cold, hard boards, my first thought will be of you, of how we walked barefoot in rivers, how our warm fingers felt, intertwined so softly together. I will think of how we laughed, how we read, how we kissed and breathed as one. Our love a pair of lungs rising and falling together.

The match that has been arranged for you by your family will bring you a better life. A life filled with all the riches that I cannot give you. A warm home filled with fires in the hearth and food on the table. I could not live with myself if you did not have those things. And so, by leaving I am giving you permission to choose them.

C

Maude had found, then, that she had no breath left in her lungs. Her head had spun dizzyingly, and she'd been forced to grasp one of the shelves to stop herself from stumbling. She'd had no idea that her sister was in love. In *love*? Constance had told her nothing of the sort. And Richmond? Who on earth did they know in Richmond?

The postal officer had not returned the envelope, which would have shown the address of Constance's original letter. There was just the note. Just her sister's handwriting. Just the words "My love," useless in identifying the intended recipient.

And so, for months Maude had plowed through every single memory, trying to work out just who her sister could have been writing to. She'd had to ignore the hot tickle of jealousy, the ugliness of being lied to, deceived by the person she had spent a lifetime protecting. It was only one day, several months later, that she finally got her answer.

*

Maude glances back at her reflection. Lady Westbury had loaned her the brocade dress, as promised. The woman had come to her in the morning to deliver it, her silver hair catching the sun's first light as it seeped in through the ruined curtains. She had asked strange questions about the fire; told Maude it was quite all right if she had known it was going to happen. Maude had not known what to make of that. If she had *known* that by trailing a new concoction in heating a blend of ethanol, malic acid, potassium dichromate, just a small one, over the fire, she would end up with a room resembling Dante's Inferno, she never would have taken such a risk and exposed herself as she did. She is appalled at her own recklessness and only grateful that she had managed to hide her equipment from Stowe just in time.

She is nervous of the evening ahead. Inebriated officers, fawning women, noisy fiddle players; the prospect of it all makes her head ache. But she has come this far to get what she wants from Edison Stowe. She will take strength from her sister. Act as Constance would have done. Become an actress herself. She needs to make him talk. A party full of Wiltshire's most wealthy and a set of ruined curtains are not going to stop her.

"It really is one of the finest houses in the county," Lady Westbury opines as their carriage trundles along the Wilton Road. The moon is fierce in the lampblack sky, the air inside the cab filled with pungent lily-of-the-valley perfume.

"The eleventh earl, the past owner, was a most extraordinary man," she recounts. *"Extremely* well traveled . . ."

Maude listens to Lady Westbury as Charlotte lowers the window to let in cold fingers of late autumn.

"A collector of antiquities, classical sculptures et cetera. I don't know much of this new chap yet, but I hear he has links to the admiralty."

Maude snaps to attention.

"I heard he has links to the board," says Charlotte. "A friend of Lady Jane Franklin's." She glances at Maude. "Very powerful."

Maude's whole body is flushing with heat. She searches Charlotte's face, but the woman has turned her focus back out of the window.

"Will there be members of the board at the party?" Maude asks, thinking of the leers and the suffocating paneled board-room. Her mind leaps to the diary, to how Mance and Stowe had spoken of a Hancock. How the clerk, Heart, had been so sure that it was all driven by corruption *inside* the admiralty office.

"Yes, don't you worry, there'll be plenty of handsome naval officers ripe for the plucking," Lady Westbury teases. "As well as anyone of repute from within a ten-mile radius of Salisbury of course."

Lady Westbury leans over to tap Charlotte on the knee.

"My dear, if you gaze too long at the moon, your eyes will turn to saucers."

Lady Westbury, true to form, was quite correct—the house is magnificent. The carriage enters via a set of gates, black iron and gleaming gold, with a Romanesque stone surround and a towering sculpture of a soldier on horseback above it.

They come to a stop just behind the gentlemen's vehicles. The footman folds down the steps, and Maude hops neatly out to survey a vast gravel courtyard lit by torches.

"Quite a place." Frank Hollis helps Mr. Westbury out behind him.

Maude can't help but agree. All around them, manicured gardens are filled with poplars and hydrangeas, a bit bare from the frosts but pretty nonetheless. A set of fountains at their center spout elegant plumes of water. Under the silver glow of the moon, guests in fine outfits stream towards the house where liveried men wait to greet them beneath gargoyles, ushering them in through the doors and into the warmth.

Once inside, Maude can see that the cloisters are indeed filled with the most exquisite antiques—sculptures, paintings, curiosities, marble busts of emperors and philosophers on colonnaded pedestals. Charlotte Hollis stands utterly enrapt at the foot of a statue of Shakespeare, chin on his fist, surveying the partygoers from on high.

"And here, the sarcophagi excavated from the columbarium of the freedmen of Livia, on the Via Appia." Stowe, his lines crisply rehearsed, leads them through the quadrangle as if they are exploring a foreign spice market.

"Such age. Such history. Remarkable."

He points out stained glass depictions of Henry VIII, of Hercules fighting Achelous, a faun with a panther, Cupid stringing his bow.

"Atys the shepherd in his goat's hair cloak," he half whispers in affected awe. "The beautiful Athena—that's a porpher relief."

"Porphyry," Lady Westbury corrects him.

They press on, lured by the hypnotic swell of violin strings and murmured voices. Maude's stomach is a clenched fist of anticipation. What will she do if she runs into Hancock? Does she have the strength, the proof, to question him about his smuggling, the death of the whaler, the fate of her sister?

The double room that yawns open in front of them is egg-yolk yellow, awash with heavy curtains, auriferous carpets and furniture that wouldn't look out of place at the Palace of Versailles. Leading off it, every anteroom is crammed with revelers. From one, the clink of crystal glasses and cutlery; from another, cigar smoke escapes like fleeing snakes. Maude cranes her neck to inspect the ceiling. A dramatic scene has been captured in fine brushstrokes: satyrs, forbidden fruit, cherubs with leg rolls, angels with swollen breasts and flaming hair.

With her head still tipped backwards, she feels someone take her firmly by the elbow and propel her forwards.

"Come, let us explore," Lady Westbury grins at her side. The woman is as plump and glossy as an otter in her taffeta tonight, an emerald-set brooch at her throat gleaming ecstatically. "But a word of advice, if you are engaged in conversation, do not tell anyone of the true reason behind our visit to Salisbury."

"Whyever not?"

Lady Westbury stops dead still. "We don't want to give anyone the wrong impression, do we?" Maude is surprised. Lady Westbury has been quite open about her macabre tastes. She had not expected the woman to be the sort concerned with what other people think. She watches as the Lady reaches up to Maude's face and tucks a hair behind her ear.

"We merely enjoy the spectacle and the theater," Lady Westbury reasons. "And . . . seeing someone deserving brought to justice."

The breath catches in Maude's throat. She could not know what she was planning, surely. She could not know of Maude's *real* reason for being in Salisbury, for being part of Edison's ridiculous tour group. She opens her mouth to speak, but Lady Westbury's attentions have already moved on. "Ooh." She tugs at Maude's arm. "A ham."

They take a turn around the refreshment room and Maude plucks at the lace of her bertha. Along one side, a table is cloaked in a crisp white tablecloth. On it: supper. A liberal spread.

"A mark of true wealth," Lady Westbury whispers.

Birds have been carved and held together with purple ribbons. A fat ham is studded with a hundred cloves and porcelain plates glisten with tongues arranged into wet, neat slices. Plates of small savouries—deviled kidneys, potted livers, Scotch woodcock—are dotted around, and at the end of the table eager attendants struggle to replenish a bath-sized punchbowl.

Next, Lady Westbury guides Maude to the pudding table, hemming and hawing over its rich offerings. At its center is an ornate cream cake, flavored, according to its small label, with orange-flower water and coconut. Garnished ices in various shapes sit like ballet girls on show—pineapples, peaches, pears, and cherry tarts. What a shame, the grand pudding has already begun to melt.

"Nnnnng!"

Maude looks up from the liquefying matter to see Lady Westbury, mouth full of trifle, gesturing wildly as an officer in a blue uniform enters through the doorway.

A cold finger traces the skin at the back of her neck.

Hancock.

She is not quite sure why her first instinct is to run. Perhaps it is because Hancock appears, quite intentionally she is sure, as if he is the most powerful man in the room. Heart had assured her that he had acted with the greatest discretion, but what if Hancock had discovered by now that it is she who has the diary? Either way, she cannot let him see her. He will surely recognize her, and she would not put it past him to have her escorted from the party. She cannot risk such a fuss. She cannot risk her true identity being revealed to Edison Stowe.

She backs slowly from the table. There are others with the lord commissioner, showy in swallow-tailed coats and gold pinstriped trousers, ceremonial swords flashing like a tiger's bared teeth. A flock of women has gathered around them, a waft of white feathers and fluttering fans. Several meters away, on the other side of the room, Maude can see Charlotte Hollis assessing the group, a glass held to her lips.

"My dear, do you not want to hear what he has to say?"

Maude hushes Lady Westbury with a frantic hand signal as she retreats.

"It's quite an occasion. Stay, listen."

Maude shakes her head, not wanting to draw attention to herself.

As she nears the wall, she sees one of the officers take a spoon and tap it on the side of his glass.

"If I might have the attention of the room." The man's voice is plummy and overloud. A fiddle player ceases with an abrupt screech.

"Your good ladies and gentlemen. The honorable Sir Hancock!"

Muttering rolls round the room. Hancock somewhat reluctantly clears his throat.

Maude shrinks into the wall, praying he will not recognize her.

"Ah, yes. Thank you, Marshall."

She recognizes that disdainful tone. The ashy, unsmiling face. She feels the walls of that office closing in on her again.

"Just a few words about a friend of mine, Sir John Franklin.

And his wife, the remarkable Lady Jane Franklin, who has worked tirelessly to raise funds to send ships, alongside our own Navy vessels, northwards to search for her husband, and his lost Discovery ships."

As he continues to talk, Maude sees, out of the corner of her eye, Stowe enter the room. She watches with interest as his attention drifts to the voice at its center, and as his eyes widen with alarm when he sees who it is that is talking.

"Lady Jane's efforts are only possible with the generous help of donors such as yourselves . . ." Stowe edges his way backwards, just as she had done, then he sidles towards the open door to the grand hallway.

". . . Just a few hundred, would aid us significantly in our efforts."

Maude steps quietly from her own hiding place, her eyes trained on Stowe.

". . . Checks can be made out to myself . . ."

He slips out of the door and disappears.

She follows, hurriedly, weaving through the rapt crowd. Is Edison fearful of Hancock because he knows Hancock had Mance killed within a week of the *Makepeace*'s return to London? And regardless, with so many concerned with the ball, could this be her chance to get Stowe on his own, to make him talk? Is she even ready for that?

The hallway is still and echoing, a chandelier burns bright above her head, making the gold wallpaper glint as if plastered with coins. On either side of the corridor, broad mahogany doors loom. She reaches her hand into her sleeve to check that the small bottle she stashed earlier is still in place. Just as her fingers brush the glass, she is seized by the shoulder and pulled, with force, into the shadows.

The Journal of Jack Aldridge

———•———

73°N, 90°W
Port Leopold, Northwest Passage
9 October 1849

REST NEVER COMES. My nights are spent out of my hammock, claiming sleeplessness so I can assist Mr. Penny in the galley. It is only there, with the glow of the stove and the man's quavering song, that I feel safe now. He refused at first, claiming he enjoyed the solitude of those early hours alone. But then he must have seen it within me: the blistering fear. He asked no questions, simply handed me a cloth and ordered me to start scrubbing. It is not uncommon for a ship's boy to be taken advantage of on long journeys like this. Penny will be well aware of that. And so he allows me to help him, my eyes growing heavy as I stir and I sift and I bake. But I never allow them to close. I cannot allow them to close.

By day, my nerves keep me awake, although I have found myself at times staggering to the sick bay as if compelled by the safe memory of Sedgewick. I'll wake twenty minutes later, chest roaring and damp with perspiration, convinced that I have been discovered, that there is a cool knife held to the soft space at my throat.

At all other times, I keep my wits about me, and my eyes trained on the two men who wish me harm.

It is a cat and mouse game.

We watch each other while up on deck. As I scour ice from the equipment, I peer up into the rigging to find Mance eyeing me like a bird of prey. At mealtimes I eat my pemmican and salt pork with one eye fixed on Stowe. He keeps one trained on me in return. It is a necessary stand-off. I will not back down.

The *Makepeace* itself has taken on the feeling of a prison. Winter is bedding in around us and the men's spirits are wallowing as low as the mercury. The daylight has shriveled up and said its sad farewells. There is no blue. No sun. No stars. Only bleak and sterile uniformity. The landscape around us has been decimated, as if razed by war. We are soldiers. So far from home.

It's a convict's routine punctuated by bland tinned meat, freezing dogwatches, and the uneasy murmur of men whose souls are fracturing here at the edge of the earth.

Men carry out their tasks, tormented by the wind, mittens strung round their necks, jumpers under their coats giving them the appearance of stuffed dolls. Everything seems without end. The polar darkness, the unreachable horizon, the snowstorms, the ice, the uncertainty, the cold hard fear. Every day exhausts me—for I know that, around every corner, lurking in every shadow, death waits with his palms outstretched. There is nowhere for me to run. No way of escape. No protection. When the wind comes, howling past ice-rimmed masts so felled and stubby they look like the fractured fingers of a giant, you would believe it is a warning from the gods. "What are you doing here?" it asks. "This place is not for you."

But still, I am here, Maude. Still, I live.

Chapter Sixteen

Edison

Edison bursts into the cool air, staggers. His clumsy arrival sets the trees spitting, birds shoot from their branches and dwindle high into the night's clear sky. His head is swimming, his heart punching his rib cage so hard he is surprised it has not fractured. He has not seen his uncle since the day of his return from the Arctic, and the man had made it very clear that if he did see him again, he would not be so lenient.

Mance had already suffered the repercussions.

His mind swills with memories from that morning, fresh off the *Makepeace*. When Hancock had summoned them to the alleyway at the docks. The ground was soft with mud, a salt stink in the air and the shriek of gulls sailing and arrowing overhead. They could still see the towering masts of the *Makepeace* above the dock's hunched buildings. Hancock had ordered them to show him the contents of the barrel. To prove the deal had been done.

"Well, I must say, I'm impressed," Hancock had drawled as Mance set about the barrel with a wrench. "I didn't think you had it in you, Edison."

Nobody ever did. But he had proven himself with this voyage. Proven he was a man not to be trifled with.

Mance seemed to take an interminably long time with the wrench. Edison's uncle had not troubled himself with small talk after that, had not asked for any more particulars about their expedition.

The barrel top heaved away eventually, and Hancock stepped in closer. Edison had watched as he raised the crook of his arm to his nose and bent to inspect the torpid oil.

Cries of industry wafted towards them from the docks, and Mance had taken Hancock's silence as his cue to roll back a sleeve and plunge a forearm in. He pulled out the first of the rocks, shook it, wiped it roughly on his trousers and handed it over to the commissioner.

The alley had seemed to fall silent as Hancock blinked wordlessly at the dun mass in his hand. Seconds dragged, smeared like the oil on Mance's trousers. Hancock turned the rock this way and that.

"Of course, they are still uncleaned, unworked." The beginnings of something hard and sharp was pushing its way into Edison's throat.

Hancock had glanced up at him, blinked once, twice. Then, without warning, drew his arm back and hurled the rock at the wall. It shattered like a cheap clay vase and fell as powder.

Edison had flinched, poised to spring forward, to stop his uncle destroying the rubies.

Then it dawned on him.

Hancock leaned over to the barrel and ducked his arm in, not even pausing to draw back the sleeve of his jacket. He stood, hurled it, again, at the wall. Then turned back to retrieve another. Threw it. Smash! Then another. A man possessed.

Mance had scarpered, then. The snake. Leaving Edison alone to face the consequences of being hoodwinked by the whaler.

"Blithering, degenerate imbeciles," Hancock roared as he continued to cast the worthless rocks at the wall. "Do you know what you've lost me? I'll be laughed at, just like Frobisher. Do you know what you've done?" Edison could do nothing but wait as the rocks exploded one by one.

As long as Hancock never discovered that he didn't pay for the trade, then he might just escape with his life. His uncle would not snuff him out, surely. Not family.

When Hancock was spent, he turned to Edison. The whites of his eyes huge. His body trembling.

"Was it just one?" The words had sliced through the air.

Edison hadn't known, at first, what he meant.

"Was it just *one*?"

Then he realized, with a quick pulse of clarity, that his uncle must know about the whaler. He did not have time to consider how.

"Yes," Edison lied, thinking of sledges and swirling sleet.

"Leave," his uncle had ordered, turning his back on him and shaking the oil from his sleeve. Edison didn't need to be told twice, scurrying from that alley like a fox that has slipped the jaws of a hound.

No money, no house, no help from family, no one to turn to. Just his cold, damned Arctic bones.

"And Edison?" Hancock had called after him.

He had turned, a small beat of hope. "I trust you know never to cross my path again."

In the courtyard, Edison stills his breathing. The sound of the party recommences behind him; his uncle must have finished his pompous speech. He spits a bitter taste from his mouth, resentful of how he'd ended up here. The gamble he'd taken in the Arctic had not paid off. Yes, he had pocketed the money meant for the whaler, but in the end, he'd lost that too. Mance took it. When Edison had gone to retrieve it from his sea chest the morning the *Makepeace* lurched back into the docks, it had gone. Mance was the only person who knew that it was there, and he took it. So, Edison supposes, he deserved what came for him too.

His eye is drawn by a movement in the bushes. A small, slender hoof steps out, followed by the wet nose and wide cow eyes of a deer. It raises its head and clocks Edison; its whole body paralyzed by fear. Edison holds its gaze and bends slowly to pick up a stone at his feet. Slowly, ever so slowly, he straightens. Then, quick as a flare, he hurls the stone at the animal's flank in rage. It strikes the small body and takes a chunk of flesh away with it. The deer catapults across the garden before disappearing into the darkness beyond. The satisfied buzz inside Edison has only just begun to ebb when someone taps him on the shoulder.

Chapter Seventeen

Maude

The room is dark, the air viscous, filled with a mechanical ticking sound.

Whoever dragged her in here has locked the door behind them and fumbles with something in the corner. They are almost imperceptible in the deadening gloom.

Maude wants to scream, to beat on the door, but her bones are glued together with fear. The sound too, the *tick tick tick*, it holds her there, a menace.

A candle flares in the corner of the room and the figure turns, its face illuminated by amber.

Her shoulders drop.

"Bit overdramatic, isn't it?"

"Is it?" Heart ponders, moving to the center of the room to light more sticks. His skin is just as pale as ever, the candlelight tossing dark circles beneath his eyes. He looks like something that has just been exhumed.

"We're in a hall in the middle of nowhere with people who have killed, people who have given orders to kill, and people who have taken great lengths to cover up their killing," he says. "That's not to mention whole troops of men who have killed to the sound of trumpets, making their killing seem far more legitimate. Plus, they've got medals. I think it rather apt that we should hide our meeting. Besides, I rather like the ambience, don't you?"

She pauses, listens. That incessant ticking. She allows her eyes to adjust to the darkness, the grainy shapes in the room slowly coming into focus. There's a large table in the middle that must be freshly polished because she can still smell its beeswax scent. Above, a large candelabra hangs inert, dozens of candles half burnt down, bubbles of wax turned solid like small, white pearls. Then at the back of the room, running almost the whole length and height of the wall, is an impressive tower of clocks. *Tick.* Dozens, even hundreds of clocks. In various styles but clearly all of them valuable. They must have been moved here to keep them safe during the party.

"What did you make of the diary?" Heart asks. He is clearly not here to waste time.

"Incontestable," she says.

"Have you got anything out of him yet? I heard about his grisly tours. Novel."

"He doesn't trust me. I haven't yet had a chance to administer . . ." She pauses.

Heart cocks his head. "I like the sound of this. Administer what?"

"Ether, chloroform, laudanum. A combination I have not yet found."

"Your plan being to . . ."

"I don't know!" Heart raises his eyebrows at her outburst. "Get him into a state where he does not care what he is saying. I need that mask to slip."

Heart nods slowly. "I suppose it could work. But it's risky. Do you need anything from me? More funds?"

"Not at the moment. I just need time." Then she remembers. "Hancock. Does he know I have the diary?"

"Of course not. But he's on the warpath. He knows it's gone. He's blaming the new maid."

They smile tightly at one another. She thinks of the book. Her sister's words. The last thing her sister touched. How could anyone think that it belongs anywhere but with her?

"And Sedgewick," she blurts out. "The surgeon."

He nods again.

"They were friends."

"I hope it's some comfort to know there were those who wished her well on that ship."

But they could not help her, in the end.

"Did you pass my letter to your brother?" she asks quickly. She had given it to him before she left for Salisbury. "Does he think he might get it to him?"

"He assures me he will do what he can."

Maude's spirits lift a little. She knows answers from the surgeon will help. Anything about the state of her sister's body, hard information, will push her further, get Stowe in a bind.

"Well, you have my address," Heart says. "Do write whenever. But for now, godspeed, Ms. Horton. May we find the answers we are seeking."

He blows out the candles.

*

She finds Stowe outside, watching a pretty deer leap across the gravel of the neat walled garden. She observes him for a moment, noticing how just the sight of him makes her flesh creep. She steps forward, eventually, and taps him on the shoulder.

He startles. She still does not know why he is hiding from

Hancock, and she has not had the opportunity to tip the contents of the small bottle in her sleeve into his drink. But if she doesn't ask questions about the *Makepeace* now, no matter how much it scares her, she may not get a better chance.

"Ms. Horton." He relaxes once he sees who it is. "Take a turn?" That mask is up already. All it took was a second.

She forces a smile and takes his elbow, sure that he must feel her pulse beneath her skin. His elbow is all bone, as if every inch of him has been made to repel. She hopes her own body is not giving her away, hopes that he cannot feel how it makes her bones shake to be so close to him.

She wonders often how Constance did such a thing, how she managed for so long hiding her true self, her true fears, beneath the coarse guise of a boy. She had become a skilled actress as she grew into a young woman, Maude thinks. She was keeping secrets even when she was at home, she knows that now. She thinks again of the letter. The declarations of love. Those words—*Do not be sad that I am gone*—meant for someone other than her. She already knew, at that point, that Constance had not told her everything about her own life. But she was confounded as to how she could have missed something so very seismic in her sister. The words drew into sharp relief a most scorching revelation—she had been foolish to believe that the two of them would always be enough for one another. She cannot remember when she'd first made that silent pact with herself. But, looking back, it must have been when their parents died. Over the years, she had not allowed herself to be tempted by marriage, nor love affairs, nor any desires that would take her away from the pharmacy. To discover that Constance had not made the same silent pact herself was the most awful betrayal Maude could ever have imagined.

The moon has cast half of Stowe's face in shadow. He smells faintly sweet, although there is a hint of something else hidden behind it. Antiseptic.

She glances around them to see if he has brought a glass with him outside. But he has no drink. Her hope falters. She is going to have to do this with words, not medicines.

"It's a beautiful evening, is it not?" He leads her down the steps onto the gravel quadrangle.

She nods, not trusting herself to speak just yet.

They begin their slow, uneasy procession around the walled garden. The moon throws their shadows across the gravel, making it apparent just how they differ in physicality: Stowe is not burly, but his shadow appears almost twice the length of hers. As if she is a child being led around the garden by someone who could easily throttle her, clamp a palm across her mouth.

"They've done a marvelous job with the decorations," Edison tries again.

She assesses the flourishes; an underwater theme, it seems, perhaps in honor of their most esteemed admiralty guests. Here and there, garlands of blue and green have been strung to assemble rolling waves. Huge clam shell sculptures, rising to the height of her shoulders, stand wide-jawed in the flower beds. Sea nymphs are cast in convincing papier maché, mouths open slightly, suggestive, as if about to reveal their own sordid secrets.

With a change of direction, Edison steers them towards the garden's far corner. At first, she panics, then sees that a grotto has been arranged there, its domed temple formed by hundreds of stacked oyster shells. A lighted candle stump, dripping with wax, has been placed at its center. The light illuminates small windows, made of jewel-colored glass and fringed with tinsel. Maude pauses in front of it, gripped by a hazy memory. She turns her head to meet it: she and Constance lighting candles at Christmas. The glow warms their faces, gifting their cheeks a full, happy flush. She lifts her fingers to her skin as if she can still feel it.

"Is Salisbury to your liking, Ms. Horton? How have you enjoyed the tour so far?"

Those rehearsed lines again.

She looks up at him, her hand still held to her cheek. It is an unusual thing, Edison Stowe's face. As if it is made of two parts that were never really meant to go together. A mouth, held in a stiff smile, and eyes that belong somewhere else entirely. She is struck by his reptilian coldness. As if, since returning from the Arctic, he has never truly thawed.

He raises an eyebrow to push her into an answer. "It's a beautiful city, is it not?"

"It is a *beautiful* city," she eventually agrees, too enthusiastically. She cannot stop thinking about the diary. Her letter to Sedgewick. What's at stake. "Such history, such age." She reaches for his rehearsed couplets. Her own words abandoning her.

"Your sensibilities are not offended by the hangings?"

Those eyes again. That ice-pick stare.

"They are not." She shakes her head as she lies. "I merely . . ." She pauses. She probably shouldn't.

"You merely what?" His eyes skim down her face to rest at her throat. This close to him, she can see where the Arctic weather has hardened his skin.

"I merely question whether the process of a hanging is just," she says.

He laughs as if surprised. Tilts his head.

"I should say in its very definition it is just. An eye for an eye. Hammurabi." When she doesn't interject, he continues as if the adage needs explaining. "Any man, or woman, who takes a life should have theirs taken from them."

He swallows after he says it.

"And what of those who are wrongly accused, those who have made mistakes, those who are pushed towards desperate things because they themselves are desperate? Do they deserve to swing?"

"Have you been reading Jameson's pamphlets?" He moves his elbow away from her. "Any individual committing a crime should know there will be repercussions." He flexes his shoulders. "If you do not agree with capital punishment, I am surprised you joined this tour, Ms. Horton." He seems to assess her face, as if eager to see her response to this challenge.

"Any individual? What about men like you?" As soon as she has said it, she has the feeling of tumbling off a very tall building. Around them, the air thickens, the wind drops, and there is no sound. No sound at all.

"What do you mean, *men like me?*"

Their eyes are locked together now, their faces just inches from one another. He is taller than she is. Stronger.

"I mean . . ." She affects a laugh; it is unconvincing. "I just mean sailors. In the Far North, on the *Makepeace?* With no police constables, no courts, nothing but ice and mountains, would a man be brought to justice for his crimes? I have often wondered."

The air rings with the long pause. "The *Makepeace?*"

She feels a hammering at the base of her throat. Had he ever actually told her the name of his ship? She knows it from the diaries, of course. From Constance. She knows he was on the *Makepeace*, but has he ever actually said it?

"Your ship. The *Makepeace*." She blinks. "Lady Westbury said that was the name of your ship," she lies. "It sounds like quite the adventure."

He does not move his eyes from hers. "I was never on the *Makepeace*." He scratches his throat quickly as he says it.

"You were not? I could have sworn that's what Lady Westbury said."

"Contrary to popular belief, Lady Westbury is not right about everything."

"I find that hard to believe." She forces another laugh. It comes out hollow.

"The *Albatross*. I was on the *Albatross*. You can look it up. Should you wish to."

"Perhaps I shall."

With a bang, the French doors burst open, and a figure comes lurching out. Maude steps back from Edison, but his eyes are still flighty with suspicion.

The figure stumbles over to them.

"They're about to sssstart the dancing sssso I got out while I could." Mr. Westbury rests an elbow on Edison's shoulder. "Save yourselves!"

Maude begs their pardon and leaves, walking as quickly as she can back to the safety of the party. The night is cool and the air is crisp, but she feels Stowe's gaze on her skin like the scorch of the sun.

The Journal of Jack Aldridge

73°N, 90°W
Port Leopold, Northwest Passage
11 October 1849

DESPIE HAS ORDERED one last sledge party out before the landscape freezes over entirely. Even though we've almost lost the light. He wants us laying cairns for Franklin, leaving final messages, anything we can do to make our presence known before winter swallows us all.

I knew I'd be selected. I knew my luck had run out. I knew as I scanned the list of names pinned to the inward hull outside the galley.

The wind howled outside, and the gray weft of the sky leered in through the porthole windows.

I knew I'd see the name under mine. And there it was: Edison Stowe.

LONDON

Chapter Eighteen

Edison

Edison's head throbs like an abscess. He'd had too much champagne at Wilton House. The sight of his uncle had him rattled, induced him to drink.

The screech of the engine is a skewer through his skull. The train shudders to a halt at the station and he leads the tour group through clouds of coal smut along the platform.

Shards of last night come back to him as they move. Daphne Westbury gleaming like a jewelery box. A room full of loud, dancing guests. Spiraling limbs and shrill cackles. Throats gulping down liquor. Glasses endlessly refilled. He thinks of Charlotte Hollis. Her plain docility. Her husband Frank. Unimpressive, but harmless enough. Then Maude, strange alluring Maude. How intoxicating. How ungraspable. Who is she, really?

Their conversation in the garden had troubled him. How had she known he was on the *Makepeace*? He was sure he had not mentioned the name to anyone. But Lady Westbury is a terrier, she will get hold of information if she desires it. Still, there are things about Maude Horton that elude him. He flatters himself that she shares his proclivities towards the darker sciences; wonders if she found herself as a child, just like him, snapping a starling's neck to slit it open at the belly, marveling at the delicate bones inside. But there must be something else. The strange fire. The questions at Wilton. Something deep within him *needs* to know more about her. It would not take a lot to follow her home, he supposes. Wait in the shadows, watch her that way for a while.

They pass a knot of railway policemen, stiff in high-necked coats, pale trousers, and stovepipe hats. Edison taps his topper down an inch.

She always seemed so unsatisfied, Ms. Horton. When they conversed, it was as if she was searching for something entirely different beneath his words. And what of that unusual tooth necklace? He imagines it glowing in her bag. It scratches at him, needles him, but he has no idea why.

He feels momentarily uneasy, but there is a delicious hint of something else there too—excitement or fear, he is not quite sure which yet.

He is still thinking about what a drop of her blood might look like when he realizes Lady Westbury is talking to him.

"Mr. Stowe," she repeats. "Do you hear that? I believe they are calling your name."

His focus heaves back to the train platform, swamped with bodies of returning excursionists.

The woman is correct. Someone is calling his name. It's faint among the hubbub.

"MISTER EDISON STOWE . . . A MISTER EDISON STOWE RETURNING ON THE SALISBURY TRAIN."

He pushes his way through the crowd towards a boy with a flat cap and battered satchel.

"I am Edison Stowe."

"Telegram." The boy thrusts a message into his hands and

before Edison has had the chance to blink, is already hollering someone else's name.

Edison unfolds the paper and quickly scans, biting his cheek when he sees the housemaid's name scrawled at the top.

The following message has been received at—London Central Station, 10 November

FROM, name and address—Harriet Black, c/o Mr. Inchbold's Bones, 17 Theobalds Road, WC1X 8TG

TO, name and address—Edison Stowe returning on the Salisbury train, 10:30 a.m.

Mr. Stowe,

His men have been round here again.
This time there was no subtlety to their threats.
Mr. Inchbold has asked me to make clear that unless you settle your debts in the next two days, your room here will no longer be available to you.

The Journal of Jack Aldridge

$\bullet$————$\bullet$

On the ice

12 *Oct.*

WE HAVE BEEN OUT on the ice for two days now and with
every passing second I have kept my eyes cleaved to Edison
Stowe.

I considered feigning illness to remain on the ship. Thought
about telling Despie what I'd seen below decks. Or even
taking a knife to myself. An injured boy could never pull a
sledge.

But would that save my life?

The wind out here is a force of its own entirely. Annihilating.
Something that screams and moans and caterwauls like a
beast. I watch my back at all times. I know the scientist's
position at every waking moment. I cling to the other men,
desperate for safety. We're given half a gill of rum and a biscuit
to eat, but I can barely manage it.

Hauling the sledge is as fatiguing as anything I have done.
I am half-witted with exhaustion, my shoulders raw from
the burn of the dragging rope. My fingers are numb. Every
meager slip of breath is snatched from our lungs and cast
into ice crystals around us. Every day we find the paw prints
of deadly white bears sunk deep into the snow.

***

13 Oct.

I don't have long to write. I stashed this journal in my
knapsack and get down what I can in the blue of polar
twilight. I do not want the men to know that I am making
a record of our journey. So, I hide, with my back against
the sledge, scribbling as fast as I can before the ice claims
my exposed skin. I do not trust the men, any of them now.
If I had a rifle or a shotgun, I'd be keeping it at half cock
beside me.

They are each loosening the ice from their beards with a
fire that crackles loudly at the center of our camp. Stowe is
kicking at it with his boot. I can hear him. It sends embers
fleeing upwards. They know there's no good to be found
down here.

On the ship, I felt his blue eyes on me at every turn. Now
he acts as if I am not a member of this sledge party at all. He
treats me as one might an unwanted dog, eyes drifting over
my head, never once glancing down to meet my gaze. It is
as alarming to be constantly diminished as it is to be beheld.
Because I know, without any doubt, that as soon as I turn
away, when I drop my guard, he will make his move.

***

14 Oct.

Stowe does not take pains to hide his true nature from the
men. Exhaustion has blunted his fine edges. He is clumsy.
Exposing. This morning, as we rested next to a narrow lead
in the floe ice, we were astonished to see tusks piercing the
surface of the water. Staggered that anything could be moving
in this place of sheer stillness. As sleet swirled around us,

the tusks speared upwards, gently tussling with one another, knocking about with the soft tap of tooth on tooth. Narwhals! Sedgewick would burn with envy. I yearned for his presence, then. His protection.

The men were agog at the sight of the whales this far into winter. There was a majesty to the creatures. Something otherworldly. As if we had been visited by magic.

It took just seconds for Stowe to act.

Without pause he lifted his gun and sent a bullet into the back of one of the whales.

The pod scattered in fear, disappearing below the sea ice in the blink of an eye. The whale hung limp in the water, leaking blood, and Edison ordered the men to help him retrieve it.

On the ice, Stowe set about hacking off the tusk. He was rougher than a butcher, raising his hatchet above his shoulder and slicing it down again and again to separate tusk from flesh. The men were nervous that the blood would draw in the bears. But they were hungry, delirious at the promise of meat.

Stowe gloried in his bounty. Ecstatic. He stashed the tusk in the bottom of the sledge among the provisions and the tents.

I was not offered the whale's flesh and would not have eaten it if I were. I have no appetite now. Only fear persists.

***

15 Oct.

This diary may outlast me after all. I hope someone finds it when I'm gone. I hope that it gets to you, Maude. Promise me this: do not believe what you are told.

Chapter Nineteen

Edison

The crow appraises him from the headstone with a stark, black eye. Its body has the wet shine of boiling tar, its head tipped ever so slightly to one side.

The bird makes Edison feel itchy. He raises an arm to shoo it away and it flaps off reluctantly, only obliging to move a few meters, where it settles on an old stone tomb and releases a raspy hack.

Above, the great dome of St. Paul's soars against the bright, gray sky. Below, the ground at Edison's feet is laced with worms and woodlice. The wet weather has lured them out of the earth, and they writhe pathetically among the soil and the ferns.

All this and he has ended up exactly where he began. Under threat of losing his lodgings. No coin. No prospects. Why does the world have it in for Edison Stowe? What has he done to deserve such paltry luck?

He had lost sight of Ms. Horton at the station, while he stood with the telegram grasped in his fist. Anger alights in his chest again. That blasted debt collector! That lowly belly worm. Will he never just leave him be? The profits from the Salisbury tour will not make a dent in what he owes Carter. Not once he's paid the train company, not if the harlot Adelaide insists on collecting her share too.

Edison had taken a detour through the chapel yard on the way back to the shop, considered making some illustrations of the tombs. Perhaps he could employ the services of a professional and use them in some clever way in his next tour pamphlets. If he had the money, that is. He had put off what he knew would be a laborious conversation with Inchbold, and instead had spent the morning scouring through piles of newspapers and broadsides, researching crimes and hangings from across the country. Calcraft had been busy—Norwich, Edinburgh, Liverpool, Bristol. Express trains from London had taken crowds to hangings at Stafford Prison, York Castle. There were countless stories of men. Men killing their wives, killing their sisters, their maids, sometimes even their own daughters. All reported in large text and florid language.

ASTONISHING DISCLOSURES! the papers promised. *HORRIBLE AND BAR-BAR-OUS CRIMES.* Narratives were always cut into three, Edison noticed: *LIFE. TRIAL. EXECUTION.* As neat as a butcher slicing up meat.

The crimes themselves were intriguing. There was the tenant farmer who dressed in a wig and whiskers to shoot his landlord and his family. The watchmaker who took an omnibus and two trains to murder his mistress in her sleep, then carried her head back to London in a velvet hat box. It was a shame, for his pockets, to see that there were fewer murderesses in action—those who laced their husbands' dinner with arsenic; young servant girls who bludgeoned their elderly mistresses to death before pocketing their jewelry. The hanging of a murderess was far better attended than the hanging of a murderer, and the newspapers had a field day when a woman was condemned. A woman is gentle and passive by nature, a woman in the very essence of her femininity is a powerless creature. Powerless creatures do not strangle their husbands with bedsheets and hide their quicklimed bodies under the floorboards.

Thirty years ago, he would have had far more options for his tours. Men and women swung for all sorts—stealing geldings, uttering, coining, hocusing. Someone could have their life snuffed out for nothing more than passing on forged documents, or for killing a cow with his cart. But Edison Stowe will not dwell on thoughts of justice today.

Executions were dwindling in London, certainly. More convicts being transported to stock the colonies; stays being granted before they even reached the scaffold.

But no matter. What could be more common than oversupply? This scarceness made his model even more valuable. You had to travel these days to see spectacle, to see justice being served, to bear witness to this declining rarity.

Which is exactly what he will facilitate.

He will arrange another tour. He has to.

Yes. His chest swells. It shouldn't be too hard, surely. But where? If he could wait for one here in London he could arrange an executioner's breakfast, a first-floor room on Old Bailey. Throw in a decent pair of opera glasses to sweeten the deal?

No. His shoulders slacken. Not London. He would be waiting a while. And it must be more exciting than London anyhow. Especially if he's to up his prices. He wonders if his previous guests might return. Bar Mr. Jameson, of course. He will ensure Ms. Horton is reserved a space. Perhaps he might find her alone one evening. A simple knock on a door after lampsout. A hand to the throat. The feel of her hair between his fingers.

That damn crow is still making a racket. He looks around for a stone to toss, and as he does, his gaze falls on someone watching him from the far corner of the graveyard. It sends a knife down his spinal cord, and he makes a show of turning his attention pointedly back to the ground. He waits for a while then raises his eyes again. Yes, the man is still there, in a thick coat that hangs down to his boots. Waiting. Watching.

Edison calls the man's bluff and moves quickly down the row of tombstones, feigning interest at a monument of a watching angel, its wings strangled by ivy, its face blighted by moss.

DUNGGGGGGGGGGGGGG.

The bells of St. Paul's almost send him leaping out of his skin. He falters, stepping backwards into a tangle of briars that spits dew across his trousers. He glances up. He hadn't seen the man move, but somehow, he is even closer now, observing Edison from behind a large stone cross.

Brazen.

Above the man, in a twisted old oak, more crows are hunched like carbuncles upon the branches. Their incessant cawing cuts cleanly through the mist, and the men regard one another, the tails of their coats blowing gently in the breeze.

Slowly, Edison feels any warmth abandon him. He does not need to see the man's face to know he is one of Carter's. He is going to have to run, isn't he? Goddammit. It is just a matter of when.

He sees the man reach for something in his pocket. Good enough. He takes off at a sprint, crashing through bushes, leaping over tree roots and exiting the graveyard at its westerly corner. Out on Giltspur Street he speeds past clusters of shoppers. His lungs, forever ruined by the ice, straining as he pelts past market stalls, tearing his way down the long intestine of the old viaduct. At the next junction, risking a glance over his shoulder, he sees, with a hot surge of energy, that the man is closing in on him. Quick as a rat, Edison changes direction and scurries down a quiet side street, glimpsing an alleyway a dozen yards ahead that he knows will provide just the refuge he needs. He bolts towards it and, with a skid, turns and ducks inside, his body enveloped by its cool, dark shadows. Then he pauses, chest heaving, and peers tentatively out onto the street.

The man is not there. The street is empty.

He falls back into the shadows, allows himself a deep, gratifying breath. The air is a balm to his ice-scoured lungs.

Then suddenly behind him: a gentle cough, and every ounce of Edison's blood freezes. Slowly, he turns.

Carter's man is taller than he is, so he finds himself eye-level with a mouth full of bad teeth. The man is grinning, a snide crocodile smile dotted with dirty gold incisors. Edison lifts his chin and tries to broaden his shoulders, meeting the man's cruel, flinty eyes.

There is silence as they inspect one another.

"Very convincing," Edison says eventually with a long release of breath, then he splutters. The cold weather is making him wheeze. "Perhaps a touch *too* convincing. My lungs can't take that much running." His palms go to his knees, and he bends double, battling to regain his breath.

The man laughs drily and reaches into his coat to withdraw a cigarette. He turns to rest against the wall next to Edison, strikes a match, begins quietly to smoke.

Silas Blackthorn is Carter's second-in-command. He is the man the most powerful moneylender in London relies on to enforce his brutal, merciless rule. Silas Blackthorn has killed more men than Edison Stowe would like to imagine. He has tortured and blackmailed, he has slipped bodies into the muddied waters of the Thames in the cold dead of night. But he will not kill Edison. He will not harm a hair on his head. Even if Lucian Carter has ordered him to. Because Silas Blackthorn and Edison Stowe have a deal.

Edison had been clever to arrange such a thing, and it had required immense flexibility of thinking. But he was agile like that, when the pressure was applied.

Silas Blackthorn had found Edison easily once he had returned from the Arctic. It can have been only a few days after the *Makepeace* had docked and Edison had installed himself above the shop. While out walking he had felt a grim, heavy hand seize his shoulder. He was eating a pie, he remembers that quite vividly, and he recalls the unpleasant visual of brown gravy dripping and solidifying on one of his best shoes. Silas had been sent by Carter to issue his first warning. Edison had invited him to join him for a drink, then made him an offer he could not refuse.

He'd thought first of the tusk, to try and pay him off that way, but someone like Silas Blackthorn does not have the nuance nor the dexterity to trade with the right people and convert something so unusual into funds. He needed to appeal to the man's baser skills, as well as his rough ambition, his yearning for control, his undoubted desire to be as powerful as the man who pulls his strings.

Edison had wanted to use his new contact at the docks for his own financial purposes. He'd had nothing else to lose when he returned from the Arctic, and after multiple scouting excursions he'd eventually made nice with a warehouse watchman who was easily tempted into conversation. The watchman seemed impressed by his scientific credentials and intrigued by his tales of adventure. It did not take a lot to loosen the tap. To see how they might work together, for mutual benefit.

The watchman, it transpired after some days of coaxing, could, for a fee, provide him with quantities of undeclared and untaxed opium. The opium could be sold directly to the dens of Limehouse, to those less discerning apothecarists, and to innumerable private buyers of questionable character. They'd undercut everything else on the market. Easy. The watchman had the access and Edison had the charm and the business nous.

He was to chip away at his debts like that. That was the plan, at least. Paying off the watchman with a percentage of everything he made. They'd never be caught; they'd only siphon off a small amount at a time. It might take a while, a *long* while, but they couldn't lose really. Yes, he did not much fancy dirtying his hands with the murky drug, and he certainly did not relish the prospect of dark hovels filled with winding smoke and the miasmic fug of the degenerate. But this had fallen into his lap. It was too good of a business opportunity to pass up.

However, when Silas seized him by the shoulder that day, he'd had to think very quickly about how best he might protect himself. How he might keep himself alive now that the money-lender had found him. In the end, it was the opium he'd had to use as leverage. If Silas agreed to keep Edison safe—while also making it appear to Lucian Carter and the rest of his lackeys that he was anything but—Edison would provide him with a steady stream of opium, which he could sell for his own lucrative profits. He knew Silas would not turn it down. This was a means to rise from his inferiority, to cement his own power, his own potential among London's criminal classes. Every second-in-command wants to usurp their boss eventually. A man like Silas—aesthetically imposing but rough of mind and manners—would do anything to take a step up that ladder. And so, they played the game: Silas ostensibly chasing Edison around the streets of London, waiting until he had left the shop to pay Inchbold a visit. Doing just enough to make it look as if he really was being pursued.

Edison chose not to see it as a way of paying for protection, but merely as another of his many shrewd deals. He was in control. He *was*. Even if he was now also late in paying the warehouse watchman his percentage. He was pulling the strings. For the moment, at least.

"He's going to push harder soon," Silas warns as a mackerel cloud of cigarette smoke wafts around them. "He knows something's not right. He's getting frustrated."

Edison sighs. He knows he is talking about Carter. Knows the moneylender will be questioning why his best man can't track him down. He's no fool. "It's not going to work for much longer," the man says with finality. "There's nothing I can do."

Silas turns to Edison and takes another deep drag. He flicks the cigarette to the dirt and squashes it with his boot, then expels a smoky breath directly into Edison's face. Edison blinks in revulsion but does not move. Silas flashes one last gilded grin and steps out of the alley, disappearing down the street.

When Edison leaves the alleyway, eventually, he starts once more to run. He is being pursued mercilessly, that's how it must look to others anyway. He continues running until he reaches Inchbold's shop and bursts through the door, breath convincingly heavy.

He turns to face the door and backs away, as if waiting for Carter's puppet to arrive. As he goes, he knocks into something large and heavy. Frederick! The bear topples, the metal dish crashing to the floor.

"For Christ's sake, Edison!" Inchbold yells.

Edison rushes to hoist the animal's body upward. It rises only an inch. "I was being chased. Pursued. One of Carter's . . ." He crouches, struggling to lift the bear. His words lose steam as Inchbold shuffles reluctantly from behind the till. Bone-weary, Edison admits defeat, taking a seat on the floor. Inchbold watches him wordlessly, hands on his hips.

When he has quite recovered, and when he and Inchbold have raised the bear, now down one eye, to its rightful position, the men stand before one another.

"Did you get the me—"

"Loud and clear." Edison turns and makes for the stairs. He cannot suffer being told what to do by those beneath him for a second longer.

"How are you going to pay him?"

"Plans are in place." He calls as he trudges up the steps.

"I will not have them round here again. Edison." Inchbold's voice rises the further away Edison gets. "This is your last warning. You've got three days. No, two days!"

Edison scowls. The man has all the courage of a blind newt. He will not eject him from his lodgings. He hasn't got it in him.

But Edison does need some money, and fast. Inchbold may be soft, but Carter is nothing but hard edges. When he realizes he is being duped by his second-in-command he will bite, even harder than before. Edison meets Hattie in the corridor, who shrinks silently into the wall. He brushes past her, merely a nudge, and the laundry she carries flies high into the air.

He reaches his room and pulls the door firmly closed.

He needs to act fast. He needs to make plans for his new tour and fill the spaces almost instantly. He must keep moving forwards. He *must* win. No advert this time then. Too slow. Private invitations. Letters to the guests from his previous tours. There is only one way Edison Stowe is going to emerge from this triumphant.

He takes a fresh sheet and begins to draft.

Chapter Twenty

Maude

"Can you just—" The clatter of metal tumbles from the room out the back of the shop. "Maude, is that you? Can you just come and give me a hand?"

She rushes to the preparation room. Her grandfather is half crouched, with a tower of storage tins balanced in his arms.

"For heaven's sake." She moves to take the weight off him. "How can you even see what's going on?"

Eventually Henry is able to straighten to his full height. He wipes his hands on the front of his trousers.

"How was it?"

Words escape her momentarily.

"The trip?" He raises his hands to inspect them, scratching at dirt sunk in his fingernails.

"Dull," she says. "Quiet. Exactly what I needed."

"Well," he says, reaching for a pot on the counter. "Someone came to see you this morning." He places a pinch of blue-green powder on his tongue. "Oof, copper acetate." He spits it out.

"Who?" she asks, alarmed. How can her grandfather be so flippant? Stowe wouldn't know to find her here, would he? She hadn't arranged to meet anyone else.

"A man," says Henry, plucking a long, dried leaf from a tube and waving it under his nose.

"To see me?"

"To see you."

Her fingers begin to tingle.

"He said he'd wait for you at The Smoked Eel down at the docks. Didn't leave a name but said you'd been expecting him."

It can't be, surely.

"Dare I ask what you've really been up to, Maude?" He fixes her in the eye, and she realizes her game is up.

"It was just a letter." She raises her palms. "I wasn't sure if it would get to him. But I had to try. You agreed! That we had to try and get a message to him. He might know something. We might get answers."

He sighs.

"How old am I, Maude?"

She tilts her head. Is this a trick? "Sixty-seven."

"I'm an old man, Maude. So, I'd like to think I will not be outliving my only grandchild."

"It's just a letter. He was a friend of Constance's."

"I need you here."

"I have no plans to leave."

"You know what I mean."

"I will be careful. I am always careful."

"I'd always thought you *were* the careful one, but now I'm not so sure."

"Who am I looking for?"

He blinks his gray eyes. "Handsome. Black hair, spectacles, brown coat. Not from round here."

She takes her grandfather's face in her hand and kisses his lined forehead.

He smiles against his better judgment, and she turns, pushes her way out of the shop, towards the answers she seeks.

*

The docks are awash with salt and bitumen. The breeze is brisk. Maude pulls her wool coat closer around her shoulders. On the water, barges cower together, jostled out of place by huge, imposing schooners. Their masts tower as tall as the clouds, ratlines tumbling from up high like threads of broken spiders' webs.

One ship is still busy with activity; it must have only recently got in. Men hurriedly denude it of its insides, stripping it of barrels and sea chests, sacks and old furniture. She watches as a chain of disoriented sheep is led down the gangway. A man in a begrimed hat wipes his nose with a forearm and strikes them forward with a stick.

The water, steel gray and whipped to ripples, makes her think of Constance. She imagines her sister, dressed in boy's clothing, looking out at the stretch of river. Was she scared before that ship cast off its lines? The question sharpens her thoughts, and she scans the surrounding buildings.

She can hear the roar of the inn before she reaches it, the roguish sound of sailors returned from a long trip at sea. She stops outside and glances up at the sign. An eel with large eyeballs puffs on a cigar.

Is she foolish, going unaccompanied to a space filled with sailors? Perhaps, but if Constance put herself into such a situation, then she can do the same.

The noise hits her like a wall, followed swiftly by the ripe and pummeling stench of sweat. The tavern is filled with men, tipping their heads back at the bar, fanning cards out on tables, roaring, cajoling, and stumbling. She swallows.

The door behind her lets in a sheet of cool light, picks out medals and epaulettes. Some men are in shirtsleeves, rolled back to reveal hairy forearms and blistered knuckles. One poor soul, she can see, has already succumbed to the drink, and is laid flat out across the sawdust as men make a game of balancing objects atop his body.

Yells come from one side of the room. Maude has to look past several sets of shoulders to see what's happening. The men appear to be inducing two small animals to race, having constructed a makeshift circuit between the tables. The animals, like none she has ever seen, appear agitated, and hop on two long flat feet balanced by thick tails. They ricochet off the tables and upend the chairs, tails thumping as the men heckle as passionately as if they were two racehorses.

She moves through the din. The men barely notice her, so fixated are they on their drinking and their games. There's something intoxicating about being among them. She wonders if that's how Constance felt, at first, on that ship.

With the next step she takes, the crowd appears to part. Then, she sees him. Just the back of him, at the bar, but she knows as soon as her eyes fall on his shoulders that it is him. Black hair. Broad. Brown greatcoat. But something else: she *feels* that it is him too. As if Constance is there, raising a finger and pointing. Without prompting, he turns, as if he has sensed that she is there too, and from that point, time seems to stutter. And when he stands from his stool and makes his way over to her, it's as if someone has wrapped the room in wool.

He stands in front of her and smiles.

"I'm Giles Sedgewick," he says. "I got your letter."

Maude feels at first as if she has tumbled into the pages of her sister's diary. As if that world has come alive around her—and this man, who she has read so much about, has risen from those scrawled words to become flesh, blood, and bone.

As they walk the docks together Maude almost wants to reach out and touch him. Just to check: he is here, he is real— a living, breathing man, his smell a musk of soap and salt.

His hands are clenched tightly against the breeze, his eyes are patient, possessed, just as her sister said, of an intelligent clarity. There's a tense strength to his body, his movements, as if he is unaware of what to do with his own physicality. The side of his mouth pulls ever so slightly upwards as he watches her talk. Is he searching for the ghost of his own friend within her too?

Around them, men stream in and out of the sheds. Hollering, whistling, and barking orders to one another. On the water, rowboats skim across the surface, some manned by single pilots, some crammed full of quarreling men. Maude wonders what these ships have brought back to London. Rare ivory, spices, sugar and rum, teas, tobacco, and mahogany. All the brazen spoils of Empire.

As Maude and Giles walk, bundled up against the cold, they speak first in only pleasantries. Maude asks him about his travels. Giles confers his deepest, gravest sympathies. But they both know why he is here.

"What do you know about Edison Stowe?" she asks eventually.

He stops, raises his eyes, studies the pale belly of a gull as it passes overhead. Nearby, a man loses control of his barrel, and it rolls with a churning, liquid sound down the slope.

Sedgewick exhales quickly.

"I know he's not to be trusted, that's for sure."

"My sister's diary suggested as much."

"I did not know she was keeping a diary, by the way." He sounds impressed. "Until I got your letter. Your sister had more mettle than most men on that ship, that's for sure."

Maude nods, still unsure as to whether her sister's note-keeping was an act of bravery or foolishness.

"Stowe features a lot, I assume?"

"You could say that."

The man is running in pursuit of his barrel now, which is picking up pace as it hurtles towards the water.

"Do you think he had something to do with her death?" She searches his eyes as she asks it.

"Perhaps, yes. The man was erratic. Paranoid. I don't think he has a grasp of his own mind. And . . ."

"Fuuuuuuuuck." The barrel has reached the side of the wharf and hurled itself into the water. "Fetch me my wine barrel. Oi. You. Fetch me my barrel back!" A man in a nearby rowboat ignores his pleas and sculls slowly onwards.

Maude thinks of the Edison she read about in her sister's diaries. Distrustful. Secretive. Mercenary. Manipulative. Then she thinks of the character he has projected since, during their tours. Authoritative. Adventurous. Reliable. As flimsy an imitation as ever she has seen. It cannot be only she who can see through the cracks, who has noticed his short temper, his fickle nature, his unpredictability.

"And?" she prompts Sedgewick. Trying to appear composed although her chest clenches at the promise of more information.

He shakes his head, as if he has not quite yet been able to make the pieces of what he is about to say fit together.

"I'd been moved to *High Regard*," he begins. "Blacklock was performing a tricky amputation and the recovery for the patient would be long. He needed an experienced assistant." A clang comes from a warehouse nearby.

Maude's eyes are riveted to his mouth as he speaks.

"When I got back a few days later, it had already happened.

The men had returned early from their sledge party, details of the accident had been relayed, and Despie had filed his report, he just needed me to do mine. Despie used Stowe's testimony as fact, corroborating his story: an accidental gunshot wound. The men had all said that bear tracks had been sighted. That a gun had been misfired in response and that Jack, *Constance*, had been struck with the bullet."

Maude fights the rising nausea in her throat. A bullet? A misfire? To hear her sister discussed in this way, to hear her death spoken about in the words of an official report is impossible to swallow.

"It's not uncommon," Sedgewick continues. "Guns misfire. Men, tense from days on the ice, think they see things, are too quick to protect themselves. But that is not what I believe happened on the sledge party. In fact, it *cannot* be what happened."

She cannot speak. Only the beat of her pulse persists.

"I asked if anyone had inspected the body." His words are more urgent now. "Despie took me aside, then. Shut the door to his cabin. Away from the ears of the other men. He wanted to swear me to secrecy. He'd discovered something about Constance that nobody else could know. I feigned cluelessness, surprise, although I knew, of course, what he was talking about. He said he'd wanted to bury the body but that he'd waited for me. That it was clear that the injuries aligned with the story, but that he'd let me have a look. As if he were doing me a favor." He almost scoffs. Their eyes meet briefly and Maude notices, with surprise, how it makes her stomach shift. "I demanded to see it immediately." He shakes his head, corrects himself. "To see her. She was being kept in the orlop. It's cold there, almost freezing, and the body doesn't . . . degrade."

She closes her eyes against the word. The orlop is where Stowe and Mance first threatened Constance, she remembers from the diary. Where they stored their rocks in a barrel full of whale oil. The fact that Constance was returned there, to somewhere so cold, so hostile, makes Maude want to wail with grief.

"Did you manage? To see her?" She gets the words out, somehow.

"There was no way I wasn't seeing her."

Maude nods gently, grateful again that Constance had a friend on that ship.

"Despie was insisting we bury the body as quickly as possible. I said I needed more time to produce an accurate report. More investigations. I told him that could take a few days. But he wanted her off that ship as soon as possible. I could sense it." He pauses, looks briefly upwards to the bleak, gray sky. "I hoped, in a way, that he was doing it for her benefit." His feet shift. "Monsters are made on ships like ours. If the men discovered that there was the body of a woman on board, who knows what they would have . . ."

Maude's head feels dizzy with the horror of it. The barbarity. The secrets. The way she must hear about her sister's body like this.

"With hindsight, he clearly didn't want people knowing that he'd been tricked, that he'd unknowingly allowed a woman on board," he continues. "Before I knew it I was, once again, called to High Regard. That's when he buried her. Without me there. Without me being able to do more investigations in order to file a thorough report." He rasps his hand over his pate. "I was so angry at him for being so hasty. So slapdash. But, at least I managed to see her. Once." He blinks dark eyes down at her.

She swallows. "What did you find?" She almost doesn't want to ask it. But she must.

"I knew Stowe was not to be trusted," he answers after a

pause. "I had already noticed strange patterns in his behavior; a lack of feeling, a manner that I found oddly cold, unnatural. And when I performed my investigations on Constance, it became clear that the truth did not, simply *could not*, align with the story he was telling."

"It wasn't an accident?"

"It wasn't a gunshot wound."

The words send her mind swilling.

"A bullet creates a very distinctive wound on a body, Ms. Horton. Stowe had alleged that a bullet had entered Constance's, or Jack's, chest directly above the heart."

She nods, although the image of a bullet in her sister's chest is abominable.

"If that were the case, I would have expected to see a relatively small wound on the exterior of the body. Internally it would have been a different story—inside a body, a bullet can pierce tissue, shatter bones, sever spinal cords, even dislocate limbs. But an entry wound, especially an entry wound when the bullet will have had to pass through a thick coat, should be quite neat, even for a heavy weapon the tissue disruption would only be about three inches or so around the wound path. There may even be an exit wound at the back of the body if the weapon used to fire the bullet is powerful, as were the muskets the men were carrying for the sledge trips. But . . ." He seems reluctant to say it, but Maude needs him to, she *so* needs him to say it. "The wounds on your sister's body were not consistent with a gunshot wound."

"What *were* they consistent with?"

"If you'll forgive me for speaking plainly, Ms. Horton, and I hope that you will."

The dread arrives with twisted fingers around her throat.

"Your sister's chest was almost entirely crushed."

Temporarily, she stops breathing.

"It had been subjected to a significant impact." He cannot look her in the eye as he says it. "This sort of injury simply does not happen with a bullet. This was the result of something large and heavy, something that narrows to a point perhaps, but still a thick point. Thicker than a spear or a bayonet or an ice pick. Blunter than that. More like . . ." He shakes his head as if he is speaking despite himself. "More like bone."

She can only watch in horror as he speaks. As he shakes his head, still trying to sift through what he saw.

"The clothing, too. I inspected it. I wanted to see the coat that she was wearing. If she had been hit by a bullet, the bullet would have had to pass through the coat, there would be evidence of that. But there was nothing. The coat was clean, and it is therefore my deduction that the coat was pulled aside before she was struck by something."

She is certain that she will faint. That she will drop to the filthy boards of this wharf to join the mud and the rats.

"I refused to sign off on Despie's report," he continues with passion. "And I could not complete my own. Not until I knew exactly what had happened. Well, he kept me at a distance after that. Moving me over to *High Regard* permanently while we were frozen in for the next few months."

She can barely hear him. She is thinking back to the pages of Constance's diary, to the passage about the sledge party, to Constance's fear, to her distrust of Stowe, to her sister's certainty that she would not come back from the Arctic alive. Then she alights on it. A thundering smash of pain, a horrible surge of certainty.

How had she missed it?

It had been there when she waited for Constance's return

at the docks with her grandfather. It had been there, swinging from chains above the till, as she first watched Edison Stowe in the bone shop all those weeks ago.

She swallows. Turns to Sedgewick, her ears roaring.

"Not a bone," she says.

His brow creases. His quick eyes search her face.

"Not a bone at all," she says. "A tusk."

His mouth falls slowly open. She knows then that she has her answer.

YORK

Chapter Twenty-One

Edison

A private and exclusive invitation to:

EDISON STOWE'S MORAL COMPASS TOURS

Excursion to York Minster and historic castle for
unrivaled sightseeing and the hanging of Matthew and
Margaret Ann Forrester, The Meat Cleaver Murderers

Leaving London (Euston Station), Thursday, 4 December

1ST CL—45s 0d

All meals, lodging, and transportation included

Accommodation at The Seven Cats Public House

For tickets, bills, and to reserve a first-class seat, apply at

EDISON STOWE, C/O MR. INCHBOLD'S BONES,

17 THEOBALDS ROAD, WC1X 8TG

*

They'd all said yes. He couldn't quite believe it, that when
he'd contacted them, sent word that he was planning another
excursion, included his invitation, complete with shrewd illustrations, that they'd all—even with his inflated prices—written
back to confirm that they would attend. Ms. Horton too.

He'd even snagged a new group member, some playboy from Kensington. Money to burn. He knew those handbills were worth it.

This was not his only coup. He had also bought himself some more time at Inchbold's by selling one of the shop's ring seals to a passing collector, pocketing the money himself—he'd use it for his rent. Inchbold would never notice it was gone, it was just one skeleton, or once he did notice, Edison would have accumulated enough money to pay off Carter and would be long gone. Although he is not quite sure where just yet. But if the man insisted on keeping the tusk for the Exhibition, then can Edison *really* be blamed for seeking trade elsewhere? It was a grubby deal, and he took far less than the bones were worth, but he could not afford to lose his lodgings right now. How would that look?

After that, York had fallen into his lap quite by chance. When returning to his room one evening, he'd found a newspaper open on the sideboard. It must have been Inchbold's. It even looked as if its pages had been smoothed neatly down as is his habit. At first, he was furious that it had been left to clutter his room, and he was sure to punish Hattie accordingly. Still, the newspaper proved useful. Emblazoned across the page was a headline, THE MEAT CLEAVER MURDERS. He quickly scanned the story—a cruel landowner, a husband and wife out for revenge. They were set to hang in the grounds of York Castle in a fortnight. A double hanging. Almost unimaginably rare. Likely to draw in tens of thousands of spectators. There'll be special excursion trains running already. *Perfection.*

The train journey, however, hadn't gone quite as smoothly as the RSVP process. The Hollises had arrived first to the carriage, followed soon after by Ms. Horton, who had chosen an oxblood dress for the occasion. It made her blue eyes shine like cut diamonds.

The playboy, Charles Arnott, had swept in after that smelling of shoe polish and ambergris. As he had sat and leaned his silver-topped stick against the seat in front, Edison had watched his eyes glide easily over Charlotte to rest on Maude.

The journey thereafter had passed, at least at first, without great incident, even when it began to rain heavily and the third-class passengers in their open tubs found themselves soaked to the skull. Such trials do not seem to impact the hearty poor much and before long he had heard them singing their merry songs.

It was not even Arnott's subsequent, and wildly intrusive, questions that had thrown the journey off course. Although the man's mouth was looser than his purse strings. "I speak as I find," seemed to be his rebuttal to any accusations of impropriety, and it took him little time to draw the ire of the other tourists. He probed Daphne Westbury first, on the provenance of her polished cherry jewels. She submitted impatiently to his questioning, batting him away with what sounded like the contents of the *Victoria Regina Atlas*.

"The sapphire?"

"Ceylon."

"The emerald."

"Colombia."

"The pearls?"

"South Sea."

When he tired of that game, he turned his attention to Charlotte, who pursed her lips and cast her eyes out the window when he began his uninvited assessment of her attire.

No, the real palaver came when the train screeched, lamps swinging from the ceiling, to a halt just outside of Birmingham.

For a while there was silence and the passengers sat patiently with their hands in their laps. Then, a great burst of activity as the guards exited from their carriages and rushed towards second. Frank Hollis and Arnott leaned across their seats to peer out the window, rubbing away the small clouds of breath that fogged the glass.

"What's happening?" Lady Westbury clambered over to join them.

"Looks like some sort of emergency," Edison muttered as he craned on tiptoes.

One of the guards was running back along the platform towards them. When he reached the group of faces squashed together at the glass, he rapped on the window with his knuckles.

"Do we have any doctors aboard? Anyone with medical experience?" His voice was muffled through the glass. "A nurse?"

Edison took a step back from the window. The rest of the group exchanged expectant glances. Hollis, he thought, might have had some first aid training. So he was not surprised when he saw him rise to follow the guard. But he was shocked to see Ms. Horton bend to retrieve her traveling bag from the corner. She stepped across to the window and raised a hand to the guard.

As far as he knew, Maude was not, and never had been, a nurse.

"I can help too," she called.

The others in the group shifted their bodies so that Maude and Hollis could weave their way out of the carriage. Edison could not discern quite why his heart was beating so fast. But he was uneasy at the prospect of anything derailing his excursion. He simply could not afford the refunds.

He whipped off his topper, smoothed his hair with his palm,

and replaced it. Then pulled himself out of the door, down onto the platform and up the steps into second.

The air felt different inside, weighed down with something heavy. The passengers had pushed themselves up against the walls to give the patient some space. It was an elderly gentleman, Edison could see, sprawled on his back on the floor between the seats. His eyes were open, glassy and unnerving. He had fallen, Edison deduced. Gluey crimson had collected beneath his head. Maude and Frank passed muttered orders between them, and he watched as Frank handed Ms. Horton a rolled-up shawl and as she lifted the patient's head and tucked it underneath.

"Water," she ordered.

A man stepped forward from the corner and offered a flask. Maude tipped it gently to the man's lips. There was a collective, uneasy averting of the eyes as the liquid rolled helplessly down the man's chin.

Maude then reached for her bag, unfastened it, and took out a smaller pouch from inside. She tipped its contents onto the floor with a glassy clink. It wasn't just bottles inside; there were balms, tinctures, pastilles, and creams. She continued tipping. There were knives, scalpels, plasters, all manner of medicinal things. How did Ms. Horton own such a collection? And why on earth would she need to bring it all with her on this excursion?

Questions wound their dark way around his bones.

"Pass me the laudanum. He'll be in pain."

Hollis began palming through the bottles until he had separated four or five into a pile. He pushed them towards her.

It was a large quantity to carry, Edison thought. Far too large for personal use.

Maude uncorked one of the bottles and appeared to weigh

up how best to administer it. Eventually, and much to Edison's distaste, she hooked her fingers into the man's mouth and prized his clenched teeth open. Then, while holding his jaw wide with one hand, she carefully tipped the liquid into the space beneath the man's tongue.

"That will keep him comfortable until . . ." She and Hollis exchanged grave glances. "Until you are able to get him to a doctor," she told the guard.

Back in first Lady Westbury was climbing the walls.

"And?" she asked, before they had even taken their seats.

"He'll be fine," Frank Hollis said quietly. Edison watched as Maude clutched her bag close to her chest.

*

And so, there is a delay to their arrival, but when York eventually presents itself, all members of the party agree that it is a fine, fine city indeed.

Their public house, conveniently close to the castle walls, has peeling paint on the frontage and a King Charles spaniel puddled in front of the fire. It's a cozy scene that makes Edison feel warm. Far too warm. Christ. Why is he sweating?

The heat surges up into his hairline, then smears back down his face to his throat. He coughs to try and relieve it. Takes a labored breath. Another.

He thinks of the contents of Ms. Horton's bag. A lifeless body. A quiet house.

At his side, Charlotte Hollis eyes him cagily. He sees her reach a hand out to him, but the image is blurred. His eyes swivel.

"Are you feeling quite all right, Mr. Stowe?"

He does not know who says it. The words slide away as if

greased by oil. He must remove some of his clothing. Why does he feel as if he is falling? The walls! Are they truly melting? He tugs at the shoulders of his dress coat, shrugging it into a pile on the floor. A lifeless, slumped body materializes beside him. He goes to nudge it with his foot, but his boot meets nothing but air. The whole group hovers nervously around him now. Oh, would that they would move away! They are stealing all the air in the room.

He pulls at the buttons on his vest, hears the echo of Frank Hollis trying to reason with him and take his arm.

But he has been plunged under water.

He must reach the surface.

He takes another breath. Deep. One, two, three. He pictures an open window; birds soar across a pale blue sky. He breathes again. Easier this time.

One.

Two.

Three.

Then suddenly, his vision sharpens, his chest stills, his breathing slows. He is once again present in the room.

"Are you back with us, Stowe?" Frank Hollis's voice is clear as a bell now.

He ignores it, rushes to grab his coat from the floor. His hat, he realizes, is in Ms. Horton's hands. She must have retrieved it when it fell. He sees her pass it to Frank Hollis and wipe her hands on her skirt.

"The weather," he reaches for something to explain. "So changeable at this time of year, one can never really settle on the appropriate number of layers."

"Quite right," Charlotte agrees generously, and the group collectively usher him towards the stairs.

*

At the foot of the staircase a slip of a man stands with an oversized ring of keys attached to his belt. He offers to show them to their rooms and the others discuss a small supper. A pretty barmaid passes by, and Edison can't help but notice that her hands are filthy with dirt, black like charcoal. He makes his excuses and departs, reminding them of their early start tomorrow if they're to beat the crowds.

He climbs the stairs behind the wispy man, a slight tremor still detectable in his hands as he grasps the banister. The keys whisper. It's impossible not to feel as if he is being led to a cell.

It takes an eternity for the man to identify the correct key on his overcluttered ring, and for him to fumble incompetently with it in the lock. When Edison is finally granted admittance to his own room, and once the man has departed at last, he drops his bag and coat where he stands and lurches to the washbasin.

He leans over it, palms splayed against the marble, replaying the scene from downstairs. It hasn't happened for a while, that alarming loss of control; that feeling of sinking, deep down into the earth. He takes the jug of water from the sideboard and bends his head over the basin. Slowly, he pours the liquid over the back of his neck. The water has teeth. It does nothing to stop the shaking. But its sharpness clears his mind of the fog. He pulls the cloth from its ring and dries his hair, rubbing hard to ward off what he knows is coming. *Rub.* Here it comes. *Rub.* Bubbling up like bilge water. *Rub.* He lifts his head and peers into the glass.

She is there. Mother.

Her presence is the unwelcome specter it always was. Silhouetted in the doorway, bird-like wrists and bony fingers giving her the illusion of a burnt-out tree. He can picture her alive now, her thin mouth and coarse hair, loose strands caught and lifted by the breeze from the open window. Once his father left, once she *drove* him out, it was just him and Mother in the house. He would never hear her approach, she made sure of that, her footfall so light she was never betrayed by the creaking of stairs. When she came to him, it was always with something she promised would make him better. Something to banish the night sweats, the cramps. He was delicate, she said, his meals needed special preparation, his medicine carefully doled out. Every sip, every forkful, every morsel or crumb was vetted by Mother. Even though, the more he ate and drank, the paler his skin became, the duller his eyes, the weaker his limbs.

It had been only the two of them for years. No housemaid, no siblings. They were so lucky, Mother said, as his body grew weaker and weaker, and she fed him. Every action he took was dictated by Mother. Every small humiliation orchestrated by her. She liked him to clean every inch of himself until no speck of dirt remained on his skin. The bathtub, too, she made him scrub until it shone, until she forced him to bow his shaking head and lick the tin clean. Eventually, he became so ill it was almost impossible for him to lift himself from his bedsheets. A doctor was never called, and Edison was too enfeebled to ever question why, lying in damp sheets, wracked with fever and pain, watching the birds sail across the sky through the crack in the open window.

He knows now, of course, that he is safe. He knows now that his mother was the one that was unwell. He still thinks though, in the cold of night when the lamps send strange shapes across the floorboards, of how she died. It was a black night. No moon, no stars, the sky hunched and threatening as a dog. The day had been miserable and filled with the sort of drowsy half-consciousness that was usual for Edison. He had watched with resentment as his mother picked around his room, touching his possessions—the books on the dresser, the small silver comb, a grand candlestick that she buffed and buffed—making it clear that they were not his possessions at all. They were hers. She owned everything in this house, including him.

It was late when he heard the noise, a shuffling sound coming from the hallway outside his room. He pulled his blanket up to his chin; it was not uncommon for his mother to come to him in the middle of the night to administer medicine, but she was not normally this noisy. He'd often feign sleep once he'd seen her shadow at the door, but she would grab him by the shoulder and shake him awake. "Just a few drops under the tongue," she'd whisper. "That's a good boy." She always made it sound like love. But in the morning, he'd inspect his reflection in the glass, the purple pools beneath his eyes more intense than ever.

This time, she did not enter his room. Edison waited, breath held, but the door did not creak open. Instead, a strange scratching came, and then that shuffling sound again. He peeled back the sheets and levered, with great effort, his frag-ile limbs off the bed. He crossed the floor on tiptoes, reached the door, turned the handle and pulled it open a crack. There was a body there, upright in the hallway, wearing the embroi-dered white nightdress that belonged to his mother. The body had his mother's hair too. Coarse and fraying out of its long plait. But the face was not his mother's. The face was slack and dead-eyed. Staring right at him but seeing nothing. The body turned and continued its corpse-like shuffle towards the staircase. Somnambulance. He had heard of people walking in their sleep before but never seen it. Never expected it to be so unsettling. Still, there was a quiet thrill in seeing his mother thus, drained of her power, unseeing, unknowing, unable to do harm.

She had continued towards the stairs, and he followed just a step behind her, silently. At the top of the stairs she paused, put her ear to the air as if listening to the drum of his heartbeat. He saw her fingers flicker, saw her begin to turn, then he held out his arms, and he pushed.

*

The next morning the air is frigid. The window had been left open all night to bang in the wind and he had not had the will to re-stoke the fire, so the bedsheets had soaked up the dawn damp. As he pulls himself upwards, they are wet to the touch.

He sighs. Pinches the top of his nose. Does he *really* have the will for another hanging? He'd heard of Calcraft's most recent attempt at Cambridge. Botched. His favorite trick of all. Leaving the prisoner dangling in agony until the hangman had made a show of tugging on the man's legs to see him off.

Perhaps he could skip this one?

But as soon as the thought forms itself an image arrives: Carter eventually arriving to exact his penance. Enraged at being deceived.

Reluctantly, he steps to the window. The street below is already busy, the city's old walls as pale as knuckles and, in the near distance, the flags raised atop their poles at the tower. He thinks of the condemned, stowed away in their damp castle cell. They must hear it all—the early omnibus rattling past, delivering indistinguishable men to indistinguishable places of work; the draymen offloading casks of ale to be drained by the scaffold crowds; the bawling costermongers and the ballad singers already staking out their plots for the impending frenzy. Above, the sky is minnow-hued and mournful.

Edison dresses and readies himself for the day.

*

Downstairs, the group is already assembled in their coats. Surprisingly, his eyes go first to Charlotte Hollis, who looks, dare he say it, almost radiant in deep emerald. Arnott rests against the wall smoking a cigar—this early!—and quickly turning the pages of his newspaper. Maude's eyes flick up as he descends the final step, but they cannot meet his. In fact, he has not been able to snag her attention ever since they boarded the train to York. She looks tired, her face pale and drawn, suspicious. He swallows dryly when he sees that she has her traveling bag with her. He pictures all her wily poisons inside. He will do it tonight. A knock on her door. Hissed questions. He knows what he has to do to get the truth from her.

"I've not seen one since the Mannings," Lady Westbury says in greeting as he arrives. "A double hanging. Have you?"

He shakes his head.

"They really are a different spectacle."

He is heartened, at least, to see that she has her black ribbon proudly fastened to her chest.

The door is open and the rumble of cartwheels lurches in through the gap. Edison leans forward and peers through. In the rainy morning murk, he can see laborers working to put the finishing touches to the scaffold at St. George's Field. The tower looms high in the background. At least they won't have to travel far today.

"Should we leave now in order to secure a favorable view? I'd like to be as close as possible to the scaffold," says Lady Westbury, looking ready to bolt. Arnott folds his newspaper away amid a puff of cigar smoke.

"If that's the consensus?" Edison asks.

"I like to be in the meat of it," Lady Westbury agrees. "Or else all souvenirs will be gone by the time we get there. I need a set of those Staffordshire figurines for my collection."

They agree to leave and Maude stoops to pick up her bag, sharing a strange look with Charlotte. Edison sees it.

There are women lined up towards the scaffold. Knots of them, draped in old red and purple shrouds, like unfashionable jewels gathering dust. They hawk brooms and brushes, clothes props and pegs, or fern roots and other odds and ends. Most of the crowd, which must number just a few thousand, surge forwards, fixated only on securing a prime view of the hanging. Members of the local church, he notices, have gathered to dole out dissuasive tracts. Good luck to them.

Below the crossbeams, a wiry hangman, too tall and thin to be Calcraft, makes a show of pawing at the equipment. He's overdressed for the occasion, in his velveteen shooting coat and billycock hat. But with this many people watching, Edison can't blame a man for wanting to look his best.

The smell of the crowd is repugnant. Festering sweat, dried lavender, blood pies, and sweetmeats.

How had he not previously noticed the sheer Bedlam squalor of the scaffold crowd? Had money alone made him overlook the full-gloated glee with which such an audience brayed for death? It's exhausting.

As he scans the sea of faces in disgust, his attention is caught by one woman. Stood a small distance from the rest of the shrouded gang, she wears a crimson headscarf, a chain of coins strung loosely around her neck. Her eyes, pale and haunting, are smudged with charcoal.

"Got eyes for the gypsies, Stowe?" Arnott jibes as he taps the ground with his cane.

"Of course not." He is ruffled at being caught. "Just rather thought I recognized her."

"Tell your fortune for a penny."

The voice lands sweetly in his ear.

Arnott raises his eyebrow devilishly. "Indulge the doxie, won't you?" He moistens his lips. "We've a while until the hanging."

They both glance towards the scaffold.

"Not really my sort of thing," Edison mutters and continues on. Although the woman's hot coal eyes have been seared into his mind.

"Oh, don't be a spoilsport. If you can't spare a penny, I'll cough up for you." Arnott strides over to the woman, extracting a coin from his pocket.

"Tell his fortune." Arnott seizes Edison by the shoulders and places him square in front of the woman. Edison sighs inwardly. Arnott is lucky he's so damn rich. The rich can easily get away with petulance.

"Anything you'd like me to illuminate?" The woman's voice is honeyed.

Edison stumbles as he's jostled from behind.

"MEAT PIES. MEAT CLEAVER PIES. DOUBLE THE 'ANGING, DOUBLE THE BLOOD."

He cannot draw his gaze from the woman's face. Has he seen her before? Does he know her?

He risks a cautious glance up at Arnott, whose wandering attention seems, thankfully, to have been drawn by a flower girl with two missing teeth. Edison seizes his opportunity. He leans in towards the fortune teller.

"Finances," he whispers, casting his eyes around for the rest of the group. He spies them, eventually, gathered loosely around a Punch and Judy show. Jack Ketch is slinging a noose around Punch's throat. "Now then, Mr. Punch," the puppeteer parrots. "You are to be hung up by the neck until you are dead dead dead."

As he starts to turn back to the gypsy, he sees Maude

watching him, still clutching her bag. Their eyes meet and she glances quickly away.

"Can you tell me anything of money," he continues, hushed. "Will I . . . Am I to come into some money soon?"

Without warning she reaches forwards and seizes his hands. If he weren't so shocked by the chill of her skin, he would have pulled them back immediately, wiped them off on the wool of his coat.

But her skin is like ice. He feels her thumbs probe his palms; it causes a twinge in his groin. He coughs, focuses instead on the young woman's eyelashes. Sooty and clumped together.

"You are certainly enterprising," she says ponderously. "I can see that."

Why does she not speak like the other urchins?

"It will pay off soon enough." She nods her head slowly; it makes the silver coins around her neck shake. "You'll come into reasonable fortune, but you must use it wisely, or others will get hurt again."

He snatches his hands away.

"Sir, I can only do the reading if we are linked by the hands."

He scoffs. He knows this trick. It's every thief's game: she keeps a hold of his hands while her accomplice has a royal rummage through the contents of his pockets. He will not be falling for such a swindle.

"Dishonest swine," he raises a finger as a smile begins to lift the side of her mouth. "Charlatan!"

"Does that sound familiar, Stowe? Hurting others? Only God and I as your witness."

"What is this?" he wheels about, searching for whoever has set him up. "You're speaking nonsense, uneducated louse."

"That's right," she laughs as he backs away in disgust, bodies knocking into him. "Best be on your way, Stowe. You've not got long left."

He halts in the crowd. He can barely see her amongst the crush now.

"What does that mean?" he orders across their heads. "What do you mean, not long left?" He will not be threatened by some harlot. He changes direction, fueled by anger, and pulls his way back through the thrum. By the time he has reached her spot again, she has dissolved into the mass of bodies.

Not long left. The words repeat, sharp like pokers. Not long left? What drivel. He rearranges his hat and sets off to find Arnott and retrieve the rest of the group.

It is only when the words come, insistently once more, that he realizes what else it was that she had said. "Stowe," she had called him. Stowe. He blinks. He is certain he never once mentioned his name.

Chapter Twenty-Two

Maude

Heads bowed, they forge their way towards the scaffold. Wealthier types have chosen to watch the festivities from the comfort of their coaches. Farmers have come in their carts or on horseback, but the overwhelming majority—dressed in the brown, black, and gray of dull garden birds—have arrived without vehicle or possessions, leaving them free to clamber onto the stands, copping a few bruises as they jostle for the best vantage points. Maude has no desire to see the hangings. She is here for something else entirely now.

Stowe had returned from the "fortune teller" suitably rattled. Good. The woman did a fine job; Maude knew she was an actress as soon as she saw her behind the bar at The Seven Cats last night. She knew all it would take to entice her to take part in some theatrics was a few pennies, a bottle of laudanum, and a slick of charcoal across the eyes. Arnott wasn't her doing. Someone else had sent him along. But she was pleased to find he was suitably pushy—steering Edison into places she needed him to be. She'd never heard of Adelaide Swan, hadn't come across her at all when she'd been trailing Stowe. But she'd been assured the woman had a keen eye for deception and knew exactly who could be employed to manipulate proceedings.

It is a thorny concept: revenge. Something she had only ever encountered before in the pages of Constance's penny bloods—husbands seeking revenge for the deaths of their delicate wives; maids enacting penance on their cruel masters; jilted lovers administering poison. It had taken a while for the want, the *need*, for revenge to crystalize inside of her. When she'd first felt it, it was like a pain, and she was sure it was just her grief growing stronger. She had never felt Constance's death as a lack. Nothing light, nothing hollow. Instead, it was a daily presence. Heavy. Something to be dragged about. But no, this was different. This was as if every single one of her bones had been set on fire. The unfairness of it all made it feel as if every fiber of her being was calling out for justice. No longer meek, no longer afraid, she wanted action.

She wants to scare Stowe. She knows now, what he did, and the hot, appalling surety of it has sloughed off any softness she had left. It had been right in front of her, all this time. The facts are brash and galling. They make her want to spit poison. Sedgewick had given her what she needed to draw all the threads together. Now she had her answers, she needed somewhere to place this unfamiliar rage. She wants revenge, and she wants it now.

The tusk had been there right from the start, swinging above the till at Mr. Inchbold's bone shop. The very weapon that was used to kill her sister. On show. A trophy. An unmistakable gloat. She had reread that passage in the diary over and over. Stowe hacking the tusk from the whale as sleet billowed and the sledge rested on the ice. Constance's fear dripped from every word. She had known it was going to be the end for her. It makes Maude want to tear her own heart out through her chest. She needs to hear the words from his own mouth. She needs Edison Stowe to admit the truth. She is going to have to make him talk, and she is going to make him pay for what he has done.

And now she has help. Beyond Sedgewick, beyond Heart. Now she has an arrangement.

*

She had been summoned just before the York excursion with a simple note card, pushed under the door of the pharmacy when she'd returned from her meeting with Sedgewick. He had not signed it with his full name. A simple C was all he offered.

The address given was in Mayfair, an unlikely place for someone like him to order a meeting. But who was she to refuse? If she did not answer his demands, he would send his men to find her anyway.

And so she tarried on a well-to-do Mayfair street, eyeing rolls of silk and sateen. Some of the material in the window was plain, some ablaze with vibrant prints. A dress shop. That couldn't be right, could it? She pulled the notecard from her sleeve and quickly checked the address.

She appraised the fabrics again, more luxurious than she would ever in her life be able to afford. They called to mind exotic spices. It made her feel uninteresting in her day dress of periwinkle blue.

But it mattered little what she wore or how she looked, she supposed.

Drawing a breath, she pushed on the stained-glass door, hoping her appearance would go unnoticed so she would have time to collect her thoughts before he arrived. The bell, pulled by a string as she entered, had more voluble ideas.

Two people, who appeared to have been deep in conversation, turned to look at her, blinking expectantly. Their expressions suggested they had been sharing a joke before her arrival. One of them was clearly the shop owner, an older woman, slim, elegant, with a long, gray braid that stretched almost to the floor. Her eyes, Maude noticed immediately, were green and hard, like a cat's. At her wrists, she wore bracelets of gold, silver, and jade. In front of the elegant woman, on the other side of the till, was Lucian Carter.

"Ms. Horton." She'd heard stories about the moneylender. Her grandfather had told her of his chilling reputation. But in the flesh, he looked so little like someone who cuts tongues from mouths.

"A fine shop, is it not?" He smiled, spreading his arms. "Mrs. Raika is the crème de la crème when it comes to the importation of quality silks."

Maude had felt that she should nod but she was finding it rather hard to move at that moment. It was an unnerving feeling, to be pinned so entirely by someone's gaze, and for a second, she easily imagined the bristling terror that must flood his victims' bodies before they die.

"Come."

She still could not move.

"*Come, come.* I need your help with something." His smile was so wholly disconcerting. Not a smile that invited joy. But one that suggested its owner knew something terrible about you that you did not yet quite know yourself.

The woman disappeared quietly out the back of the shop, and after a short while the sound of her singing filtered out through the silks.

"Now. Let me get a good look at you. Yes, that's it."

Carter took her by the arm and spun her slowly, assessing every inch of her as she turned. It was a slow and excoriating action, giving Maude the sensation of being forensically peeled.

"Perfect. Now, if you wouldn't mind. Hepzibah! The oxblood."

The woman emerged with a roll of red fabric under her arm. Her pursed lips were stuffed with pins.

"I have been following you, following him. Quite the caper."

Maude could do nothing but blink wordlessly in response.

"And when I saw you, I realized you have the exact same proportions as my wife, almost a mirror image. Same hair. Same figure," he continued. "I like to surprise her. I thought you wouldn't mind acting mannequin for a while."

He was toying with her. He was making her his puppet.

"And I must say, I am impressed. My top man seems conveniently incapable of getting close to that rat before he scarpers. A risky game, on his part. Thinks he's been clever. My men should know better, of course. They should know that I see everything, I *know* everything, that there are consequences for forgetting just that. But anyway. No matter." He waves his hand as if swatting a fly. "We need not worry about that any more. He cannot continue such double-crossing from the bottom of the Thames."

Maude swallowed quickly.

"But *you*, well, he seems rather more comfortable in your company. Although, I suppose, beauty does lubricate social connections rather nicely. My men don't quite have that appeal. Do measure her up, H."

Hepzibah took her measurements briskly. Moving Maude's arms left to right, up and down. She had no choice but to obey. All the while, Carter watched, appraising the fit, how many buttons, how much lace.

When Hepzibah had almost finished, and when Maude was so trussed up, she felt like a poppet doll bristling with needles, she decided to ask him if he was going to kill her.

He barked with laughter, as if she had suggested something absurd. More games. More toying.

"What is it that you want from me then?" A pin dug into her rib, but she could not move to free it.

"Oh heavens, I thought that was quite clear," he smiled. "I want you to give me Edison Stowe."

There was a long pause. Hepzibah took it as her cue to disappear once more.

Carter could get to Stowe easily if he wanted to, Maude knew that. He'd still have loyal men who would follow any orders he gave them. Shearing off thumbs, trailing debtors, enforcing his power at every possible turn. But the man had a strange energy about him that day. He seemed . . . excited, that was it, at the prospect of some grander scheme, something that would send a message to the whole city.

"What do you want from Edison Stowe?" she asks.

"Money. Among other things." He said it as if there could be no other answer. "What is it that *you* want from him?"

She met his eye, fully for the first time. It was like being stabbed through the pupil.

"I want revenge," she said.

He grinned. "Delicious."

He took a hand and plucked a loose thread from her chest. She eyed his fingers, pictured broken bones and blood. Twisted thumbs and gouged-out eyeballs.

"Why do you need me?" Again, Carter was powerful. He knew where Stowe lived, he could get to him. But that was seemingly not enough for him. "How am I supposed to get you the money?" She knows, of course, that cannot really be what he wants.

He smiled again, raised his eyebrows, as if she has been naive in her misunderstanding of his instructions.

"I am a patient man, Ms. Horton, but even I have my limits. I have watched his silly little shows and his tours and his spectacles and my men have proven themselves utterly inept in getting the job done. I do not want you to get *money* from Edison Stowe." He briskly smoothed down the material of her skirt to signal the fitting was completed. "I want you to help me kill him and I want it to be the greatest show of them all."

She had fought to keep her jaw from dropping open. She could not join forces with Lucian Carter. Could she?

"Oh," he'd chuckled and tapped his head as if he had forgotten a valuable piece of gossip. "I dropped in on your grandfather the other day."

She bit the side of her mouth.

"Such a pleasant man." He stepped around her to assess the final fit of the gown.

She knew, then, that he had her.

*

Elbows jab into Maude's ribs, and she is brought back to the quarreling crowd. The crush will help her in her task. She had agreed to assist Carter. She'd had no choice, of course, and he'd already helped her—introducing her to Adelaide, who'd been supplying information to Carter for months, sending Arnott to bolster their plans. Yes, she would help the money-lender, but not before she had got what she wanted herself. Death would mean finality, no more talking, no more truth. And she still owed it to Heart, and to herself, to find out what she could of Hancock's conspiracy. It may not work, she is well aware of that, but she has to give it a try.

Now she just needs to find a way to separate herself and Stowe from the rest of the group.

She pats her bag, in it all the things she needs. There are dozens of taverns lining the square. She needs to ensure she and Stowe are separated so they can drink alone, so she can do what she needs to do without Lady Westbury or anyone else butting in.

"Here we go, The Meat Cleaver Murders." Mr. Westbury has secured a broadside and is regaling the tour group with the particulars. "A cruel landowner, a glorious revenge, a body stuffed between the hay bales et cetera et cetera . . ." His wife stands grinning at two pottery replicas of the murderers grasped between her fists.

Maude watches as Edison loosens his cravat. He must have been truly rattled at hearing his "fortune'.

The crowd quickly quietens. A hundred mouths hiss as the condemned pair is led up the scaffold and hoods placed over their heads.

"Mr. Stowe," she turns to him, drawing her face into a troubled frown. This is her chance, if she can only coax him away, she can finally compel him to talk. Whatever drug, whatever method she has to use.

She feigns a swoon, stumbles, grips his arm.

"I am feeling quite faint, I wonder if we might . . ." Bodies barrel into them. She lifts her head—a skirmish nearby has sent the spectators into a churn like cattle. Raised voices volley above their heads. Stowe stands on tiptoes, cranes his neck to see; she does the same, but she is sure to keep her hand clasped to his forearm. This is her chance. She *must* take it now. Constance needs her to. But her waters run cold when she sees what it is that has caused the fuss. A young woman, dressed in little more than rags with a baby at her breast, is struggling to keep her footing. The crowd around her staggers back and forth, clamoring and grabbing, intent on gaining a better view of the hanging. Over the din of it all, the red-faced infant howls.

Maude pauses, wondering briefly if this is just what she

needs in order to steal Stowe away without the group noticing. But almost immediately she is washed in a flood of shame at having had such a thought. She whips her hand from his arm, steps forward, pushing hard against solid backs and thighs. She pushes and pushes, trying to squeeze through the crowd. It is immovable.

"Help that woman!" she calls, waving her arms towards the slowly sinking mother.

The surrounding crowd stops, reaches in unison for their hats, and holds them reverentially to their chests. The hanging is about to take place.

"There's a woman with a child, she needs help!" Her throat rasps with the words.

There is a hush as the hangman takes his place on the platform.

"There is a baby. Please." Hers is the sole voice now. She looks around for a policeman, someone, anyone, who can help.

"She needs assistance," Maude cries desperately. "Save her. There's a baby. They'll be crushed!"

A bell rings. A most abominable sound.

Her hand goes to her mouth as she watches the woman about to fall, but before she does, Maude sees her raise her arms above her head, offering up the child. At the scaffold, the doors drop, and the crowd erupts, but Maude's eyes are still on the woman. The baby. Her heart lurches as a man leans over and takes the infant from the woman's outstretched palms. He then passes it backwards over his head to another stranger, who does the very same. And so on and so on, until the child has been handed over the heads of dozens and placed, by a quick-thinking tradesman into the straw bed of a cart.

Overcome with relief, Maude turns back to seek out the tour group. Lady Westbury appears to be demonstrating the effects of the short drop execution method on her husband; Charlotte Hollis stands patiently beside them; and Arnott is already cloaked in a caul of smoke from his post-swing cigar.

Edison Stowe, she notices with a bitter sting of regret, is nowhere to be seen.

Chapter Twenty-Three

Edison

He'd barely noticed getting in the cab, the words rattling around his head. *Not long left. Not long left.*

They come with smeared visions. Hot and blurred. The bottles in Maude's bag. Bodies dropping to their deaths. Crowds howling. Icy fingers and wolfish eyes cloaked in charcoal. He needs a drink.

"You feeling all right now, Stowe?" Frank Hollis asks. Edison rubs his forehead in response. The man had found him on the outskirts of the crowd feeling quite queasy indeed. He suggested they take a drink at a nearby tavern together and Edison had been grateful for the chance to escape the rest of the group.

"A hanging's not for everyone, is it. Got to have a strong stomach." Hollis reaches across and lowers the window.

"Hmm." Edison is too distracted to reply. Why does he feel as if things are starting to unravel? He reminds himself: he is a man of reason and science. He will not be troubled by the words of some whore with painted eyes. He leans and looks out of the window, tries to gather his bearings. He can't seem to shake the unsettling feeling that he is being taken somewhere against his will. He leans his head out the window again to look behind them, but there are no other vehicles.

"You should come and see some of the death masks at Tussaud's," says Hollis. "See how they were made. It's quite the process. That will strengthen your stomach."

"My stomach's quite all right as it is," Edison snaps, but the good-natured Hollis doesn't seem fazed. He places his calloused hands in his lap and turns his attention to the window.

They are quiet for a while and the carriage lurches through the narrow lanes.

"Quite a goldmine, is it not, Tussaud's?" Stowe asks by way of making amends, remembering an article he had read in an old issue of *Punch* while researching his tours. He had cut it out with a pair of scissors, kept it on his dresser. "Good MADAME TUSSAUD," it said, "devoting art to homicide, turns to the pleasantness of profit the abomination of blood. With her so much murder is so much counted money."

"It's very popular, yes. The crowds can be quite something, especially if there's a new exhibit."

The carriage judders as it crosses cobbles.

"Speaking of which, we're thinking of doing something on the Arctic. You should get involved? It would be an honor to cast your likeness."

Edison considers it, nods. He can see himself in an exhibition. And if he can get past this bout of . . . whatever it is—weakness?—Tussaud's could help promote his tours to a wider audience.

Hollis seems pleased. "I'll write with the particulars as soon as we're back in London."

"Of course." Edison grabs his seat as the carriage lurches round a corner. "I read that Grosholtz rummaged through piles of corpses to make her death masks in France. I should imagine this would be a far more pleasant experience."

Hollis laughs. "A formidable woman, Grosholtz. Well, Madame Tussaud, as we called her. Tiny as a wren, guts of an ox. She'd not blink twice at a hanging, I'll tell you that. Now where is that other cab?" He peers again out of the window. "Ah."

Edison is briefly irked that they will not be able to drink alone, as he'd hoped.

"The Westburys?"

"They chose to walk. Maude and Charlotte shared a carriage. There they are now. I said we'd meet them at the inn."

Perhaps begrudged companionship is better than no companionship when it comes to drinking.

"Hmph. I'm glad we're not in that carriage." He gestures backwards with his head. "Small mercies."

Hollis smiles questioningly.

"The tension! Jealousy on Charlotte's part. Apologies. No offence intended. But it's a very feminine thing, is it not? Being envious of another's appearance."

The cab stops at a crossing and a jarring screech comes barreling through the window. Edison watches as a woman puts her nose to the glass and hooks her filthy fingers in through the opening. She cannot be beyond twenty years of age, but she has the appearance of a hag.

"Can I inchrest you gentulmun in some eggs?"

The men share a dubious glance.

"You!" She raises a dirty finger at Edison. "I've got something very special just for you."

He huffs and reaches over to slam the window shut.

"Friendship extinguishes such mortal jealousies, I'm sure," Hollis posits after a while. "Charlotte doesn't feel like that and, anyway, in my profession, you become far more interested in an unusual face than a beautiful one."

"What?"

"A face is far more interesting to mold if it has singular qualities to it—the hook of a nose, a scar upon a lip, eyes slightly wide set. Our flaws are what make us unique."

"No, what do you mean their friendship?"

"Charlotte and Maude's friendship. There is no ill will between friends. No jealousy."

Edison scoffs. "I am amazed that women declare friendship after mere hours spent together. It's as if clasping an embroidery ring and exchanging asinine thoughts about the weather entitles you to the sort of bond shared by men who go to war. So very vacuous, so very female."

Hollis pauses before he answers. "They have known one another for a lot longer than that." Edison frowns, confused. "Charlotte told me the other day," Hollis continues. "I was surprised too. But I gather they've been in contact for some months now. That's enough foundation for a friendship. I'd like to think you and I were friends even though we haven't known one another for too long."

He turns to Hollis. Mortified to find that he is not jesting. But what's that? An inscrutable twitch of the mouth. Does the man hold his gaze for just a beat too long? Something cold wires its way into his veins. Creeping slowly, insidiously through his blood. He doesn't like this. He doesn't like this at all.

Maude Horton is a liar. What else is she hiding?

Chapter Twenty-Four

Edison

His head is turning cartwheels. Someone is striking a very large gong next to his ear. He opens one eye and immediately winces it shut. Why does the ceiling appear at such an obtuse angle? And why, on God's blasted earth, does he have sawdust tickling the back of his neck? He risks opening an eyelid again and groans. He is on the floor. How did he wind up on the bastard floor? Gingerly, he stretches his arms out, sweeping through piles of sodden, filthy sawdust . . . the horror! He jack-in-the-boxes upwards, his vision smearing slowly after him.

He pinches his brow as his eyes roam the room. It has darkened to pitch black outside, yet it was light when they arrived. Only a few candles flicker within the pub now, casting everything in a dull, treacly glow. No one seems to be paying him much attention, ergo he must have been on the floor for quite some time. And speaking of time, where in Christ's name did it all go? One moment he was in the cab with Frank Hollis, the next . . . he wakes up here, sprawled like a sot on the floor of some sordid inn. What sort of gentleman leaves another in such a position?

He rolls onto his knees and draws a breath, then staggers to his feet. The pain in his head is merciless. He wets his lips—his mouth feels as if something has crawled inside it and died—then goes to rest his elbow on the table in front of him. Somehow, it leaps two feet away from him, and he crashes forwards onto his hands and knees once more. Without thinking, he groggily flexes his fingers into the damp sawdust and then, as if an alarm bell sounds, he recoils. Filth! Squalor! What interminable repetition. Why does he keep ending up on the floor! He half stands, rubs his hands on the back of his knees, then wipes his sloppy mouth with the back of his palm.

Something taps at the side of his vision and enters. A memory. From earlier in the evening. He can't make out all the details, but he squints into the near distance to find them. Arnott. Ambergris and shoe polish. A beer, just one mug of beer, held in his hand. But then a strange feeling coming upon him. Voices that sound as if they are coming from very far away. He blinks heavily, shakes his head, it leaves something else imprinted on his vision: a face, looking over him. It is quite beautiful. Dark hair falls in ringlets across a pale forehead. The face is speaking, or at least its mouth is moving, although he cannot make out what it is saying. The face leans further and something cool and hard trails across his cheek. The face retreats at a jerk, but as it does, he sees what it is that has touched him. A tooth, two parts of a tooth, on a string. And that is when he remembers.

The Arctic air blasts his skin with the scorch of a cinder burn. The sawdust begins to swirl and shift and from it rise piles of snow warped into hills and hummocks. The air swarms with sleet, the howl of the wind tormenting his ears.

One two, one two. A regimented march slowly forwards. A trudge through the snow. The heavy sledge moving only inches with each step.

Their party has been going for days, depleted by hunger and

fatigue, but Edison's belly is full. He had feasted last night on the flesh of a narwhal. He'd hacked the tusk from the creature's mottled body and stashed it in the sledge, he would be taking it back to England. It would make him rich.

It was a hopeless sledge exercise. He knew that. They all knew that. They were not going to find *Terror* and *Erebus*; they were laying cairns that would be uncovered by no one but the Esquimaux. Yet Edison needed to be a part of this particular party, away from the ship. There was something he had to see to.

It was not safe to carry out the extermination on the *Makepeace*. Although he'd wanted to. Once the boy had seen them in the orlop, he'd wanted to slash his throat as he slept; creep upon him on watch and toss his body overboard to be fractured by the ice. But Mance had convinced him to wait. Away from Despie, away from Cook and those who had eyes on the boy, he'd be free to act without suspicion, punishment.

The boy was stronger than he looked; he certainly pulled more than his weight when it came to the sledge. The other men seemed grateful for the boy's efforts, impressed by his determination, his duty.

Edison hoped it did not mean he would fight back when it happened.

Regretfully, the boy had seen too much, heard too much. But the other men seemed protective of him and his small size. To do what he needed to do he was going to have to get him away from the rest of the party, on his own.

Edison had made a show of seeing the bear prints, he was clever like that. He had spent the whole afternoon telling the men just how big they were, how it appeared that the bear was stalking them, it must be hungry. There were no prints of course, but the men were too spent to realize. They were easily coaxed into agreeing that they should keep their muskets to hand at all times.

When they'd hauled the sledge as far as their limbs could take it, they'd set up camp at the foot of a vast mountain. A fire would not light in that night's weather. They would have to huddle in their tents to try and generate some warmth.

A storm had set up its wailing and the sky was an eery, soulless navy blue. Sleet danced and swelled around the tent, but inside it was calm. The men were setting out their sleeping bags, their breath fogging the air. The boy announced that he was going to retrieve his satchel, which he'd stored inside a safe compartment of the sledge.

Edison knew this would be his only chance.

He waited for the boy to leave, then stepped out of the tent after him.

The wind had strengthened, and it buffeted the comforter around his face. The land was white for as far as the eye could see, the snow settling in droves on the interminable ice.

He could just make out the shape of the boy, trudging away from him towards the sledge. It had been left some twenty meters from the tent. Edison glanced behind him: the men were tucked inside their bags already, unlikely to want to leave them, unlikely to stick their heads out after him. His musket was already loaded and prepped, so he raised it to his shoulder, pointed, and held it there as he ran to get closer to the boy. The knowing snow muffled his footsteps. As the boy reached into the sledge, pulling back the tarpaulin, Edison put his eye to the sight and rested his finger on the trigger.

The boy froze then, as if he could sense the gun on his back. He turned, slowly, and while Edison expected to find a look of terror on his face, he saw something else entirely: resignation.

A look passed between them. The circumstances were as

the circumstances were. The boy needed to be extinguished. And so Edison pulled the trigger.

The gun did not fire.

Edison tried again.

The gun did not fire.

By now the boy's resignation had been replaced by panic, confusion, and as Edison downed the musket in anger the boy turned and began to run.

It did not take long to catch up to him, he was just a boy after all, no match for Edison's long strides. No match for the barrel of a musket which Edison swung against his skull to knock him to the ground. The boy half turned as he fell, landing in a twisted position in the snow.

Hell.

Edison was going to have to beat him to death. Not as neat as he would have liked. But nevertheless, he raised the barrel.

Then he paused.

If he struck the boy on the head again, how could he pass it off as a misfire? He needed something else, something that would make his story believable.

Just a simple accident. A bullet gone rogue. Happens on expeditions all the time.

The boy began to groan, to raise his hands in front of his face in paltry self-defence.

Then another noise.

Edison's head whipped round.

One of the men was calling from inside the tent. He was sure of it. He couldn't risk them coming out here. He couldn't risk being caught. He had to act quickly.

That's when he glanced into the sledge, the tarpaulin pulled back and laid along the bottom: the tusk. He placed his musket on the tarpaulin and leaned in with both hands to retrieve it.

The boy moaned girlishly, louder this time, as Edison knelt and pulled back the boy's coat, wiping away the sleet that had collected heavily on his own eyelashes. He needed to give himself a clean shot, he only had one chance, but the sleet continued to swirl and blur his vision. He raised the tusk and just as he jammed it down with a violent jerk into the boy's chest, he got a glimpse of something strange. Gleaming weakly through the thick flakes of white that swarmed in the air. Yes, he remembers it now. Can make out the details. Two halves of a tooth, strung together on a piece of cord.

Straightening to his full height in the pub, he staggers backwards to his stool. Confused and yes, he will say it, afraid. How does Maude Horton, a woman he had never met until a few weeks ago, have that necklace? A necklace so strange and so distinctive, worn by the boy he killed, *out of necessity may he add*, in the Arctic?

He needs another drink to steady his nerves. He gestures to the barman, although his hand does not follow his mind's orders. Does Maude Horton know what happened on that ship? Does she know about his uncle's plan too? Of his failure? Does she know that a whaler is dead because of him?

Is he going to have to dispose of her too?

His drink has still not arrived.

"Barman." In his head he says the word clearly, but the sneers around him suggest otherwise.

"BARMAN." He makes sure his voice carries across the taproom. A large man wearing an apron and an expression of noticeable disdain glances up from the bar. He holds a cloth in one hand and a glass in the other. He looks exhausted.

When he sees who it is that is calling, he returns to his cleaning.

"Oi." Edison stands, sways, staggers across the room. A few gray faces, late night stalwarts, turn to watch as he crashes into a table. Then, in recoil, as he upends a stool with his backside.

He reaches the bar eventually and clears his throat. He will be served by this imbecilic slug.

"Another beer."

He slaps a palm onto the wooden bar top. It lands in a puddle of something brown which splashes up to his chin. He leaps back from the bar in horror, then pauses. It is unlike him but his urge for another drink outweighs his disgust at the establishment that serves it.

"I said another beer. Now."

The barman refuses to meet his eye.

"You've had enough. Best go home and sleep it off. Again."

Edison gasps theatrically, then turns his head left to right to assess the reaction of an invisible audience.

"I think you'll find it's my job to decide when I've had enough," he slurs. "It is your job to serve me."

The barman gives a wink to an enormous man sat reclined by the door, large fingers linked across his stomach. Edison doesn't see the human mountain stand and stride over. He only feels him as he is seized by the waist, hauled from the countertop, and carried kicking and jeering out of the pub.

The next thing he knows, his cheek has met the cold wet cobblestones of York. Then: a knock as his topper is hurled out the door behind him and strikes him on the shoulder.

"Piss off back to London," the man mutters. Edison raises his head and wipes the grime of the street from his face.

LONDON

Chapter Twenty-Five

Edison

As he makes his way out of Euston Station, he feels it might be better if he himself were at the end of Calcraft's rope. At least that would mean he did not have to deal with Maude Horton, or the infernal pain that had his skull in its grip.

The memories congeal inside his head, he can't find a way through. He'll walk back to Clerkenwell, he decides. He must try and order his thoughts.

He had got the early train back to London; the others could find their way home and if they didn't, he cared little.

Maude Horton *knows*. She knows what he did. But how?

And, hell! What is it to her? They do not share the same name. They are not family. It was just a ship's boy. Nobody anyone would miss.

He walks. Inchbold will let him in. He knows he will. He'll give him a few more days' grace, the man just takes a little persuading sometimes. As Edison goes, the stink of the city comes to greet him head-on. He presses a handkerchief to his nose to ward off the miasmic reek of the Thames, resisting the urge to spit.

A nurse maid rattles past pushing a two-seater perambulator. He thinks of the servants, the maids, the cooks, the street cleaners. People like Hattie who survive only by tending to the needs of those above them.

He will never be like that. He will never be like *them*.

He crosses the river and pauses on the bridge. A pair of steamships patrol the horizon and wherries wind their way through what choked space they can find. The contrast between ice and mud yawns into his mind. That godforsaken landscape that gifted nothing but dead whiteness.

He lurches forwards, hoping that motion will invigorate him, and as he goes, meandering along the river embankment, across Fleet Street and the old viaduct at Holborn, he finds his shoulders starting to lift. Eventually, his chin tilts up towards the watery sunshine. Edison Stowe is an explorer, a business-man, and an entrepreneur. He could have been one of the greatest minds in science were he not scuppered by ill-fortune and debt. He will not be cowed by a woman. Edison Stowe is above those who seek to destroy him. It is he who will win out, it always has been and always will be thus.

By the time he reaches Clerkenwell, the scent of baked potatoes and roasted chestnuts fills his nose. He is feeling positively hopeful about the months to come. So hopeful, in fact, that he almost doesn't notice that the door to Inchbold's shop has been left ajar.

He pauses at the threshold. *Strange*, he thinks, *Inchbold always keeps it shut.* A scratching sensation takes hold of his neck, then scuttles to his scalp like a beetle.

He pushes on the door and calls out for Inchbold.

No reply.

He steps into the shop and pauses. The air is gray and dim. No oil lamps have been lit and the specimens are trapped in their own unnerving shadows. He steps in farther, the room ringing with silence as if holding its breath.

He calls Inchbold's name again. Then Hattie's, louder.

He scans the room, squinting through the darkness.

What he sees fills his heart with dread.

The bones have been obliterated.

To his left, the chimpanzee skeleton stands without a skull. Across the floor, femurs and fingerbones have been smashed and scattered. He swallows dryly, the blood appallingly loud in his ears. He moves quickly to the oil lamp on the wall. A matchbox rests in the cradle of the bracket. He takes one out and strikes it. It lights easily and hisses into flame, so Edison can better see the detritus of the room.

"Shit." What is Silas playing at? This should not be happening.

At the center lies the body of Livingstone, the lurcher. Momentarily, Edison allows himself to hope that the dog is simply sleeping. But as he steps over it, he notices the pool of dark blood that has leaked from the animal's slit throat. His mind flashes back to the week before he left for York. He had not seen Silas, nor spoken to him. Not hugely uncommon— they could sometimes go for a while without contact; Silas dealt directly with the watchman now, mostly. But something feels very odd about all this. He kneels beside the dog and places a hand on the wiry fur. The body is cold. This doesn't *feel* like Silas's work.

He hesitates. There is something between the dog's teeth. He bends and peers at it. Yes, a piece of paper, small and folded. Wincing, he pulls it out, then stands and moves towards the light. When the words are illuminated, he knows that their luck has run out. That their deal has been uncovered. That Silas Blackthorn is dead.

The end is nigh.
Lucian Carter

His head swoops frantically side to side, terrified that the moneylender is lurking in the shadows. A flash. His heart slams itself against his chest. Is that the glint of a knife he sees? He stuffs the paper into his pocket. Inchbold will not forgive him for this one, but without that evidence, perhaps he can pass the whole thing off as a burglary. Nothing to do with him.

Then, he hears a strange noise.

It comes again, a muffled sort of groan, just like the noise the boy made out on the ice. He rushes towards the back of the shop, holds his ear to the air. There it is: a human sound. Male. Fear wires its way in.

The strangled sound comes once more, and this time Edison can trace it to the space behind the counter. He leans his body over the desk.

Inchbold is on the floor in the fetal position. His hands and feet have been bound and his mouth gagged. His eyes dart up to Edison's in fear. Then, he begins to groan urgently. Edison flings himself around the counter and crashes to his knees.

"It's all right," Edison whispers, setting about quickly untying the gag. His fingers are shaking, and he fumbles over the knot, but eventually it is loosened and Inchbold thrashes his head to free himself. He gulps in air, gesturing with wide eyes at the binds on his hands and his feet. Edison unties them.

He must have been here all night.

When the binds have been removed, he helps Inchbold up to a seated position. The man's breathing has slowed ever so slightly but his whole body is trembling. Edison can see in the half-light that his face has been badly beaten. His right eye is swollen and bloody and there is a blue-black bruise spreading across his chin. He pictures the scene—Carter and his remaining loyal men barging in through the door as Inchbold quietly shut up shop for the night, as he carefully dusted each of his specimens, ensuring the wooden shutters were secured and no coins left in the till. He imagines them stalking the room, destroying immaculately arranged bones, demanding Inchbold tell them Edison's whereabouts.

Did he resist? Is that why they have done this? Did he try to protect Edison as a friend would?

Perhaps he should apologize. He risks a glance up at Inchbold. He is surprised to find the man staring at him, his countenance glassy and drawn with fatigue.

When he goes to speak, Edison knows, in his bones, what he is about to say. He knows the words will signal an end to any hope for him.

"Get out." Inchbold says it quietly. There's no malice to his voice, only sorrow. "Gather your things and get out."

Chapter Twenty-Six

Maude

Gas lamps cast angular shadows across the pharmacy floorboards. In the fish tank, small silver bodies dart and ripple. She can hear her grandfather out back moving bottles and packages, but she ignores him, tearing down the narrow hallway to her room.

Once inside she draws a breath, pauses, then hurls her traveling bag to the corner where it lands with a crash of broken glass.

She tips her head back, tears breaking free from her eyes. She thinks of how many nights she's gone without sleep, trying to find answers. She thinks of the agony of sharing a train carriage, an inn, with the man who killed her sister, the man who had treated Constance as if she were nothing more than an animal to be destroyed.

She had got so close to getting what she needed from him but, once again, she had ruined it, fumbled her chance.

She'd given him too much. Or had it been mixing the mescal with the laudanum that had caused the reaction?

She cries out, hot with fury at her failure. She owes Constance so much more. She has ruined it all. This is exactly why Maude had always favored a restrained approach. She'd lost sight of that, got ahead of herself. She does not even know who she is any more, and it has cost her.

After the hanging, she'd been desperate to find another opportunity to get Edison Stowe alone. The message had soon come, and she'd found herself at a tavern with Stowe, Arnott, and the Hollises, who had made their polite excuses and left. It had started off so well, the tincture slipped into the drink, the glaze coming over his steely eyes. She had experimented with something innocuous, asked him about the weather and he had smiled in a strange lopsided way. When she'd asked him what he'd thought of the day's events his eyelid began to twitch quite violently. She had fought to keep her frustration hidden. He had begun slurring his nonsense about staircases and sleepwalkers, long before she'd asked any of the questions she wanted to ask—about tusks and sledge parties and rubies and ship's boys. At one point he began to drool and then he slid slowly, like a snake's discarded skin, from his stool. When he hit the sawdust, he had curled up like a violated woodlouse, lost consciousness, then started loudly and obnoxiously to snore.

Her chance was gone.

Now, she raises her fingers to her brow, noticing how they shake, then presses the hard tips of them against her temples. Her body feels like a burnt-out building. The fumes from the broken vials in her bag causing an ache behind the eyes.

There is only one thing left now. To fulfill Carter's demands, to protect her grandfather. And this business, she knows, shall be conducted in the manner that Stowe has conducted his own—with farce, with spectacle, and with sheer, determined annihilation.

That's it, she thinks, picturing Constance's smiling face. *It's time.*

Chapter Twenty-Seven

Edison

He is ruined! Unmoored! He has nothing left! No money, no lodgings, no dignity. He has been left to scrabble in the dirt with the pigeons and the rats.

Edison Stowe is a man of *quality*, why is that so hard for people to understand? He does not belong alongside the malodorous of London. He does not belong in a place like this.

Carter had killed that dog as he knew that was what would get Edison finally hurled out of the shop. Not sly threats. Not torture. Not the desecration of bones. A dog's slit throat is what had flushed him out onto the streets.

He needs money. He needs money to stay alive and he needs it right now. If only he can get his hands on money, even a small amount, he might be able to hold off Carter for another day. He can stay alive.

He eyes the room: damp, gray and moribund. The bed is a woebegone excuse for such a thing. The whole of last night, after he'd arrived fresh from the carnage at Inchbold's, he found himself tossing and turning, rusting springs at his ribs. The floorboards were rotting and there was an unsightly black stain the size of a dress hoop stretching across the middle of the room.

It's cold, too. There are holes in the window glass and every few minutes, the wind hooks its fingers in and shakes the panes. Still, at least he'd managed to find a place to shelter. Or should that be hide? He'd made a clever choice; The Black Dog is a flash house, exactly the sort of place Carter and his men would frequent. They would never think to search for a man of Edison's standing in the rooms upstairs.

His eyes go to his trunk, the battered leather and groaning buckles. It's a shameful collection of all that he has left. A few coats, shirts and trousers, some old books about jellyfish.

He stands to assess himself in the looking glass, hands flickering unthinkingly to his face. Such hollow cheeks. Such disheveled hair. And is that grime caked into the lines around his eyes? Disgusted, he rushes to his suitcase and rummages for a clean handkerchief. When he finds one, he steps back to the glass, spitting into the material then leaning into his reflection to scrub.

He pauses as his stomach bleats with hunger. He has not eaten since yesterday lunchtime. Surely he must still have a tab open somewhere. Yes, The Dancing Bear! They're never to know he's no good for it. He'll wear his hat pulled low, one of his older coats. If Carter's men are waiting, he could still slip past them unnoticed.

Downstairs, he scours the busy pub, keeping his eyes peeled for men with tattooed scalps or bruised knuckles. There's a knot of undesirables clustered around a game of blind hookey, and a man with a large gold earring and an air of barbarity taking hushed meetings at a table in the corner. A sudden roar erupts and one of his lackeys seizes a man in a chokehold. There's a flapping sound as the man attempts to find purchase with his feet. The man with the earring removes a cigar from his pocket and lights it. None of them turns to watch Edison as he walks by. He realizes, with a dull spasm, that he is disappointed. He has become invisible. Just like them.

The Bear is some distance away, but he knows he won't have trouble getting served and he really does need to eat.

He is almost at the door, almost outside, when he is halted by a voice.

He turns, resisting the urge to squeeze his eyes shut against what he is sure is going to be one of Carter's brutes.

"Yes, you. Fancy man. Get over 'ere." It's the barman.

It crosses Edison's mind that this could be a trap. The very moment where it all catches up with him.

The barman is waving and calling persistently, making a scene. He goes over just to shut him up.

"Stowe, isn't it?" the barman asks. By the depths of his sunken cheeks, he can barely have a tooth in his head. He eyes Edison expectantly.

How can he know that? Edison had given a false name on arrival and hadn't spoken to anyone since he got here last night.

"Message for you." The man reaches out a thin arm. At the end of it, a note. There's a drunk's tremble to his fingers and the paper flaps slightly, until Edison snatches it and stuffs it into his coat pocket. He glares over his shoulder. No one is supposed to know he is here; how can there be a blasted note for him behind the bar?

He turns from the barman, who mutters something pointless about manners, and strides back to the staircase, taking two at a time. He'll have to go hungry again tonight.

It is only when he is back in his room, and when the doors are locked that he takes the note out to read it. His shoulders slacken in relief.

Dear Mr. Stowe,

I write, as promised, with an invitation.

As previously discussed, we are working to create an exhibition, a showstopper that we anticipate will draw in immense crowds here at Tussaud's. HEROES OF THE ARCTIC, it is to be called—waxworks of those brave men who have ventured into the frozen north in search of Sir John Franklin and the mysterious Northwest Passage. There'll be snow, there'll be bears, there'll be ships. We hope it will appeal to those traveling to London for the Exhibition next year.

We would be most honored if you would pose for the exhibit.

I know you are a busy man, so we have a slot available this evening. The studio is just off the Separate Room, which I think you will find quite interesting.

I shall send a carriage for you. Seven o'clock. You will be paid for your contribution, of course.

I am very much looking forward to adding you to our collection, Mr. Stowe.

With great respect,
Frank Hollis

Edison folds the paper and glances at the clock. Then inspects his face in the mirror again. A bit haggard still but no bother, he has plenty of time to get ready, now where is his jar of pomade? He knew an opportunity would present itself. He needs money and he needs it now. He cannot set out his hat to beg, he has not time to establish another tour, and a return to his old habitual gambling parlors would prove too risky at this stage. But posing for a waxwork? Posing for a waxwork seems like an easy way to get what he needs. Posing for a waxwork will be what saves him.

There is a question he must address, though: how did Hollis know he was staying at The Black Dog? It needles him briefly, tossing a puff of suspicion into the air, until he realizes that, of course, Hollis must have stopped by Inchbold's shop first. Edison had told Inchbold and Inchbold only that this is where he'd be. If Inchbold sells any of his specimens, Edison is still deserving of his cut, no matter what's happened. George should not have told anyone of his whereabouts, not even Hollis, but Edison supposes he is still weak from the beating by Carter's men. He will not begrudge him too much.

He wonders, as he rubs his fingers over his hardened cheeks, how much he will be paid to pose. Perhaps he should have asked that in the carriage in York. Still, it will be something to stave off Carter and, at present, Carter is his biggest threat. He will deal with Maude Horton later. One pest at a time.

Chapter Twenty-Eight

Edison

It is jarring to see Tussaud's stripped of its crowds. Madame Tussaud herself had only recently died, and her self-portrait, cast in wax, had been positioned at the front doors of the exhibit. The newspapers had reported record numbers: members of the quality with their canes and embroidered waistcoats, come for the effigies of kings, queens, and emperors as well as to ogle the dead woman's likeness.

Now the street outside is silent, a few rats scratching about but no human souls on the cobbles. The carriage Hollis sent has departed, leaving Edison alone in the dark under the grim, spitting rain.

He regards the posters on the building's facade, illuminated by a faint streetlamp glow. *NAPOLEON!* reads one in enormous lettering. Another: *Distinguished characters, royals, poets, beautiful women.* Below it, in smaller font: *Heads of the French Revolution (inc. scale model of the famous guillotine, with real blade—THE TOOL THAT TOOK TWENTY-TWO THOUSAND LIVES!).*

That's what this is, isn't it? A business built on beheadings. He purses his lips and blows out the air. Just *imagine* the profits.

*

Hollis has left the door to the exhibit ajar for him. He feels somewhat bruised that the man has not welcomed him in from the street. But he supposes he must be busy preparing the wax.

He pushes on the door and steps in. The entrance hall is vast and screaming with silence. All lamps have been extinguished; the exhibits lit only by the weak moonlight that bleeds through the high, narrow windows. Edison shrugs off a shudder. Alone like this he feels quite as if he is in a room filled with corpses.

The ceiling is cloaked in drapery, giving the impression of a dark and unforgiving sea above him. The room is colonnaded around its edges, and huge plaster casts of Roman vases spew dark, sculptured garlands along the coving rail. Something large and heavy hangs at the room's center. Ah yes, two huge candelabras suspended from long wires.

Edison's eyebrows lift a touch. He knew Tussaud's was popular, but he hadn't expected such a fine room, for he can see that it is fine even through this Stygian gloom. The walls are covered in gilt-mounted portraits. And of course, on huge ornate plinths, are the likenesses of some of the world's most impressive citizens.

"Mr. Hollis?" Edison words ring around the cavernous space.

The silence roars even louder in response.

He feels a prickling in his palms, then turns, momentarily alarmed. The figures, he sees, arranged around the room are all watching him. At least, on his own like this, that is how it feels.

He'll find Hollis.

He steps towards Alexander, Emperor of Russia. Even in the dark, see how the medals at his breast dazzle! How glittering the gold of his fringed epaulettes. He leans in closer to inspect the face, fancying that he can make out a little of his own likeness in the features.

"Mr. Hollis, it is Edison Stowe. Thank you for the carriage."

He crosses to the opposite side of the room where Louis XVI and Marie Antoinette stand on guard. His footsteps echo as he goes. There is Count Bismarck and Garibaldi, Emperor of Mexico, although he has to squint to read the plaque.

"Hollis," he calls out again then startles. Was that one of the figures crossing the wall at the back of the room?

He shakes his head to rattle out the thought. The silence is getting to him.

The Separate Room. That's right. Hollis had said the studio was off the Separate Room. He'll find the staircase. He'll ignore the panic that is clawing upwards from his toes. He will carry out his sitting as quickly as he can, he will pocket the money, and the money will be what saves him now.

There is a candle, flickering, at the top of the stairwell. Next to it, a note—*STUDIO DOWNSTAIRS! F. H.* Edison sighs in relief and picks up the brass holder.

The air is even thicker below ground. The walls appear entirely black, cloaked in heavy velvet drapes. Low lighting gives the whole cramped space the morbid feel of a dungeon.

Another money-maker, he thinks. The Separate Room, or the Chamber of Horrors, as Tussaud shrewdly nicknamed it before she died, has always drawn in the crowds, with its "murderer's corner", its death masks, its poison boxes, and its grisly souvenirs. It's not dissimilar, he supposes, to what he was achieving with his tours. Royals and murderers. He does not decide what makes money.

He appraises the exhibits quickly, announcing himself to Hollis once more. On one side of the room, a series of disembodied heads have been displayed like prized antiquities. In the corner, a roped-off procession of tatty-shirted figures looms—British murderers cast from life at their trials; men who slit people's throats celebrated just like the statues of poets in an abbey.

If he were not trying to shake off the distinct and foreboding sensation that he is being watched down here, he might be distracted by Tussaud's attention to detail. On the French Revolution figures in particular, the marks of violent death have been rendered with vivid accuracy. Severed heads staged to highlight the exact circumstances of the victim's death. Immortalized with a noose around their necks, a bullet lodged in their temple, a dagger above the heart, in a bathtub drenched in blood.

At the center of the room is Tussaud's most impressive exhibit, a scale model of the famed guillotine. Next to it sit small reconstructions of the Bastille, before and after its destruction.

"Hollis! Are we to do this or not?" He's getting rankled now, he will not have his time wasted.

Then, he sees her.

A woman. Standing with her back to him. At first, he fancies it a statue, then he realizes the statue is breathing. She is assessing a wax figure on a plinth. Her shoulders are slight, her hair corvid dark, and as she turns, his breath catches to find the face that so captivated him the first time she stepped into his train carriage. It is the face he saw in a flash at that first hanging at Newgate. There are those rosebud lips, the eyes like Arctic ice. Skin pale and soft as a child's.

He knows, then, he has been had.

"Ms. Horton," he whispers.

Chapter Twenty-Nine

Charlotte

Ten miles away, in Richmond, Charlotte Hollis holds a well-thumbed note in her hands and wonders if the deed has yet been done.

Frank, her husband, is pottering around downstairs—drawing or sculpting, or whatever it is that he does with his time in their shared studio. They are quite content living separately but together under one roof. Theirs is an easy companionship, a partnership based on respect and peaceful tolerance of one another's lives. It is not a companionship based on love. But that was always the agreement.

Frank Hollis, of course, did not write a letter inviting Edison Stowe to pose for an Arctic exhibition. Charlotte Hollis did. Frank Hollis did not furnish Maude with a key to Tussaud's so that he could be lured down to the famous Chamber of Horrors. Charlotte Hollis did.

They realized they would never really get him to talk, they knew that no poison or intoxication would induce him to admit to his crime, no matter how long they persisted with such a plan. But they were certain he would be foiled by two simple things in his possession: arrogance and greed.

Edison Stowe, much to his misfortune, had paid Charlotte

Hollis little attention during his tours. He had eyes only for Maude, and she cannot blame him for that; the woman is incandescent, just like her sister. No one really seemed to notice Charlotte with her plain face, her unremarkable hair, her staid clothes. People rarely did. That's where she found her power.

She runs the note between her fingers again, soft as suede now. She has caressed it so often, shed tears over it, committed its words to her mind so that they dance around her head as she sleeps.

My love, the words say. *Do not be sad that I am gone. Do not trouble yourself with anger. Do not shed a single, salty tear.* This letter is her most treasured possession. *I think of how we laughed, how we read, how we kissed and breathed as one. Our love a pair of lungs rising and falling together.* Those words provided comfort, assuaged the grief and the white-hot confusion that she'd felt for so many months after she left.

She'd first met Constance in St. James's Park three years ago, while Charlotte was strolling arm in arm with her father. They'd passed a young woman on her backside in the undergrowth, and her father had rushed to help, certain that she must have swooned and fallen into the bushes. Constance had looked up at them both and beamed, dirt smeared across her cheeks and soaked into her hems. Charlotte's father had raised his eyebrows as she explained that she was foraging for mushrooms, would they like to take a look?

"My grandfather is a chemist," she had explained as she'd stood and wiped her hands on her knees. Her voice was young, boyish, and beguiling, and Charlotte had felt as if a pair of fingers were pressing on the skin at the base of her throat.

Charlotte went back. Making that long journey from Richmond every day for two weeks, searching for the girl who scratched around in the dirt for mushrooms. Until eventually she found her, filling her bag with white fluffy Lion's Manes. Constance had patted the dirt next to her; tentatively Charlotte sat.

After that, every second of spare time was snatched and placed in one another's company. Charlotte may have been plain, but Constance's friendship illuminated her like a stage actress under a spotlight. To be with Constance was not like being with any other person she knew. She felt that she was in orbit of some bright-burning planet whenever she was around. That merely by being with Constance was to be warmed by the force of something inextinguishably good. Charlotte had spent her life, until that point, quietly preoccupied with her own insular interests. She liked to paint, to sketch, to create sculptures with the doors of her workshop firmly closed. She had never shared her little passions with anyone else; they wouldn't have been interested in her humble talents. But Constance was.

They walked often, marveling at London's frozen rivers, the patchwork patterns left on the ground by falling sycamore leaves. They would lie on the grass together and look up into the branches, listening to the whisper of the wind through the leaves and closing their eyes against the dappled sun. Just as they had different ways of viewing the world, they had different ways of viewing the trees—Constance would run her hand over the bark, speak of purgatives, teas for colds, measles, and other ailments; Charlotte would grasp the leaves between her fingers, twist them by their stems like dancing dolls, take them home to sketch them. They did not always agree. Charlotte thought Constance impatient, erratic, and far too bold. Constance rebuked Charlotte for not being stronger in her beliefs, more ardent in her opinions. There was something about Constance that scared her a little. Something wild and reckless. A glimmer of threat. But the women could not deny that there was something solid, just like the roots of the sycamores, that bound them together. She cannot quite remember when her feelings of friendship grew into something else entirely. Although she supposes, when she thinks of it, her thoughts were never really of friendship at all. Her father had questioned the time she spent with her new companion. He had arranged a marriage match for her, someone interested in the arts as she was. He implored her to accompany him to dinner so that they might meet one another, he was sure she would be quite content with his selection. But she made her excuses, feigned illness or pains whenever the date swung around. She knew that in Constance she had found her contentment. With Constance, she knew she had come home.

But then, it was gone.

For so long, Charlotte had not known the real reason behind her heartbreak. She had spent more than a year believing that Constance had simply left her, without word, without cause. She had not known where she was, or why she had gone with no explanation, no parting words. That was why Charlotte had not had the strength to reject the marriage her father had secured for her. That was how she'd ended up as a wax maker's wife.

It was only when Charlotte had come to terms, in some way, with the fact of her abandonment that she went looking for Constance's sister. Constance had spoken of Maude with such fondness and pride. Charlotte was spurred by the quiet injustice of her abandonment; if Constance would not speak with her then perhaps her sister would. She would not reveal who she was, not at first, and she was a married woman by then, anyway. But she would ask after a Constance Horton, to see where she had ended up, to see if that might help her put their love to rest.

The pharmacy was just as Constance had described, crammed with jars and spirit lamps and strange equipment, a wall of drawers looming high like so many sets of false teeth.

There was a woman there, behind the till, inspecting the faded labels of bottles, an apron pinned neatly over black bombazine. Her face, like that of a royal courtesan, appeared entirely out of place amongst such a setting. She should not have been so surprised to see such beauty. Constance had always said her sister was like something from a painting. But it was hard for Charlotte to look at. It distracted her, momentarily, from her questions.

Maude had been suspicious, at first, when Charlotte had asked after Constance, whether she was still living in London, whether she might be accepting visitors. Then, the woman's face had crumpled, and her shoulders had dropped inches, as if the strings that were holding them up had been snipped. An old man stepped from a room out back and took his quiet place beside Maude at the till. He put a hand on the base of her spine, gently coaxed her upright again. He had a kind face and eyes veiled with age. She knew, immediately, that this was Constance's grandfather.

She had not taken in every detail of what he had said, as a strange sound had wound its way into her ears and would not cease its whining. She remembers only snatches, even now, just single words: voyage, dream, stubborn, died.

She had run. She hadn't known what to do with the words, how to place them in any order that made any sense and so she had fled the pharmacy.

But she soon knew she had to return, she needed to know more of Constance's strange and ambitious voyage, and she felt compelled, through her heavy, confusing blanket of grief, to tell Maude that her sister had been loved.

Maude had lost her temper at first. Accused Charlotte of lying in order to create a scandal for their family, of seeking money. It stung, but Charlotte had gently countered that she would have nothing to gain by admitting such a tryst. She is a policeman's daughter. An affair with a woman is hardly something that's going to lead her to great riches.

She'd left her address at the pharmacy, unsure if she would ever hear again from the other Horton sister.

Until one day, Maude arrived, knocking gently at her door. She came with a letter. She had seemed reluctant to hand it over at first. As if she did not want to relinquish a part of herself. But she had told Charlotte softly that the letter was for her. The words inside changed everything.

After that, Maude came back. Then again, and again, and slowly the women forged a deep friendship. Charlotte had been delighted to find in Maude a quick mind and a strong ally. They allowed one another to speak of Constance when they needed to; Charlotte recalling her soft, impish way of being, Maude describing how they had never needed to speak in full sentences. Charlotte had watched as Maude slowly rebuilt a part of herself from the rubble of grief, watched it happen as one might watch a master complete a painting—in awe of the skill, dazzled by the process, and certain that you could never achieve such a thing yourself.

Then one day Maude came to the house with something else. She rushed in through the door and slammed a book on the table.

"I need you to help me trail this man. Look! We need to make him talk." She had tapped the pages of the book. "He had something to do with what happened to her." Charlotte picked it up. Two words underlined again and again and again. *Edison Stowe, Edison Stowe, Edison Stowe.*

They were to join the tours, all of them, Frank included; it would be too irregular for two women of their age to appear on that train unchaperoned. Frank's eyes had widened in their sockets when Charlotte brought back a handbill, told him what the man from Clerkenwell was offering. Her husband saw death as a day in the office. It had not taken much persuading to convince him to accompany her on the tour. He did not know, at first, of her friendship with Maude. Did not know the true reason for their attendance at those hangings. But she'd had to tell him everything before York, to ask him for assistance, to beg for secrecy. He had paused and she had watched the familiar lines of his face shift as he considered it. Eventually, he had met her eyes, answering wordlessly.

Theirs might not have been a partnership of love or lust. But there was respect there, a strong devotion of sorts. So, she had not been surprised to find that his eyes said yes.

By the time Maude and Charlotte took their seats, quite separately, on that first excursion train, taking care not to reveal their friendship, or even acquaintance, they were bonded by so much more than their grief. They were chained together by their determination to get the truth from Edison Stowe.

Now revenge would be theirs. Hattie, the maid, had been easy to recruit. She had seemed terrified of Edison, Maude had said, but also strangely determined to help bring him down in any way she could. She relayed information to the women. Helped Maude track him. Planted newspaper articles, provided insight into Edison's moods and proclivities.

The use of Tussaud's as a location, the staging of the waxwork, now those had been Charlotte's ideas and she was really rather pleased with them. Maude and the moneylender had agreed. Stowe, in a room full of murderers, where he belongs. He had always reveled in a spectacle, had he not—barely blinking as people were hanged; caring more whether he was charging his guests as much as he could for his tours.

A spectacle he would get.

There were plenty of spare wax heads to be found in their basement workshop collecting dust. It had not taken much work with her sculptor's eye to find one that could be warmed and manipulated into the pinched features that resembled Stowe's. The blond curls she had chosen from the wigs that her husband had discarded in a basket in the corner. A brush had taken the knots from it, and she had scraped it into the severe side parting that Stowe favored. A rough metal comb run over the cheeks and a spot of rouge had recreated his Arctic-hardened skin.

Edison Stowe was a man of countless faces, of ever-changing masks. This was just another to add to his collection.

Chapter Thirty

Edison

H is first inclination is to run.

"I wouldn't recommend that," Ms. Horton smiles as he begins to back away. "A woman like me would never come to a place like this unchaperoned." She gestures to the waxwork on the plinth and he quickly considers who else might be in the building. "Do you like it?"

Edison's eyes climb upwards, his mouth slackening in horror.

How is it possible, how can it be that the figure that stands on a plinth in front of them, with its waxy face and its grotesque, inanimate body, is a mirror image of his likeness.

It is a joke. It must be. A horrible, dreadful joke.

"Come see, come see!" Maude apes the enthusiastic tone of a child. Forget the model of Sarah Siddons in the entrance hall, London's greatest actress of all is in the Chamber of Horrors downstairs.

Terror compels him forwards. Maude gestures to the plaque. Insists that he bends to read.

Edison Stowe, it says. *The Arctic Killer.*

"What is this?" His head swerves, searching for others in the shadows, searching for a sign that this is all a set-up, that the curtain will come down on this damned, preposterous farce.

"You have always loved a show." Maude's face is still frozen in that horrifying smile. "You live for the spectacle! We all do, do we not? That is why you run your tours. And now you are part of the show too!" She nods at the waxwork.

She has the tooth strung around her neck. His eyes cling to it, a horrible heat surging through his body.

He shakes his head again, quickly, mutely.

It angers her.

"You killed a boy in the Arctic." Maude's words come out shrill. "With a tusk. You speared him through the heart, crushed his chest, crushed his organs. Took the life from his lungs."

He cannot swallow. A boy, yes. Just a boy. A necessary euthanasia. Just a boy. Who would miss him?

"Jack Aldridge," Maude says.

Edison would not have recalled the full name.

"Although it was not Jack Aldridge. It was not a boy."

The woman is mad. That much is clear. He must find a way to escape. He could overpower her, easily. Crush her skull, snap her neck. She is just an animal—flesh, blood, bone.

"It was not a boy that you killed, it was Constance Horton. My sister. Someone far cleverer than you, someone braver, a far greater adventurer than you'll ever be." She is spitting now. It does not become her. The details of her face are starting to blur into an ugly smear. He tries to capture the thoughts that swill. He tries to focus on her face, her mouth, what she is saying.

A sister. A woman on the ship? There was no woman on the *Makepeace*. He'd have known. But he had heard of such things before. Wanton women disguising themselves to- to- to . . . He swallows. Lady Westbury had mentioned that Ms. Horton was bereaved. A sister, was it? That means the person she has been mourning all this time was on the *Makepeace* with him. The sister she so grieves was the "boy" he snuffed out. The boy he was so sure nobody would miss.

He realizes, then, with dizzying horror, that Maude Horton must have been after him all this time: the strange questions in the garden at Wilton House, the looming face he recalled when he came to at the inn at York. The conniving shrew! The audacity of it. The bold and improper scandal of it all. A woman? His fingers twitch. He will not be bested by a woman. He will not lose this fight.

"Does that surprise you?" Maude continues as he moves his hand slowly towards his coat pocket. He knows what he has there. He was not so foolish as to leave The Black Dog unarmed. "Does it anger you to have been deceived, for so long, by a woman?"

Is she talking about herself or her lying sister? Either way, he will not answer her. Not with words anyway.

"Look around you." She gestures to the waxworks of murderers and criminals and revolutionaries. Oh, how she continues the farce, unknowing of what is about to come for her. Sad. Sad, that she believes, even for a second, that she can win out against him. He reaches his fingers into his pocket as she blathers. "Costumes, masks, illusions, faces falsified in wax," she continues. "Nothing is really as it seems. My sister was not really a ship's boy, and you are not really human."

His fingers settle on cold steel.

"You are a monster, a body made of poison, driven by greed and malice and self-preservation at all costs. And what is it you said?" Her voice rises with passion at the end. He can see the pulse ticking at her throat, he can see just where he will pierce the skin. How pathetic that she does not know that. How embarrassing that she continues to uphold these theatrics. He takes one last look at the room filled with blood and knives and instruments of torture, and glances up one last time at his likeness. They have, at least, captured the handsomeness of his face, his noble air, a man who watches those beneath him from his rightly raised position.

"*An eye for an eye*, you said. You said that to take someone's life means yours, in turn, should be taken. Well, I think we can arrange that."

No. In one quick motion, he withdraws the knife and rams his whole bodyweight into her. It is a feeling he is familiar with now, the hot immediacy of being about to end a life. It does not faze him, just as it does not faze him to club and flense a seal, or to pull out the innards from a gray fox belly. It has all been leading to this, he sees, and with her out of the picture he will be untouchable again.

They land together heavily, his body on hers, she helpless under his weight. He has her pinned but will not slit her throat, not quite yet.

She blinks slowly, confused, those blue eyes rolling, the breath snatched from her lungs. She groans in pain, just as her sister did. She must have hit her head as she fell. Good. He wants her groggy.

He pauses, briefly, luxuriating in the moment, holding off the delicious release for just a few seconds longer. Something stirs in him to know that he is so close to her face that he could bite her, kiss her, do anything to her and she would be powerless to his touch. He considers slowly licking the skin of her neck, to see how she tastes. Then, he realizes she is trying to talk.

It's what her sister did too. He recalls it now. The boy, for he *did* think him a boy back then, out on the ice, had pursed his lips around a word as he died. He almost laughs when he realizes what it is that the boy must have been trying to say.

Ms. Horton's blinking grows slower as she murmurs. The sound is getting weaker, more rattling with every breath. A pool of blood is forming around her head like a dark halo. A black corona. Strangely, it becomes her. Gives her the look of a saint.

"I thought she was trying to say 'Mother,'" he grins, allowing a small bark of laughter to escape. Her eyes go immediately to his, wide, lit with fear.

"When it happened," he continues plainly, "I thought the boy, well, I thought *she* was crying out for her mother."

Maude's eyes close against what he is about to say, her body going limp. He is sure he can see a fat, wet tear forming at the corner of her pretty lashes.

"M-m-m-m-m-m-m." He makes a simpering impression of Constance Horton's final moments. "M-m-m-m-m-m." He takes the knife, lifts it, trails it across the white skin of her throat until her whole body shakes.

"But it was not 'Mother' was it, Ms. Horton? It was 'Maude'!" Her face crumples in response. "But even you couldn't save her."

A click in the darkness wrongfoots him and, without thinking, he jerks his head to the side. As it goes, it meets cool metal, something hard and unnatural is pressed into the space just above his right ear.

"I think you should stand. Don't you, Mr. Stowe?"

Hell.

Gingerly, he turns his head further and the gun moves with it. When he sees who it is, every inch of him freezes. The pain of it worse than the scourge of any frostbite. Standing above with a freshly loaded pepper-box revolver pointed at Edison Stowe's skull is Lucian Carter.

"Time's up."

Epilogue

She watches from a distance as the coffin is lowered into the ground. She tries not to imagine the state of the body inside. It must have taken a while for an affordable plot to become available. The sky is a gloomy mackerel gray, but the birds are in high spirits, their chatter lending levity to the grim proceedings.

She can see the man, Inchbold, hunched at the graveside. Forlorn in his gray coat and flat cap, he takes a handkerchief from his pocket and dabs at his nose. At one point, he glances up and she wonders if he sees her, but she shrinks slowly backwards into the foliage.

Her sister is here too, hiding with her in the trees. She is in the beetles and the birds, the smell of rain on grass, the gentle kiss of the cold in the air. This is how it is and how it always will be. Wherever Maude is, Constance will be too. Just as summer follows spring.

She hadn't seen what Carter had done with Stowe back in Tussaud's. But she'd heard it all. Slipping in and out of consciousness, the screams had sounded so very far away, but she knew they could not have been more real.

When she'd come to as she was carried out of the heavy doors by men she did not know, as her body met the cool night air and she found her face bathed in the silver glow of the moon, she had felt a peace come upon her that she hadn't known since she and Constance were together, mixing potions and chattering together with their grandfather in the pharmacy.

Weeks later, once she had recovered, she returned her sister's diary to Heart, along with Sedgewick's official autopsy report, which he had written and certified now they knew the exact circumstances of Constance's death. They'd taken them as a package to Charlotte's father, a chief constable, confident that their findings and all those links to murder and fraud would be enough to bring down Hancock once and for all.

Giles Sedgewick himself had decided to tarry in London. Maude flushes a little now, thinking of his face, his gentle way of being, his bond with Constance for which she will forever be grateful. Their grandfather is enamored with the surgeon, and the two spend long evenings discussing advancements in chemistry. Henry pushes Sedgewick for stories of his travels and Giles quizzes her grandfather on the contents of his cabinets. Maude sits with them sometimes, lulled by their amiable chatter. She catches Giles watching her, his face lit by candlelight. When their eyes meet, she knows good things are yet to come.

This morning, she had risked a stroll through the crowds that had gathered for the hanging. There were tens of thousands assembled at Newgate, record crowds no doubt. All of London had been enraptured by the story, newspapers leading with the crime, in all its gory details and dramatics, for weeks.

She had paused briefly at one point to catch the refrain of

the ballad singer, dropped her gaze at the sound of the familiar name.

There was a frenzied excitement about the scaffold crowd. The sort of energy reserved only for the most sensational crimes.

She pulled her way through it all, faceless and unnoticed.

When she reached a cider stand, there was a slum child selling broadsides. She stepped forwards, put her hand out with a coin, soon found it replaced by paper. She shook out the sheet, lowered her head and studied the words.

THE CRUEL MONEYLENDER AND THE WAXWORK MURDERS

Fraud! Scheming! Torture in Tussaud's!

On the tenth of December the most despicable and horrid crime took place deep in the bowels of Madame Tussaud's Chamber of Horrors.

Adventurer and entrepreneur Edison Stowe found his remarkable life cut short by the actions of the condemned, Lucian Carter, and his scurrilous accomplices. Stowe—who in 1849 gallantly traveled to the Arctic to aid with search efforts concerning Sir John Franklin and his Discovery ships—was enjoying an inquisitive stroll around the "Separate Room" when he was set upon, unprovoked, by Carter and two of his henchmen.

For years, Lucian James Carter has struck fear among Londoners with his violent acts of retribution. He had, until now, remained at large.

The details of the torture enacted upon Stowe before he was killed are too heinous and too gruesome to be reproduced in print, but the instruments used for the macabre activities were all themselves taken from the Chamber of Horrors exhibition itself.

Once the horrid deed had been done, wily Carter escaped from Tussaud's and continued to elude police for several days. But under questioning, his two stooges easily gave up the details of their ringleader and revealed details of dozens of similar murders, making the deranged Lucian James Carter one of London's most prolific killers.

He will hang at Newgate at 10 a.m. today.

Now, on the hillside, Edison Stowe's rotten body is finally interred. Still a hero, for now, but Maude knows the truth will out eventually. When it does, no doubt it will sell a thousand newspapers, filling many pockets, stocking many coffers. Murder, after all, is still the story that London likes the very best.

As the coffin sinks down into the earth, a loud roar goes up from the crowd at Newgate, signaling that Carter has swung. The sun gives a flash of its warmth through the London sky, and Maude Horton, her sister beside her, pulls tight the shawl around her shoulders and disappears into the trees.

Historical Note

Hangings were popular public events in the nineteenth century, attended by all tranches of society—the wealthy, the poor, the celebrated, and the disdained. Occasionally, a hanging was so headily anticipated it was felt that it warranted a public holiday. In May 1820, the boys of the esteemed Westminster School were awarded an extra day's leave so that they could watch the spectacle of five Cato Street Conspirators—political dissidents who had concocted a harebrained scheme to assassinate the entire cabinet—meet their ends outside Newgate Prison.

Edison's (fictitious but grisly) scheme has its roots in truth. There *was* money to be made in executions, lots of it, and many exploited such demand. The trade in printed broadsheets (or "broadsides") began as early as the seventeenth century, starting as "dying confessions" or "truthful accounts" of those about to be hanged. They were originally produced by Henry Goodcole, the first full-time chaplain of Newgate Prison, and described in great, often wildly embellished, detail the enormity and heinousness of each criminal's offences. These "confessions" found a lucrative market among a public hungry for sensationalism, and eventually evolved from broadsheets into multi-page pamphlets covering the trials, the sermons preached to the condemned, and accounts of their lives and crimes. They were most often, though, a single sheet, printed on one side and sold on the street (they found their readiest market at the gallows with a body still swinging) for a half penny or one penny. For those who could not afford it, the broadsides were pinned up by pubs, coffee houses, or in shop windows, where groups of children would gather and gawp at the woodcut images of the condemned.

When husband and wife Frederick and Maria Manning were hanged at Horsemonger Lane Gaol on 13 November 1849 (an event to which Daphne Westbury and Frank Hollis both refer), they attracted the largest crowd ever to attend a public execution. It is estimated that between thirty thousand and fifty thousand people turned out to watch the spectacle, and it was equally popular with the "swell" upper classes as with the poor (many fashionable ladies eagerly waited to see what Maria had chosen to wear for the occasion: black silk). Two and a half million broadsheets were sold. China figurines of the murderous couple went like hotcakes and basketmen sold "Manning biscuits" and "Maria Manning's peppermints."

Space surrounding executions could be monetized too. At the hangings, nearby coffee shops and pubs opened their doors to the highest bidders; first floor rooms opposite the scaffold could be hired for as much as £12. At the execution of the Mannings, entire memberships of many of London's most fashionable clubs hired rooms and housetops to get the best views of the "drop."

The hangings that took place outside Newgate offered a plum opportunity for the governor of the prison to cement his social standing too. When a hanging came around, he would lay on exclusive social events, to which he would invite a small, select group of distinction. An unimpeded view of the proceedings could be had from the prison, and after the execution, the party would withdraw to take breakfast and brandy.

At 18 Old Bailey The Magpie and Stump public house still stands. During 1783–1868, when public executions took place in Old Bailey (the street running alongside Newgate Prison), hospitality packages were offered to rich patrons with macabre inclinations, just like Lady Westbury. For a substantial fee, guests could stay overnight, feast on an "execution breakfast," and then obtain a privileged view of the gory proceedings in the street below from their bedroom window. The pub dates back several centuries but is now glass-fronted and much flashier. It overlooks the Central Criminal Court (the Old Bailey) which was opened on the site of Newgate Prison and the old Sessions House in 1907.

The main function of public executions, as far as the authorities were concerned, was to demonstrate to the assembled spectators the dire consequences of breaking the law. But many questioned their dissuasive effects. In 1791, *Gentleman's Magazine* acknowledged the ineffectiveness of public hangings, commenting that "instead of damping the feelings of the lower orders of people [they] only served to heighten their wickedness." Public sentiment surrounding hangings was largely mixed, but many, like Jameson, were opposed to the grisly spectacle.

Charles Dickens attended the execution of François Courvoisier, the valet who had murdered Lord William Russell, and subsequently wrote in his account that the crowd displayed "No sorrow, no salutary terror, no observance, no seriousness; nothing but ribaldry, debauchery, levity, drunkenness, and flaunting vice in fifty other shapes." (Readers will notice echoes of Dickens's words in Jameson's ardent protests.)

Dickens publicly declared that he hoped never again to see such a thing. However, he did attend the hanging of Frederick and Maria Manning at Horsemonger Lane Gaol in 1849, insisting that he went with the sole intention of observing the crowd. It led him to conclude in a letter to *The Times* that the sight was "inconceivably awful [in its] wickedness and levity."

A subsequent *Times* editorial disagreed with him:

> *The scene is doubtless the most horrid, and apparently the most hardening, that can be imagined. We are not prepared, however, to follow Mr. Dickens to his conclusion. It appears to us as a matter of necessity that so tremendous an act as a national homicide should be publicly as well as solemnly done. Popular jealousy demands it . . . The mystery of the prison walls would be intolerable, for, besides mere curiosity, popular indignation would ask to see or learn the details of the punishment.*

Many, however, saw the gallows as an effete institution, unfit for its purpose, arguing that solitary confinement, hard labor for life, or transportation to the colonies would be a greater and more deterring punishment.

The abolition of public hanging eventually came after the report of a Royal Commission of 1864–6 which led to new legislation in 1868—twenty years after Dickens's letter to *The Times*, meaning hangings could only be conducted within prison walls.

I have fictionalized Edison's excursion company, but similar tours did exist in the nineteenth century. Some sources even allege that, alongside their trips to temperance events, country fairs and industrial towns, the early tours of travel company Thomas Cook involved excursions to public hangings. When the Lightfoot Brothers were executed in 1840 for the murder of philanthropist and shipping agent Nevell Norway, it is estimated that a crowd of around twenty-five thousand people gathered to watch the executions. This included passengers on nearby trains, which were laid on especially and halted below Bodmin Gaol wall to allow spectators to watch without leaving the wagons.

It wasn't just hangings that excited the macabre sensibilities of the Victorian train traveler. "Murder sightseeing" was quite a popular pastime too. While awaiting execution, murderers who had garnered headlines with their "barbarous" crimes were often ogled in their cells by the nobility and paying members of the public, and it was not uncommon for people to spend an afternoon traveling to the site of a well-publicized murder (a house, a barn, a tavern) to have a good snoop around. Sometimes the decomposing bodies of the victims still remained in situ.

At the same time as this "Murder Mania" was in full swing, the disappearance of British naval officer Sir John Franklin and his men launched the golden era of Arctic exploration. More than thirty sea and overland expeditions would search for clues as to Franklin's fate over the course of two decades, charting vast areas and mapping the completed route of the Northwest Passage in the process. While many of these search expeditions were funded by the British Government in response to public demand that Franklin be saved, others were raised by public subscriptions following appeals from Sir John's indomitable wife, Lady Jane Franklin.

The gloomy fate of Sir John Franklin was eventually discovered by the Hudson Bay Company's John Rae and reported on Monday, 23 October 1854 in the *Toronto Globe*, under the headline: "Startling News: Sir John Franklin Starved to Death."

The newspaper reported "melancholy intelligence" that Rae had uncovered while surveying the Boothia Peninsula:

From the Esquimaux [Rae] had obtained certain informa-
tion of the fate of Sir John Franklin's party who had been
starved to death after the loss of their ships which were
crushed in ice, and while making their way south to the
great Fish [Back] river, near the outlet of which a party
of whites died, leaving accounts of their sufferings in the
mutilated corpses of some who had evidently furnished
food for their unfortunate companions.

Just like public hangings, the general public followed the often grisly fate of these polar expeditions with unrelenting curiosity. One of Franklin's would-be relief ships, *Resolute*, was frozen in on such a journey in May 1854 and abandoned in latitude 77°N. In September of the following year, she was found by an American whaling ship rigid with ice, floating some 1,200 miles away. The US Government spent $40,000 bringing her back and even more in repairing and refitting the ship, after which they presented her as a "Floating Pompeii" to the British Government, the scene of "disaster" carefully preserved inside, down to the officers' musical boxes and pictures of ballet girls on the walls. A desk made using timbers from the ship was gifted by Queen Victoria to President Rutherford B. Hayes and installed in the White House. It has been used by nearly every US president since.

I have taken an author's liberty with many things in this novel. The year 1850 was actually a quiet one for hangings, so I hope I will be forgiven for creating my own set of murderers and putting a noose around their necks. In fact, by the middle of the nineteenth century executions in general were relatively uncommon (executions of women were extremely rare). But this was a fact that only seemed to stoke enthusiasm for their grisly theatricality when they did take place.

The *Makepeace* and the *High Regard* are fictional ships, their crews are fictional, and the ranks of those on board may not comply with the traditional make-up of naval or Discovery Service ships at the time (if an author cannot tweak these things, then who can?). But in plotting their path into the Passage I took inspiration from James Clark Ross's 1848–9 (failed) Franklin relief expedition.

Tussaud's Chamber of Horrors is real and existed as a sort of arena for murder. Those who would never have dreamed of attending a public hanging could sate their darker inclinations at Tussaud's. The exhibits drew in huge crowds throughout the nineteenth century—over thirty thousand catalogues a year were sold, which could indicate attendance levels at ten times that number. The establishment knew its audience well and was quick to move at any moneymaking opportunity, displaying relics from murder scenes, death masks of famous criminals, weapons, poisons and clothing. In the run-up to the Mannings' trial, popular magazine *Punch* began to voice its distaste for "Murder Mania" and the role that Tussaud's played. "The rag-pickers of crime are at work," it published in an article recalled by Edison in this book. "London reeks with the foulness of the Bermondsey murder. There, in words of ink-black blood, it stains the walls; there it is gibbeted in placards, and is carried shouting, in the highway . . . Good MADAME TUSSAUD, devoting art to homicide, turns to the pleasantness of profit the abomination of blood. With her so much murder is so much counted money."

Most items are now in the exhibition's archives, although

a new Chamber of Horrors has recently opened, giving the general public—whose appetite for the gruesome has not been dimmed by 170 passing years—a chance to ogle some of the objects mentioned in this book, and to join Edison Stowe, Maude Horton, Charlotte Hollis, Frank Hollis, Charles Arnott, Mr. Jameson, and Lady and Mr. Westbury in becoming tourists of the macabre themselves.

My desk was piled high with books, pamphlets, and diaries during the writing of this novel, but I'd like to acknowledge a few resources in particular that aided me greatly in the long (and occasionally arduous) research process. *London: The Executioner's City* by David Brandon and Alan Brooke provided fascinating insights into William Calcraft and other Victorian hangmen, while *The Invention of Murder* by Judith Flanders proved an endlessly helpful, and entertaining, account of the "Murder Mania" that gripped England in the nineteenth century. Owen Beattie and John Geiger's *Frozen in Time: The Fate of the Franklin Expedition* was indispensable when it came to Sir John Franklin's ill-fated expedition and the ships that set out in search of it. I'd also like to thank Jane Sherwood and the Sherwood family for loaning me their precious copy of the diary of George Brown (1826–80), who sailed out to the Northwest Passage on HMS *Investigator* in 1848 in search of Franklin's ships. His tales of life on board and activities in the Arctic helped illuminate Constance's diaries. I'm so grateful to have had the privilege to read them.

Acknowledgments

A second novel is an interesting beast, and I sometimes felt like I'd never see the day when *Maude Horton's Glorious Revenge* was published. But there was an army of people who propped me up during the higgledy-piggledy process and to whom I owe a huge debt of gratitude.

To my wonderful, eagle-eyed, unshockable editors, Orla King, Carina Guiterman, Bev Cousins, and Sarah St Pierre, whose editorial suggestions made this book immeasurably better. I was quite sure you would show me the door when I sent you a bonkers manuscript about hangings and Arctic exploration. But you didn't. Thank you, so much, for embracing Maude and co.

Thank you to my indomitable agent, Maddy, whose support never wavers. I will always be so incredibly grateful. And to the rest of the team at the mighty Madeleine Milburn Literary TV & Film Agency for your enthusiasm and kindness.

It takes a village to publish a book, and I'd like to thank the sales, marketing, production, PR, and design teams (and anyone I've missed!) at Picador, Penguin Random House Australia, Simon & Schuster US, and Simon & Schuster Canada. I may not have met you all in person, but I'm bowled over by the work that you do behind the scenes. Thank you also to Mary Mount, Lucy Hale, Siobhan Slattery, Rosie Friis, Laura Carr, Sam Humphreys, Alice Gray, and Bella Bosworth.

Special thanks to Frieda Ruh and Lucy Scholes for creating a fittingly glorious cover for this book.

Thank you to Nim Singh at Destination Canada for all your help during the long and far-ranging research process, and to Tessum Weber and Kylik Taylor for speaking with me about life in the High Arctic (when can I move in?). Thank you, again, to Jane Sherwood and the Sherwood family for loaning me George's diaries. What a remarkable man. Thank you to Megan Berrisford at the Salisbury Museum and the staff at the Haunch of Venison pub for being so welcoming while I had a poke around the rooms up top.

An author's job can be a lonely one, but I am blessed to know so many fellow writers who simply make my life better. To my writerly soulmate Nikki May. We started as agency siblings and ended up like real sisters (even down to the bickering). To the magnificent Saara El-Arifi and Amy McCulloch. It scares me to think that if we'd published in different years, I might never have got to meet you. You truly mean the world to me. To Emilia Hart and Ally Wilkes (co-founders of the Book Two WhatsApp Support Group—formerly known as BOOKS ABOUT SHIPS). I am staggered daily by your brilliance and friendship. (Thank you also, Emilia, for accompanying me to the Chamber of Horrors at Tussaud's and screaming at absolutely everything.) Thank you also to Collette Lyons and Emma Stonex. Two women of immeasurable talent whose kindness and support I'll never forget.

Thank you to the Kirbys and the Arnotts for the enduring love and enthusiasm. To Laura, Robin, and the rest of the SWGS crew, and to Tom, Lucy, and Sam for being there, always. To the niblings—Phoebe, Max, Martha, and Rufus. You are astonishing. I love you. Stop growing up so fast!

To my dad, who'll never get to read this book, but without

whom I would never be writing books in the first place. I miss you every day. To Mum, the strongest, most wonderful, self-sacrificing person I know. I love you. Thank you for everything that you do.

And to my two guiding lights: Bobby, simply the very best there is. How did I get so lucky? I love you, I love you, I love you. And to Rose, the other half of me. The center point of my compass.

About the Author

LIZZIE POOK is an author and award-winning travel writer whose work has appeared in *The Sunday Times*, *Lonely Planet, Rough Guides, Condé Nast Traveller,* and more. Her assignments have taken her to some of the most remote parts of the planet, from the uninhabited east coast of Greenland in search of roaming polar bears, to the foothills of the Himalayas to track endangered snow leopards. Her first novel, *Moonlight and the Pearler's Daughter,* was shortlisted for the Wilbur Smith Adventure Writing Prize and the HWA Debut Crown, and longlisted for the Author's Club Best First Novel Award. *Maude Horton's Glorious Revenge* is her second novel. She lives in London.